Luke

The A**hole Club Series

Tiffany Patterson

TMP Publishing, LLC.
San Antonio, Texas

Tiffany Patterson/Perceptive Illusions Publishing, Inc.
PO Box 5253,
Bayshore, NY 11706

www.TiffanyPattersonWrites.com

Publisher's Note: This is a work of fiction. Names, characters, places, and incidents are a product of the author's imagination. Locales and public names are sometimes used for atmospheric purposes. Any resemblance to actual people, living or dead, or to businesses, companies, events, institutions, or locales is completely coincidental.

Cover designed by Covers by Combs

Ordering Information:
Quantity sales. Special discounts are available on quantity purchases by corporations, associations, and others. For details, contact the "Special Sales Department" at the address above.

Luke: The A**hole Club Series/ Tiffany Patterson. -- 1st ed.
ISBN 978-1-941924-07-5

"Perfect people make for boring romance novels."
-Tiffany Patterson

Everything Changes

Luke

"Step aside, Double Ds. The winner of this race is coming through," I commented as I pushed my way through the crowd around Lenny and me.

I heard a loud sucking of the teeth in my peripheral as I spotted long brunette hair whirling.

"Luke, what the hell?" An offended female voice shrilled. It sounded familiar.

I turned to look into the face of the chick I brushed past. My gaze narrowed. I vaguely recognized her.

"Seriously? You're going to pretend like you don't know who I am?"

I raised an eyebrow, staring her in the face, still unable to discern her from a hole in the wall. That was, until I dropped my eyes to the cleavage she had hanging out of the sleeveless top she wore. I tilted my head to the side, observing. There was some familiarity.

"Shelly?"

"Cheryl," she corrected with her hands on her slim hips.

I shrugged. "Can't remember them all." I turned my back on her at the same time she sucked her teeth again. She started to say something, but I didn't have time for her hurt feelings or whatever the fuck she was trying to pull. Not my fault I forgot her name as soon as my dick dried.

"Luke, man, are you sure you want to do this?"

I pushed out an exasperated breath as I stopped at the driver's side door of the vehicle I was preparing to race in. I turned to look over my shoulder and directly into the worried hazel eyes of my best friend. Correction, my only friend. I don't like most people.

"Tighten up, Lenny, you're starting to sound like Stacey over there." I nodded my head toward Double Ds, who was still glaring at me from the distance.

"Cheryl," he corrected.

I shrugged. "Whatever."

"I don't have a good feeling about this race. Jeremy has been giving all of the drivers dirty looks." Lenny gestured his head in the direction of Jeremy, who stood among a few of the spectators.

"Aww, does he look like he's going to call me bad names and take my milk and cookies at lunch time?" I fake-whined, rolling my eyes and lifting my middle finger in Jeremy's direction when he shifted his gaze to mine.

He scowled, causing me to smirk.

Lenny frowned. "Come on, man, take this serious."

"Fuck that and fuck Jeremy. In fact, fuck everyone in this damn race. I didn't come here to befriend these dipshits. As long as they cough up the money once I win, I've got nothing to say to any of them."

"You don't even need the money."

I snorted. "Fuck no, I don't need it, but I want it."

I let that sentence be the final word on it. He was right. I didn't need the money from this race. The underground fights I got into were my main source of income these days. The money wasn't why I was out here in the dead of night as spectators made bets and cheered in the background of my proverbial dust.

I was doing this because I wanted to. Plain and simple. Finally, doing shit I wanted these days. Out in the open and not giving a damn what anyone had to say about it. Anyone who didn't like it could kiss the innermost part of the crack of my ass. And yes, that even included my best friend.

Looking over at my Mustang, a current of anticipation rushed through me. Though fighting was mostly my thing, the opportunity to join this race came up and I was game.

"I'm doing this," I said to Lenny.

He looked as if he wanted to argue his point but didn't say anything more on the matter.

"Anything goes wrong, you know the drill."

He began shaking his head. "I'm not—"

"You bail and we'll meet up later. You know where."

"And what if…" He didn't finish his sentence.

And what if you die?

I knew that's what he was thinking. Lenny was always thinking the worst of the worst type of shit would happen. Comes with the territory of our respective backgrounds, I guessed.

"Then it was nice knowing ya." With another shrug, I turn away from Lenny, and look toward the rest of the drivers mingling about.

One voice rang above all others, though.

"She's not racing with us. She has no business out here," I heard Jeremy growl from my left.

I narrowed my gaze.

"Doesn't matter either way. Your ass is still going to lose," Kelex challenged back at Jeremy.

Apparently, Jeremy was up in arms 'cause some chick had the audacity to enter the race. I caught a glimpse of her earlier. She was hot with her smooth looking brown skin and fat ass. I would've definitely fucked her, but she'd have to get in line. I was an equal opportunity type of asshole.

Anyway, Jeremy, Kelex, and Pit talked shit back and forth between one another. The noise of their shit talking began to get under my skin.

"Hey," I called from afar. "All of you can shut the fuck up and let your engines do the talking for you. Fucking pansies." I rolled my eyes as I noticed Pit headed in Jeremy's direction.

They better not fuck up my chance at this money. But before Pit could reach him, Jeremy backed down by getting in his car.

Finally, I climbed in my own car and started her up. Revving the engine a few times, I waved Lenny off with a two finger salute, and lined up with the rest of the vehicles.

"Let's get this shit over with," I uttered to no one in particular as I saw Seth signal to the two chicks he had flagging this race.

I angled my head to the side. I was pretty sure I fucked one of them before. The blonde's face didn't conjure up any distinct memory, but I vaguely recalled the small butterfly tattoo on her ankle as I watched her swallow my cock.

Not a bad memory but I shook it off nonetheless. There would be plenty of time for ass later.

The two chicks strutted to the front of the cars, holding up the black and white checkered flag. For the briefest of seconds, I took my eyes off the flag and glanced to my left, taking in my competition.

Pit was at the far end. Deacon, the new girl, Jeremy, and Kelex were behind the wheels of the four cars between Pit and me.

I took in the scene for a second too long. Before I could turn my head front again, the distinct sound of screeching tires and the smell of burning rubber hit my nostrils. I didn't have time to accurately put my fucking foot on the gas.

"Idiot," I berated myself for being distracted.

In this race every second counted. I hadn't finished blinking before, Pit, Jeremy, Kelex and the new girl were ahead of me. I floored it and soon was on their tails. I shifted gears, looking for that extra advantage and in an instant my back pressed against the leather seats, momentum holding me in place. That adrenaline rush I always sought out took ahold of me.

Everything outside of my car became a blur. The spectators' cheers, the lights, even the other cars in this race fell away. Nothing else mattered besides getting over that finish line.

However, just before I made it to the line, Jeremy's car swerved. I inhaled sharply, bracing for the impact of Jeremy's car hitting the new girl's vehicle. Yet before he could, Kelex thwarted him.

The screech of metal on metal crashing into one another couldn't be mistaken. A half a second later, a car rolled right before me. At the last second, I turned the wheel to avoid hitting someone's car by mere inches.

"What the fuck?" I yelled as I stopped my own vehicle. There was no time for true assessment. All I heard was screaming and chaos.

I pushed my driver's side door open and saw another car on fire. The driver was still inside. My feet were moving before I even realized I was running in the direction of the flames.

Pit was already there along with the new girl. They weren't my concern. The fact that Kelex's fucking car was on fire with him trapped inside was. I pulled open the dented passenger door.

"Shit," I cursed, realizing how bad it was. "We need to get him the hell out of here," I yelled to the other side of the car. Kelex's right side was on fire and the noises coming from the front of the vehicle sounded like we were all going to be lit aflame if we didn't move it.

"This isn't working," I grunted, realizing my efforts to beat back the flames while trying to undo Kelex's seatbelt were for naught. I remembered the blanket and kit in the trunk of my car.

I was gone in an instant, sprinting back to my car and popping open the trunk to pull out the blanket I kept inside. Leaving the damn thing open, I turned and hauled ass back to Kelex's vehicle. Seconds later, I arrived in time to help Pit finish pulling Kelex's large frame from the car. As soon as his body hit the ground, I covered his leg and right side with the blanket to beat out the flames.

Kelex yelled and writhed in fear and pain. As the flames on Kelex's body died off, a loud noise behind us had us all taking cover. I laid across Kelex's body, trying to protect him from anymore damage. A second later, I glanced back over my shoulder to see Jeremy's car had exploded with him still inside.

"This is all bad," I murmured as the crowd who was so thrilled and anxious to watch the race, scattered like the fucking cockroaches they were.

"We need to get him to the hospital," the girl called.

"You need to get the fuck out of here. Anyone connected to this shit is going to jail. Go," Pit barked.

I rose from Kelex's body, watching as Deacon and Pit worked to place Kelex's now unconscious body in the back of Pit's car.

"You're bleeding," I told the chick, looking at her for the first time since all this shit went down. She had a pretty deep gash on her forehead and the blood soaked through the T-shirt she held to the wound. I silently berated myself for removing most of the first aid supplies I had in my trunk just days earlier.

Taking off my own shirt, I held it over the blood soaked cloth in her hands.

"Hold this on top of that," I instructed, helping place her fingers around my shirt.

Pit moved in, asking if her car was drivable.

"One of you follow her to somewhere safe," he ordered, looking between Deacon and me.

"You on the call list?" he asked her.

I assumed he was talking about Seth's call list. Seth, the organizer of these races had us all on a list by nicknames. Mine was Skullcrusher. My fight name.

"Yeah, I'm Skittles," she answered as sirens blared in the distance.

My heart began to race anew at that sound. Nothing good came from the sound of police sirens. We needed to speed this shit along.

"I'll get someone to you for your head. I'll have them text you. All of you, get your cars out of here. Lie low," Pit said.

"And you?" she asked.

"I'm going to be the low life my father says I am. None of you were here. None of you know what the fuck happened. I'll get him to the hospital. This is all on me, I'll take this one."

I don't know what the fuck he meant by that, but I didn't give much of a shit either. It was time to fucking go.

"You can't do that," she argued.

"Already done, sweetheart. Now get your ass the fuck out of here before I change my damn mind."

"Let's go," I demanded, as the sirens grow louder.

When she appeared as if she wanted to stay or follow Pit, I took her by the arm. "There's nothing you can do for him now. Let Pit do whatever the fuck he's gonna do. You need to get that shit taken care of before you become the next casualty of this mess." I dipped my head in the direction of her wound.

My words seemed to scare her enough that she acquiesced, still looking concerned, but following my lead.

"Wait." I stopped her right before she got into the car.

"Follow my finger." I held up my pointer finger and moved it from left to right. I watched for any signs of pupil dilation, inability to concentrate, or any other indicators of a concussion. I couldn't be too sure, but she looked okay enough to drive the short distance to get medical treatment.

"The drive is only a few minutes from here. Stay on my ass. We come to any red lights blow through 'em. Can you do that?"

She looked again to Pit's car.

"Hey." I shook her by the arm. "Can you do that?"

"Yeah… yeah."

I nodded. "Get in your car."

Once she did, I ran back to my vehicle. Shit was about to get real. *I hope Pit knows what he's doing*, I thought as I pulled off, glancing in my rearview mirror ensuring the girl was following closely.

For whatever reason, when I saw she was, I let out a sigh of relief.

I was not expecting the night to end up like this. Hell, I bet Kelex wasn't either.

CHAPTER ONE

The Loss

Luke

Thirteen years later...

I watched the pretty little thing turn and smile at me over her shoulder as she lowered the fruit tray onto the coffee table. We were in one of the holding rooms of the stadium, where we fighters waited for our turn to get in the cage. I continued with my warmup stretches to keep my body limber all while allowing my gaze to travel down her svelte frame. I paused, staring at the long legs that led to the six-inch stilettos she had on. How women could maneuver in those things was beyond me.

"Is there anything else I can get for you, Mr. McConnell?" The seductive lilt of her tone made the implications of her question clear.

"Yeah legs, you can get me—"

"Are you sure you want to do this?" Lenny's question interrupted me as he pushed through the door.

Rolling my eyes at his disruption, I responded with, "For fuck's sake. You couldn't wait five more minutes to barge in here?" I gestured with my head to the chick who'd brought the fruit to my room. "I was just about to share with legs here what she can do for me." I tossed her a half grin.

Lenny grumbled and mumbled something inaudible as he moved further into the room. "Legs, was it?"

She knitted her eyebrows and looked over to me, a question in those brown eyes of hers.

"Yeah, well, Mr. McConnell has a big fight in about fifteen minutes, so he doesn't need to be distracted. Thank you for the uh… fruit."

I watched, smirking as Lenny took the woman by the arm and escorted her to the door.

"I'll catch ya' later, legs," I called while moseying over to the coffee table, surveying the fruit tray she left but not touching anything.

"Man, what the hell are you doing?"

I shrugged and folded my arms across my chest.

"Are you sure you want to do this fight?"

I rolled my eyes toward the ceiling and dropped my arms. "You wait until ten minutes before I have to go out there to ask an asinine thing like that?"

"You know this isn't the first time I've asked you this."

"And what did I tell you all the other times?"

Lenny sagged his shoulders and sighed.

"Yeah, I thought so. I'll be fine. I'm gonna go out and beat the hell out of this fucker and then go off and bang that pretty little thing who you so rudely escorted out of here. And you're going to head home to that wife of yours and stop riding my dick about this fucking fight."

Lenny, didn't respond, used to my outbursts by now. Instead, he simply grunted before pulling out his phone and typing something into it. Probably texting his wife, Constance.

I didn't say anything else as I gazed in the mirror, avoiding making contact with my own eyes. I knew what I'd see lurking there and didn't feel like being confronted with it at the moment. Not when I could hear the dull roar of the crowd in the arena. It was a mid-sized venue I was fighting in tonight, but the fans still showed up.

You're doing more fights than you need.

Lenny's words from the previous day continued to echo through my mind, but I shook them off. Sure, most fighters at my level only did about two to four fights per year, but I opted for more. Fighting felt like all I knew how to do sometimes, so that's what the hell I did.

"All right, so tell me what you know about this guy?"

I inwardly flinched as Lenny walked behind me while we headed toward the main arena minutes later. He, with Marshall, the cutman who'd been assigned to me during this fight, trailed behind me. The question had always been something Banks, my former trainer, would ask me as we headed toward a fight. It was his signal now was the time to lock it in and focus.

Hearing Lenny say it didn't feel right. I wanted to tell him to shut the fuck up, but I bit my tongue. A testament to how good of a friend Lenny was. As much shit as I gave him, it was still only about half of what I gave anyone else.

"He's got a mean left hook and loves to use it."

"And?"

"He's got sloppy footwork."

"And?"

"His mother wants to bounce up and down on my cock."

"Shit, Luke. Will you be serious."

I chuckled at the expression on Len's face. "Chill out. I've got this shit under wraps." I pressed my fist into his chest and pivoted, heading down the aisle toward the ring. As soon as the spotlight hit me, the crowd cheered.

That shit used to send my adrenaline pumping. It still did, though not as much.

I didn't acknowledge the crowd to my left or right who called my name. On the outside, I took it all in stride as I undid the belt of the silk robe that hung around my body. Lenny stepped behind me to remove the robe. I nodded at the ref, known as Big John, because he was just as big as most of the fighters in my weight class.

All around me, I could hear the noise of the crowd, gathering to cheer on their favorite contender. The chants used to energize me, get me pumped up and ready to go to war. They would drown out the garbage in my own head and allow me to concentrate on the guy in front of me. Now, I found myself needing to drown out the audience as well. I shifted my gaze around the cage in front of me until it landed on my contender for the night.

Ronaldo Lee Caldwell.

What the hell kind of name was that? I didn't know but whatever. To each their own, I guessed. I gave Caldwell a once over, letting my eyes move over his entire frame from head to toe, sizing him up. I went over everything I knew about him and his fighting style.

He's quick off the jab but has sloppy footwork.

His right hook is deadly.

He loves a chokehold.

He's a hell of a grappler.

Has had a total of three knockout wins over the last three years.

Don't let him get you on the ground. I reminded myself.

I continued to stare at Caldwell as I entered the cage. The spotlight shined on the both of us, while the rest of the arena remained shrouded in darkness. Except for the cellphone lights. The cheers from the audience would've been deafening to an untrained fighter.

Angling my head from one side to the other, I cracked my neck and rotated my shoulders, making sure my muscles stayed loose and ready. I'd done plenty of warming up in my waiting room, but needed to stay that way. I began shadow boxing at my side of the cage while I watched Caldwell do the same. His eyes drilled into me as he swung at the air, apparently this was his attempt at intimidation.

Whatever, dumbass.

"And fighting tonight we have…" the announcer at the center of the ring began speaking into the microphone, while the camera guy and ref circled Caldwell and myself. The audience roared and applauded as our names and stats were read off. I glared at my opponent, drowning out the white noise.

"All right gentlemen, let's have a clean fight. You know the rules," Big John declared as we closed in on the center of the cage. "Ready?" he questioned looking at me.

I nodded.

"Ready?" he asked Caldwell who also nodded.

"Let's fight." He clapped and stepped back, moving out of our way.

Caldwell moved in closer, and we began circling the cage, fists up, bouncing on the balls of our feet. Caldwell made the first move with a front kick. I easily side-stepped it and made a move of my own, trying for a right hook. I missed, but he was a few steps slower than me. A grin crossed my lips as my confidence mounted. This win might be easier than I suspected.

I easily ducked the left hook he sent my way and landed a left jab of my own right to his ribs. He grunted and attempted a head lock maneuver since I was in so close. He was almost successful.

That was until I aggressively made contact with his right ribs with my left elbow, forcing him to release me. I moved in quickly with a left uppercut and then a right. Caldwell's approach was slowed down by my punches. Yet, he continued to swing at me, I dodged it and landed another blow to his left ribs. My minor victory was short-lived however. He dipped low, somehow able to wrap his arms around my legs. We both went down with me on my back and him over me.

Fuck no. I wasn't going down this easily. I began elbowing in the head, and flipping both of us over, pushing away from him enough to break his hold on me. I leapt to my feet, keeping my eyes locked on his every move.

Breathing heavily, I continued to dance on the balls of my feet, staying out of his reach so he wouldn't be able to get me to the ground again. I wasn't an idiot. He was better at grappling than I was.

Still. I wanted Caldwell's ass. I wanted this win more than I wanted my next breath.

The only thing standing in between me and the W was this fucker. For that reason, he had to be taken down. Nothing mattered more than the W once I stepped inside the cage.

I moved in quickly, more determined this time. I rained blow after blow, ignoring the pain from the punches he was able to land to my mid-section. Yeah, I'd have some bruises in the morning, but Caldwell would be limping away from this fight.

Right when I felt Caldwell's energy waning, the bell signaling the end of the first round went off. Stepping back, I found myself surrounded by Lenny and Marshall.

"Ah fuck," I grunted when Marshall pressed the cold enswell to the side of my face. The reduction in swelling would allow me to keep fighting, but I always hated those fucking things. "No." I shook my head, frowning, when Lenny offered a bottle of water.

"How're you feeling?"

Deepening my frown, I glared at Lenny. As far as corner's went, he sucked. He was a hell of a lawyer and manager, but sucked as a trainer. It was moments like this where I missed Banks' presence more than ever. I didn't let myself dwell on that. I went over what I knew about Caldwell and his fighting style. Replaying the first round of the fight in my head, I chose what minor adjustments needed to be made.

"All right, minute's up," Lenny said as the bell ending our break sounded.

I nodded and clapped my hands in front of me before moving to the center of the cage, on guard.

"Ready?"

I tipped my head.

"Ready?"

Caldwell did the same.

"Fight." Big John jumped back.

Caldwell charged and moved in, right into my left uppercut, followed by a right hook to the jaw. He went down. Again, I moved in to begin pummeling him into submission.

I was ready to end this fight, but Caldwell's legs were strong. He wrapped me up in a leg lock. I struggled to land my blows where I wanted them to go. I thought to do a spin move that would land me on my back, and reverse the leg lock he had on me. It was a risky move, but one I'd practiced in training, though never used in a fight.

Just when I made the decision and began to execute it, Caldwell moved again. This time, twisting me up in some locking maneuver I was a stranger to. Somehow, he'd left my right arm free and I pummeled him with right arm strikes, causing him to break the hold. The bell for the second round went off and we separated.

The one minute break felt like an eternity. I was antsy to get this motherfucker wrapped up and have this W under my belt. As soon as Lenny and Marshall exited the cage, I advanced to the middle, arms up. My aim had been to end the bout early, but I could just as easily put Caldwell on his ass in the third round as I could in any other.

We circled one another. I watched as blood from a cut on Caldwell's lip dripped to the floor. Caldwell dipped his upper body and attempted to wrap me up for a takedown.

I sent an elbow to his back, breaking his tenuous hold and causing him to stumble forward once I leapt out of the way. He quickly recovered before sending a right hook in my direction. I narrowly missed the assault. We ended up on the ground again, both of us striking and kicking. The bell for the third and final round sounded in the distance and we pulled apart from one another.

Once the points were totaled, Big John raised Caldwell's arm, declaring him the winner of the bout.

"What the fuck?" I demanded. *I should've won this fight*, I kept telling myself. Caldwell was skilled, but I was fucking better. I knew it in my bones.

Pissed off, I stomped out of the cage, pushing past Lenny and heading straight for the back room to get my shit and get the hell out of here. Of course, luck wasn't on my side that night because a fucking reporter with a cameraman behind him came barreling down on me.

"Luke, do you want to tell us what happened in there tonight? Is it true what everyone's been saying about you? That, at thirty-four, you're washed up and need to retire? What about the loss of your trainer—" The motherfucker couldn't get whatever question he'd been about to ask out before I lunged in his direction.

"Luke, man, don't," Lenny urged in my ear as he held me back. "Your career," he reminded me.

"You don't want to do this man," my cutman added on top of Lenny's pleas.

The pounding of my own heartbeat in my ears nearly drowned out their voices. I wanted blood and was ready to take it from anyone at this point. Fuck my career.

"Banks wouldn't want you to do this," Lenny said.

That's the comment that finally gets me to calm down.

"Stay out of my way." Glaring at the reporter, I pulled away from Lenny and my cutman and proceed to the back of the arena.

"Luke, man. What the hell was that?" A breathless Lenny blurted out as he raced behind me.

"I'm leaving."

"Leaving? What the hell? How could you—"

"Look, Len, I don't wanna hear shit right now. I'm getting the fuck outta here." I looked around the room for my belongings, in particular the keys to my Maserati. I began undoing the Velcro from my fighting gloves, throwing them off. I clawed at the tape with my teeth, spitting it out onto the floor.

"We have to—"

"I don't have to do shit but find that brunette with the legs from earlier."

"Luke—"

"Not another word, Len. I'm fucking serious," I growled, pointing directly at him before snatching my keys, wallet, and clothes from the chair where I'd left them earlier.

In three long strides I was back across the room, yanking the door open and low and behold, the woman from earlier stood at the door, arm raised as if she was about to knock.

"Am I interrupting?"

I looked back at Lenny before turning back to her. "You're right on time, legs. Let's go," I answered, wrapping my arm around her neck. I proceeded out the back of the arena, uncaring about the after-fight interviews that were expected, the reporter with his dumbass questions, or the L I just took.

CHAPTER TWO

Lean Into It

Luke

"What the fuck?" I groaned at my ringing phone as I lifted my head from my pillow. Damn near knocking the phone to the floor, I caught it in time before it hit the ground and flip it over to see who had the nerve to call at this ungodly hour.

PITA. The phone read.

"Aw, fuck no," I grumbled, hitting the ignore call button and tossing the phone back onto the wooden nightstand at the side of my bed.

"Mmm," a feminine voice murmured to my right. I winced, nearly forgetting Legs from the night before.

"Shit," I grunted, pushing out from underneath the heavy comforter and rising from the bed to stand, stretching.

"Wow, he did a number on you last night," the woman said as she stared up at my body from the bed, eyeing me seductively.

I looked down at my body and noticed the bruises around my ribs and abdomen, visible even with all the tattoos that covered those areas. Compared to other fights I'd been in, this was nothing, but I didn't need to explain that to Legs. Especially since she had a one-way ticket out of my fucking house, departure time within the next five minutes.

"Yeah, whatever. Look, it's time for you to high tail it outta here."

Her forehead wrinkled in confusion as she sat up in the bed, resting her arms on the tops of her knees. She allowed the bedsheet to slide off the top of her body, exposing her very round, perky, and fake tits.

"Leave?" she purred, now fully moving from underneath the bed linens, crawling across my spacious bed to my side. "I thought I could stay for a little while and we could hang out. I'm sure there's something we could do... a little trouble we could get into together." She lifted up onto her knees, wrapping her arms around my neck.

I'll admit she did make a pretty picture and she sucked cock like she was trying to suck blood from a fucking stone, but I rarely ever double dipped. Broads get too attached.

I took her wrists in both of my hands, unlocking them from around my neck, taking a step back. "Is that what you thought?"

She nodded, hopefully.

All hope was extinguished when I shook my head, dropping her hands from mine.

"That's not gonna work out, Legs. I've got shit to do. It's time for you to leave."

Her face immediately morphed into a pissed off expression. "So, you're just kicking me out?"

"Pretty much. Don't fret, doll."

I paused, glancing down at my nightstand and retrieved my phone from it.

"I'll order you an Uber. Even pay for it to take you wherever the hell you want to go. As long as it's away from here." With a swipe of my thumb, I pull up the car service app.

"What's your address?" I ask without looking up from my phone.

When I don't get an answer, I peered up. Laughter was my first reaction at the affronted look on her face. Unbothered, I picked up the panties, shoes, and short band dress she wore the night before and tossed them on the bed at her.

"Luke, I thought—"

"You thought wrong. Your Uber will be on its way as soon as you let me know what address to put in," I said, eyeing her with a lifted brow, waiting.

When she didn't respond, I shrugged. "Fine." I typed in the address of a random restaurant. A minute later, I turned my phone screen to her with the app opened on it so she could see. "Clarke is your driver's name."

That's when she let out a string of profanities any National Fighting Association fighter would be proud to have strung together themselves. It took a total of six minutes to get Legs dressed, down the stairs, and into the Uber. I informed the driver to drop her off wherever the fuck she wanted to go and slammed the door in her face. I heard her yelling something as the driver pulled off, but I didn't stop to think much of it. Like I'd said, I had shit to do.

Heading up the stairs back into my bedroom, I removed the sheets from my bed and bunched them up on the floor by the door to remind myself to take them down to the laundry room for my part-time maid to clean. I shuddered at the thought of sleeping on sheets I fucked some random broad on the night before.

Next, I made a beeline to the shower to rinse off the previous night, before dressing in a pair of running shorts, a T-shirt, and my running shoes to head out for my usual five mile run along the beach.

I lived only a block away from the ocean and I did my best to take advantage of the picturesque scenery daily. While running, I replayed the night before. Going over every moment I could recall of the fight.

I wasn't on my A game at all. Caldwell had a strong grappling game, something I'd always been weak on. This had been especially true after Banks died and I began mostly training myself. Caldwell wasn't a better fighter than I was. He was just better trained. That fact punched me in the gut as I ran, knowing I should've won that damn fight.

Yet, maybe the truth stared me in the face.

Were the articles right? Was I over the hill?

The reporter's words from the night before echoed in my head and I picked up my pace, running faster. My legs stung from the tiny granules of sand pelting the backs of my calves. My heart beat rapidly the quicker I ran. My chest expanded with every pull of air as my lungs fought for enough oxygen.

Relax your muscles. Lean into it.

I heard Banks say over and over as he used to do whenever I went through one of his extreme workouts or a hard fight. The more difficult the challenge, the more he'd tell me to relax, to lean into it. "Don't resist," he'd say. "It only makes it worse."

"Fuck off," I yelled out to no one in particular since I was all alone on the beach. Breathing hard, muscles aching, and sweaty after five miles, I completed the beginning part of my workout and headed back to my place to eat and head to the gym for the day.

CHAPTER THREE

The Woman for the Job

Luke

"How'd I know you'd be here bright and early?" I snidely remarked to Lenny as he approached while I unlocked the door to the mixed martial arts gym I owned about twenty-five minutes from my home.

"Because I'm always here. Especially the day after one of your fights."

I stiffened, hating he had to mention the fight right off the bat. I knew he would want to go over it to analyze what happened in the fight. Me? I just wanted to forget all about it.

"Whatever. Don't start with all your lawyer talk so early in the morning. I haven't had my coffee yet." I pointed the key at him before pushing through the door and strolling through the empty gym.

"You don't drink coffee."

I shrugged. "I'm thinking of starting."

"No, you're not."

I turned to Lenny, holding out my arms and replied, "You never know."

I flicked on the light switch located outside of my office, illuminating the entirety of the gym. We were surrounded by a large space, at the center of which is a boxing ring, of course. To the right of the boxing ring was the open mat space where classes such as Aikido, Jiu-Jitsu, and Krav Maga were held. At the far side of the gym were three doors that led to rooms where other martial arts classes along with kickboxing and some yoga classes were held.

"Anyway, I'm not here to talk to you about coffee."

"And don't start giving me shit about last night's fight either." I entered my office that was mostly encased in windows from three different sides so I could look out at the gym from my desk, tossing my keys onto said desk.

"Fine, then let's discuss trainers."

My body went rigid with tension. "For fuck's sake."

"You knew this conversation was coming, Luke. It's been—"

"I'm the last person you have to tell how long it's been," I said while glaring at him.

"Fine. I won't tell you how long it's been. I will say it's time you seriously consider taking on a new head trainer." Lenny's voice grew louder as I pushed past him, out of my office and over to the area where we kept the punching pads and hanging punching bags.

"Luke, we've gotten at least ten different inquiries over the past month."

I didn't say anything as I stood with my back to him, pushing my fingers through a pair of fighting gloves.

"The trainer who called about the job last week would be a great candidate. There are three resumés on your desk right now. Hell, even Greyson has been vying for the position since he started here."

I grunted, knowing Greyson, my newest Karate instructor, wanted the position as my head trainer.

"The kid's too fucking wet behind the ears," I said.

"Fine. And the three local trainers who've been calling? Any one of them would be perfect for you."

"How the hell do you know that?" I refused to look in Lenny's direction.

"I don't, but if you give them a shot they could work out. At least try one."

"Or, try me instead."

I spun around on my heels at the intrusion of a woman's voice and came face to face with the deepest pools of brown eyes I'd ever seen. Not deep as in dark—which they were—but deep as in a fucking oasis lived in them. I immediately grew angry at the invasion.

"Who the hell are you?"

She didn't appear alarmed or thrown off at my demanding tone. Instead, those very full, plump lips that were coated in a warm pink color spread into a smile.

"My apologies for interrupting and surprising you both." Her gaze shifted to Lenny before moving back to me. "But the front door was unlocked, and I assumed that meant you were open for business."

I waved a gloved hand her way. "Sorry, sweetheart, but you're about an hour early for the women's kickboxing class. It doesn't start until nine-thirty. Shelly will be here around then to get you signed up and all of that." I turned to Lenny, thinking this woman would go on her way.

"Oh no, I'm not here to take the kickboxing class."

Again, I moved my annoyed gaze to her, lifting an eyebrow. "Then?"

"My name is Syd Quinn and I'm interested in training. More specifically, being your head trainer," she said with a straight face.

Pausing, I looked this woman over from head to toe, making sure to avoid her eyes. She stood at about five-foot-six. Her hair was pulled back into a bun that displayed her long neck and impeccably clear tawny brown skin that damn near glowed.

She wore a navy blue pants suit that, while professional, did absolutely nothing to hide the small waistline, flared hips, and thick thighs many of the so-called models on Instagram had to go under the knife to achieve. One look at this woman and forget about alarm bells. An entire fucking orchestra of warning sounds exploded in my head.

That was when I looked at Lenny, who remained silent the whole time and finally I got it.

"That's a good one," I stated before bursting out in laughter. I laughed until my stomach muscles tensed up and tears sprung to my eyelids. "You almost fucking had me with that one."

I pulled the gloves I'd been wearing off and tossed them onto the pile of other gloves before moving around Lenny to head back to my office.

"I'm proud of you, Len. I didn't think you had it in you to prank me like that."

"Um, I don't."

"Hey, I don't know what you're thinking, but I'm not here as a joke," the woman added, obviously following behind the both of us.

I paused at the door of my office, spinning around, eyeing her. "Sweetheart, you wanna quit playing games and tell me what you're really here for?" It wasn't an anomaly for a groupie to show up at my gym under the guise of taking a class to find their way into my bed.

Chicks.

"I just told you. You need a new trainer, as evident by what your friend was just saying, and I'm a trainer."

Again, I observed her from head to toe, this time noting the high heels she wore.

"You want to be my trainer?"

She nodded.

I tilted my head to the side. "What are you really looking to train?"

Her forehead wrinkled as she looked between Lenny and me. Realization must've donned quickly because her eyes widened and she answered with, "Oh no, no, no." Shaking her head adamantly. "I'm really here to train you, Mr. McConnell. As in, for the cage.

Not anything else." She held out a piece of paper, but I simply stared at it in her hand.

"Do you have any experience training fighters?" Lenny inquired as if this was something more than a joke.

"Well… not as a head trainer but—"

"Pssh, doll, it's time for you to go."

"Wait, I know that didn't sound too convincing, but if you'll just look at my resumé."

"According to your own lips, you don't have any fucking experience. In case you didn't realize, I'm no up and coming fighter, looking for anybody to come along and train me for free or whatever you were hoping for."

"I'm well aware of your history and record, Mr. McConnell."

I didn't know why the hell her saying my name like that pissed me off, but it did.

"Good. Then you knew when you walked your ass in here you were most definitely not going to get the trainer job… or any other job you were looking for." I eyed her knowingly, because no way in hell did she come here looking to be my trainer.

"Look, I know my experience is light but what I lack in experience I can promise you I more than make up for in hustle and creativity. I—"

I grunted and turned to my desk, grabbing the three resumés that had been sitting on top of it for days. "You see these?" I held up the papers. "These are three top of the line trainers, begging me to take them on and give them a shot to train me. One of them is an Olympic gold medalist in boxing. Another has two heavyweight champions under his belt, and the third has trained fighters up and down the West Coast, but you want me to overlook these three for… you?"

She lifted her chin, looked me square in the eyes and replied, "Yes."

I'd taken a gut punch from Caldwell the night before that had less of an impact on me. Her one simple response from that full mouth with a beauty mark an inch above its right side, nearly knocked me the hell over.

However, I wasn't budging.

"Look, sweetheart, I don't know what type of games you're playing but I'm not in the damn mood." I brushed past her to head toward the boxing ring, needing to get some space between myself and this woman.

She followed me into the main space of the gym and into the boxing ring.

"Syd."

"What?" I questioned, turning to her, in spite of my better judgment.

"Syd. That's my name. In the..." She paused, checking the gold watch on her wrist. "Six minutes I've been here, you've called me sweetheart twice and doll once. Condescendingly so, I might add. And I'm sure other women you encounter enjoy the pet names and all, but my name is Syd. If we're going to be working together, you should get that straight right now."

"We're not going to be working together."

"Are you sure about that?"

I lifted my eyes to stare at Lenny over her head, sure this still had to be some kind of a joke, even though Lenny was the least funny person I knew. He gave me a blank stare, telling me he was as clueless as I was as to what was happening right then.

"Look, Luke. Can I call you Luke since I allowed you to call me by my first name? Thanks. Anyway, I'm sure those trainers you mentioned are great and all, but they don't have what it takes to train you, which is why their resumés were left sitting on your desk, idle. You haven't called any of them even with their stellar credentials. You know why?"

I parted my lips to ask why, but apparently this chick didn't need my permission to keep going.

"I'll tell you why, because none of them will tell you what your real problem is."

"And what the hell is my real problem?" I folded my arms across my chest.

"You're unfocused. The last eighteen months have been hard on you, I'm sure. It's spilled over into the cage. Your footwork could use some serious work, your grappling *definitely* needs improvement, you try to choke out sports reporters because you're bitter and it shows and…" She paused, looking over her shoulder to Lenny before turning back to me. "You're sort of an asshole. For some fighters the asshole vibe works in their favor. Not so much for you. Not if you're trying to get where you want."

"And where's that?" I asked with folded arms.

"To the top. The belt. You want the number one spot. You're holding yourself back."

I opened my mouth to give her a scathing response before I tossed her out of my gym on her ass, but nothing came out. Words failed me, even as I heard the smothered laughter coming from across the room. I glared at Lenny who covered his mouth with his fist, but the wrinkling around his eyes told me he found that shit funny.

"Get the hell out," I ordered.

Syd shrugged. "You still need some time to think about it. Not a problem. I'll be back tomorrow."

"Don't fucking bother."

"The day after tomorrow, I guess. That's not a problem, either. Besides, you probably haven't done any sort of ice bath or massage down after last night's fight, considering that minor encounter with the reporter after the fight. You'll need a day or two of rest. I'll be back, but I'll leave this with you."

I watched silently as she lowered the paper in her hand to the floor of the boxing ring she'd stepped in after me and then turned on her heels and headed out the door she entered through. I fought my base self not to let my gaze fall to watch the sway of her hips as she exited.

What the fuck was that?

"I think I like her," Lenny finally stated after nearly sixty seconds of pure silence.

I didn't say anything as my eyes remain locked on the now closed door, watching for what, I had no clue.

"Yeah? Well, let her train you," I finally responded to my long-time friend before heading into my office, slamming the door shut behind me. I could still hear Lenny's laughter as he picked up his belongings to head out.

Syd

"Good morning, Vince," I sing-songed, pushing through the glass doors of my office, feeling chipper with my extra-large black coffee in my hand.

Vince raised his head from his computer and a smile crossed his lips. "Good morning, Syd. How's your morning going so far?"

"I can't complain, but I still have that important call in about thirty minutes. Ask me again later."

Vince gave me a playful frown. "The NFA contract is going to go through seamlessly. I can feel it," he stated proudly.

"Let's hope," I responded a little more pessimistic than he was. While I knew my company, ParaSquad could deliver on everything we'd promised the National Fighting Association over the months of back and forth negotiations, I didn't trust anything until the documents were signed and the money had been exchanged.

"Did you have breakfast this morning? Tanisha brought in some scones and pastries from that place across the street you both love."

My eyes widened. "I was in a rush and forgot to get breakfast when I ordered my coffee this morning. Thanks for letting me know. Do I have any messages?"

"A few." Vince handed me the phone messages and I proceeded down the hallway toward the small kitchen and staff area.

The delicious smell of freshly baked pastries hit my nose as soon as I entered the room. I headed straight for the counter where Tanisha, my best friend and business partner had placed them. Opening one of the cupboards, I pulled out a small plate we kept on hand specifically for occasions such as this. Having skipped my breakfast and missed dinner due to the fact that I worked late the night before, I decided to go with the cherry, cheese-filled turnover. It was my favorite, but I only allowed myself to have it once or twice a month, otherwise I'd eat it daily.

"I see you sniffed out the baked goods."

Twirling around with the turnover in my mouth, I nodded at Tanisha who began laughing at me. Wiping my face with a napkin and swallowing my first bite, I responded. "Vince told me about them as soon as I arrived. I missed breakfast and am starving."

Tanisha raised a perfectly arched eyebrow. "You actually did it?" she questioned, folding her arms over her chest.

I rolled my eyes. "Have you ever known me to not do something I said I was going to do?"

She shook her head. "Not even senior year, when you said you were going to bribe Professor Michaels so you wouldn't have to take the final for our biochemistry class."

"Exactly. Of course, I went to McConnell's gym this morning."

"And how did it go?"

I lifted my chin, looking my best friend in the eye. "Better than expected."

She stared at me for a moment before doubling over in laughter. "Girl, he threw you out on your ass, didn't he?"

I sighed and waved Tanisha off, passing her with my plate in one hand and coffee in the other to head to my office. Naturally, Tanisha followed me because she's not one to drop the subject easily.

"Did he call the police to kick you out or did you go peacefully?" She joked as I sat down behind my desk.

I didn't answer as I pressed the button to boot up my desktop before continuing to eat my pastry.

"No, of course the cops weren't called. You would've called me with your one phone call to come bail you out," my best friend concluded, sitting in the chair across from me.

I frowned, swallowing my second bite. "I don't think that's how it works."

Tanisha shrugged as she sat back in the chair across from me, crossing her legs. Unlike me, Tanisha opted to dress in a more casual look for work. She wore our black polo-style short-sleeved shirt with our company name ParaSquad across the left breast. The 'Q' formed the caduceus sign, making up our company's logo. She matched the shirt with a pair of blue jeans and flat Vans shoes, her typical style.

Tanisha and I were both former paramedics who once had dreams of going to medical school after college. However, our interests changed, and she completed her Master's in Public Health, while I went on to get my MBA. Together, after grad school and dissatisfied with our jobs, we put our heads together and formed ParaSquad. A company that hired part-time paramedics to work local, state, and even some national fairs, concerts, and sporting events. Basically, anywhere large crowds gather and there's a potential for injury.

Our list of clients included everything from local 5k walks and runs to citywide marathons, collegiate sporting events such as basketball and football games, and soon, if all worked out, we'd have a three year contract with the NFA to work all its city fights, which would serve to increase our annual revenue by a third.

"Have you thought about the possible conflict of interest if, by some miracle, McConnell actually takes you on as his trainer?"

I tilted my head to the side. "Obviously you have."

"We're about to sign a contract with the NFA to work their events for the next three years, correct?"

I nodded. "Assuming all goes well."

"Let's assume that it does. How is it going to look with you running not only the emergency services component for the local NFA fights, but also training one of its top fighters?"

I shook my head, dismissing her argument. "Of course, I've considered it, Tanisha. There's no conflict. ParaSquad will mainly be working to ensure the safety of the spectators and guests of the arena. The fighters have their own team they bring with them to fights to see to their health concerns. If, by some chance, we have to step in to aid a fighter, our staff is trained to do so. If I'm there and need to assist a fighter if they get injured, I will have no compunction in doing so. No conflict whatsoever."

Tanisha eyed me carefully. "Have you spoken to Randy about this?"

"Yes," I responded, assuring Tanisha that I had sought out the counsel of our company's attorney on the matter.

"Okay… I'm not trying to get sued."

"Nor am I."

My friend eyed me. "Did you watch the fight last night?"

I nodded. "After I got in. He lost to Caldwell." I sighed, frowning.

"You sure you want to train this guy? He's lost how many fights in a row, now?"

"Only two, but only the last one counts against his official record."

She shrugged. "Sounds washed up to me."

"Don't say that," I replied, feeling strangely defensive of Luke. "He's a hothead and his grappling sucks, to be honest, but he's not done."

"How do you know?"

Shaking my head, I let out a breath. "The man's got a chip on his shoulder. He lost his head trainer two years ago and has had a hard time since. They were together since his debut." My heartstrings tug, thinking about what Luke must be feeling after the loss. I can only speculate, but they seemed close.

"I'll take your word for it," Tanisha said.

"Do that," I replied before taking the final bite of my pastry. I closed my eyes and whimpered, willing myself not to go back and get another. "These are so damn good. That's the second time I've had one this month. Time to cut myself off."

Tanisha sucked her teeth and waved me off. "Girl, as much as you work out, why are you even stressing about a little pastry?"

"Easy for you to say, Miss. Can Eat Whatever She Wants and Not Gain Weight. Even with a five day a week gym habit, it's a struggle for me to remain in these size twelve clothes."

"Whatever," she says, rising from her seat. "You want to complain about all that thickness, give me some. God was rude as hell when he was giving out ass and thighs the day I was born."

I laughed at my friend. "Aww, Nish… lil' booties matter too," I joked.

"If we weren't at work, I'd curse you out. Let me go to my office. I have a call to make before our conference call."

I nodded and took a sip of my coffee before turning to my desktop to open up my emails. Checking the clock, I noted we still had another twenty minutes before our meeting with the NFA team who'd been working on our contract. I went over all the notes I'd prepared, the contract they'd sent over, as well as printouts of the latest emails that'd been sent between the NFA, Tanisha, and myself to have everything at my disposal during this meeting.

By the time that was finished, I still had another ten minutes to kill. Somehow, I found myself pulling up the website to the main sports news outlet and looking up articles and write ups on the previous night's NFA fights. The results of the fight between Luke McConnell and Ronaldo Lee Caldwell had made the front page.

Many of the reports implied he was washed up, same as Tanisha had. I knew better. McConnell wasn't washed up. He needed the right people in his corner, the right trainer, and I was the woman for the job.

CHAPTER FOUR

You Got the Job

Syd

I woke up in an extremely good mood. The day before Tanisha and I sealed the deal with the NFA, ensuring yet another long-term revenue stream for our company. I was certain I had the answer to Luke McConnell's problems. I only had to convince him of it. Lucky for me, I was great at talking and negotiating.

Pushing the sky-blue bed linens off of my body, I peered at the clock, noting it was five twenty-six am.

"Perfect," I murmured to myself, standing from my canopy bed and reaching my arms overhead for my first stretch of the morning. Moaning, I flexed the muscles of my neck and back one way and then the other, waking my body up and preparing it for the workout I was about to put it through.

While brushing my teeth and then changing into my workout clothes, I strategized how I wanted to approach McConnell that morning. I seriously doubted he'd taken a look at the resumé I left the day before. Though, that might be a good thing. Admittedly, I didn't have much experience in training other fighters at his level, but I meant what I said about making up for my lack of experience in hustle and creativity. Plus, Luke needed someone and something outside of the box.

I contemplated all of this while driving the five minutes to the gym right up the block from my house. I took my usual sixty-minute body pump class, and then headed back home to get ready for the day. This time, I didn't skip breakfast since, if all went according to plan, I'd have a few hours at Luke's going over my training strategy with him. I was hoping to at least finagle my way into a tryout session with him. Then I could demonstrate what I knew about his sport, training, and specifically what his needs were.

By the time I finished dressing in a pair of black dress pants that stopped just above the ankle, fully displaying the mauve colored stilettos that matched the short sleeved, satin top I'd tucked into my pants, I was ready. Giving myself one final look over, I grabbed my black handbag that carried my work laptop, tablet, planners and other important files I needed and headed out to my garage.

Piling all of my belongings into the backseat of my Porsche SUV, I then got into the driver's seat and pulled out, heading in the direction of Peak Performance Martial Arts, Luke's gym. The same one he owned and trained at. The gym was about a thirty-minute drive from my place, especially with this southern California traffic.

I pulled into the back of the strip mall where the gym was located, and got out, walking around the front. A few minutes later, I spotted Luke approaching the front door to unlock it. Rushing to nearly a run but making sure I remained as quiet as possible, I closed in on him.

"Hey."

Quickly, I jumped back as Luke spun around, fists in the air.

Folding my arms across my chest, I smirked. "Good. Quick reflexes. All's not lost with you."

He narrowed his dark syrup eyes. A frown marred his face, evident even underneath that thick brunette beard of his.

"You again. You're like herpes, never fucking go away."

"Thank you." I grinned.

"That wasn't a..." He broke off, shaking his head before turning back to the door and pushing it open.

The door nearly slammed in my face. Without some fast reflexes of my own, it would've. Yet, I quickly grabbed the doorhandle before it shut, allowing me to follow him inside.

About halfway to his office he paused and turned to me.

"I didn't invite you in."

I shrugged. "If I waited for an invite, I'd be waiting all day. I don't have that kind of time and neither do you."

"What I don't have time for is more of your bullshit. What the hell do you want?"

"I've already told you what I want, but it's not about what I want, it's about what you need."

He raised one dark brow. "What I need," he repeated, folding his arms over his chest. I nodded. "And what is that exactly?"

"Me." I hold out my arms wide as if the answer was obvious.

He rolled his eyes and turned away from me, heading in the direction of his office. "I don't like women." He waved a dismissive hand in the air.

"It doesn't matter to me that you're gay."

He halted abruptly, spinning around to face me, his face stormy. "I'm not fucking gay."

"Oh, you're not?" I questioned, a surprised expression covering my face.

His lips firmed and his nostrils flared, and a small bubble of satisfaction rose in my belly. For some reason, it felt good to rattle him a little.

"Get the hell out."

I shook my head and continued following him as he turned on his heels in the direction of his office, flicking on the lights of the gym.

"You tried that yesterday and it didn't work. Say, did you get any sort of ice bath or massage work done since we last spoke?"

"What? Why?"

"Because as your trainer, I need to know these things. I'm certain you're well aware of the need to properly take care of your body after putting it through such a grueling activity. You don't need me to tell you that."

His frown deepened. "Go back to the part about you being my trainer."

"As your trainer—"

"Yeah see, that's the part that doesn't work for me." He pushed past me and headed in the direction of the punching bags, but I followed.

"Well, seeing as how you don't have any other head trainers and—"

"Did I say you were like herpes a few minutes ago?" He spun around asking.

"I believe you did."

"I was wrong. You're more like a boil on the bottom of an ass that refuses to get better until it abscesses, and you have to go into the fucking ER to get it treated."

I folded my arms over my chest. "Now, I do believe *that* was an insult."

"You catch on quickly."

He turned and began straightening up the pads that had been left on the floor around the crates they belonged in.

"Quicker than most. Which is why I know you're going to be taking me on as your trainer. And the sooner the better. You're in negotiations to do that Rodriguez fight in six months, right?"

He paused, finally lifting his head to stare at me. "Just because you know a little about the fighting world, doesn't mean you're cut out to be a trainer, sweetheart."

"And now we're back to the pet names."

"See? And offended easily. The last fucking thing I need is a trainer who'll pop up and sue me for sexual harassment or some bullshit like that because they couldn't take being called sweetheart one too many times."

"Then you won't hire me because I'm a woman and you don't know how to control yourself around women?"

"That's not what the hell I meant." He tossed the boxing pad in his hand into the black crate.

"Sure sounded like that's what you meant. Also sounds like something Harvey Weinstein would say."

"Don't you dare compare me to that fucker." Luke charged, angrily, pointing his finger at me.

I held up my hands. "Wouldn't think of it."

Slowly he lowered his hand, glaring at me before turning and heading to the other side of the gym.

"You're still following me," he said over his shoulder.

"Indeed I am. We need to work out your training schedule. I notice you've been taking on about five or six fights per year over the past two years. Frankly, for someone of your experience and at your level, I think that's way too many fights. We'll likely have to cut the amount of fights in half, so that you can have more time to train and recover, and—"

"Why are you still talking like this is a done deal?"

I slumped my shoulders and pushed out a heavy breath. "Tell me something? Did you ever call any of those trainers you were bragging about yesterday, who are beating down your door to train you?"

The narrowing of his eyes told me his answer before his lips even parted.

"I was busy."

"I'm sure. The truth is you don't want to take on a new trainer. You're pissed you have to, but you do. That's just the reality of it." The entire NFA world knew Luke's trainer of more than a decade had died nearly eighteen months ago. Since then, he'd been training himself and it wasn't working out for him.

"You know what they say about people who try to represent themselves in court?"

"Of course, I do."

"They have a fool for a lawyer."

"I said I fucking knew what the saying is."

"It's the same for any fighter who tries to train himself. You think you know all there is to be taught, or what's good for your body, but you don't. It's my job as the trainer to be up on the latest research about recovery, best ways to enhance your workouts and build the type of body that will withstand the grueling three rounds inside the cage, five if we're aiming for the championship bout. Which we definitely are. I know all of that. It's my job to collaborate with you and help reign you in when you're going too far or push you when you're getting lazy. Right now, you're spinning your wheels and while it hasn't cost you much except a few fights, soon enough you'll be losing ground. And do I even need to get into your poor groundwork?"

Luke stood there, arms folded over his broad chest, staring at me for a few uncomfortable heartbeats. My mind told me to keep talking, to keep using my words to persuade him I was the right person for this job, but I bit my tongue to keep my mouth from opening. Words wouldn't suffice in this situation. Luke was a fighter, a man of action. If I talked too much, I could talk myself right out of this position.

"How old are you?"

Tilting my head to the side, I replied, "You know it's rude to ask a woman her age?"

"How old?"

"Thirty-one."

He snorted. "Young as shit to be a head trainer."

I nodded, knowing he was right. Most NFA fighters had head trainers who were in their fifties or even sixties.

"Young in years but old in spirit," I said, grinning and wiggling my eyebrows.

"You talk a lot of shit," he said. "What're your top five fights of all time?"

"What?"

"Top five fights. List 'em. Off the top of your head."

"Uh," I stuttered, caught off my game. "I never stopped to think to rank them."

He sucked his teeth. "Exactly. Full of it. You came in here with a few one-liners you read off the internet about my fighting and thought you could pull some slick shit over on me."

"Sugar Ray Leonard versus Thomas Hearns in '81; Ali versus Frazier in '75 is a classic; Diaz versus McGregor back in 2016; Definitely can't leave out Royce Gracie versus Gerard Gordeau in '93, the fight that utterly changed the sport of MMA. Lastly, my own personal favorite is Chael Sonnen versus Anderson Silva back in 2010. That one was a thing of beauty. I still can't believe Silva was able to pull that one out. I go back to it—"

"Enough," he said, cutting me off. "You've watched some fights. Cute. Doesn't mean jack shit where training comes into play."

"It does mean I know fighting styles."

"Fine." He shrugged and then pushed past me.

"Great, I think we—" I stopped when the front door of the gym opened. A younger man wearing a pair of black gi pants and a black T-shirt that read 'Peak Performance Martial Arts' entered.

"Morning, Luke, ma'am." He waved at both Luke and me.

Luke nodded and I smiled at him before turning back to Luke. "We'll have to start by coming up with a schedule."

"Hang on, I never said you had the job."

"But you just said fine. I assumed that meant I was hired."

"Never assume, sweetheart. You want to be my head trainer?"

"Yes, that's what I'm here for."

"Cool. Greyson," Luke called and waved over the guy who'd just walked in. He placed a hand on his shoulder.

"Greyson here is one of Peak Performance's newest instructors. Well versed in self-defense and is a black belt in karate. Any good trainer should know how to fight themselves. You want to be my trainer. Last two rounds on the mat with Greyson."

My eyes bulged. "Are you serious?"

"As a heart attack, sugar."

I frowned. "We're really going to have to do something about you and these pet names."

"Last two rounds and you might get the opportunity to try... sugar." He winked at me condescendingly. The glint in his eyes told me he knew he had me with this proposition. He obviously expected me to back down. Clearly, he had no idea who I was.

Right then, I kicked off my heels and strolled across the gym to the area where the large blue mats were set up.

"Greyson, was it? Let's get this over with since I've got a fighter to start training," I called across the room, noticing both men looking somewhat stunned. Greyson more so than Luke.

"Ma'am, I don't think is a good idea."

"Please call me, Syd. You'll get used to seeing my face around here soon enough."

Greyson narrowed his eyes for a brief moment. "Luke, what the hell?" He questioned, looking bewildered.

"You heard the lady. She wants to be my trainer. And since she won't go the hell away, I've decided to see if she's worthy of the position."

Greyson turned back to me. "You're serious?"

"As a heart attack. I last two rounds with you, and I've got a new job. Let's get started, huh? We've all got work to do. Luke, make sure you keep time."

"This is bullshit," Greyson mumbled.

"Giving orders already," Luke grumbled. "Just like a fucking woman."

I shook my head, turning to my opponent. He didn't look too happy to be going up against me. "Let's get this started."

"Your call. The sooner we get this over with the better."

"If you want to keep your job, don't go easy on her, either," Luke insisted.

"Please, don't go easy on me," I repeated.

"And... fight," Luke called at the same time the buzzer on his phone went off, signaling the beginning of a round.

With a focused gaze, Greyson moved in quickly with a side kick. I easily avoided the strike but caught his leg and brought him to the ground. "Ah," he yelped and grunted, trying to get out of my hold.

Lucky for him, I was in a forgiving mood and let him up without pinning him. Once he rose, I nodded and watched his midsection to see what direction he would move in. When he shifted right, I went left, and vice versa.

Moving in closer, I pushed at Greyson to throw him off his center of balance. That worked and he quickly came back at me with a move of his own, which was exactly what I wanted. When he lifted his leg in an attempt at a leg sweep. I shifted my body, hooked my leg under his and grabbed one of his arms, pulling him forward until he hit the ground.

Again, I let him up. A mask of anger blanketed his face. The looks of it told me he hadn't anticipated this beatdown. I smirked and tossed him a wink.

Moving with greater purpose this time, Greyson went in for a punch. Again, I used his body's leverage to throw him off balance, and soon enough he went crashing to the ground. With that, I landed a jab to his stomach. Not a hard one, just something to let him know it wasn't all fun and games.

Before I knew it, the buzzer signaling the end of the five-minute round went off.

"You fucking took it easy on her," Luke bemoaned.

I laughed in the face of his frustration. "You obviously didn't read the resumé I left with you yesterday. I've done more than read a few articles and watched a couple of fights. Fifth dan black belt in Judo with over fifteen years of mixed martial arts training. I talk a lot of shit because I can back it up, Luke." I winked again. "I'm not new to this. Hey, Greyson, ready for that second round?" I called, still laughing.

Greyson didn't respond as he stood at the center of the mat looking pissed. I laughed some more. Most men had a rough time being bested by a woman.

"If I'd known I was going to end up fighting this morning, I would've worn something a little different," I commented, laughter still in my voice as I turned to Luke. He didn't say anything as he moved from the mat to his office. I followed and leaned against his office doorway. I watched him for a minute before I said, "Guess that means I'll be seeing a lot of you. We'll get started tomorrow since you're obviously in shock over it all. Bright and early tomorrow at seven a.m."

"I don't get here until eight thirty most days."

"Well now, it's seven since we have to train before I go into work."

He frowned, his forehead wrinkling in confusion. "Work? Ain't that what this is? Your new job?"

I shrugged. "This, yes, but I also own my own business. Anyway, see ya' in the morning. Wear comfortable clothing," I told him, eyeing the dark T-shirt and jeans he wore.

I grinned again when his response was an irritated grunt.

"Oh hey?"

"What?"

"What's your favorite fight? I told you mine."

"Thrilla in Manila, '75," he answered, not even looking in my direction.

I nodded and pushed away from the door. "It is a classic. See ya' later, Greyson," I called as I padded across the gym floor on my bare feet to get the heels I'd stepped out of earlier. Strolling out of the gym, I felt like I was ten feet tall, having gotten the position I wanted so badly. But now, the real work began. I needed to follow through on all my bravado.

Luke

"Hey, was that that Syd woman from yesterday, I saw pulling out of the parking lot as I came in?" Lenny questioned as he stood in the doorway of my office.

"I don't know, Len, since I wasn't out there with you and I don't have fucking x-ray vision. I don't know who you saw, pulling out of the lot," I snarked.

Lenny frowned in the way he always does when I give him one of my smartass answers, which was pretty frequently.

"Anyone told you you're a jackass lately?"

"Not in the last…" I paused to look up at the clock. "Twelve hours. That also could be because I haven't spoken to very many people in the last eleven and a half hours, either."

"Consider yourself told. Asshole," he mumbled.

"I'll jot it down in my fucking calendar."

"Anyway, what was she doing back here? You didn't… did you?" He frowned.

I cut my eyes in his direction as he moved inside my office, shutting the door. "No, I didn't. Not that it's any business of yours."

The fucker actually had a nerve to let out a sigh of relief.

"I hired her as my trainer. I think."

Lenny was silent for a heartbeat before he said, "That's great."

I wasn't surprised by his reaction. He'd made it clear the day before when she first showed up, he was a fan of hers. But I wanted to yell at him to fuck off because the very thought of working with Syd had me feeling off balance. The absolute last thing any fighter wanted was to feel like they weren't on solid footing, or they couldn't orient themselves. In a fight it could mean total disaster. In life outside of the cage, the consequences were the same.

"Yeah, whatever. I'm sure Syd will quit after a week anyway."

"Syd?" Lenny questioned.

I frowned as I gave him a scathing look. "Yeah, that's her damn name." He'd just used it himself. "Shit Len, I'm the one who's been getting knocked in the head all these years, don't tell me you're already losing your shit, going senile or whatever the hell is happening."

He shook his head. "I'm just surprised. I can count on one hand the number of times I've heard you call a woman by her actual name."

I glared at him, giving him a dumbass expression because he couldn't be accurate. "Get out of here, man."

"I'm serious. What was the name of that woman you took home after the Caldwell fight?"

"Who, Legs?"

"See? You don't even know her name."

I opened my mouth to argue because I knew I'd ordered the chick an Uber and had to put her name in the app for that, hadn't I? The words never came as I recalled that I'd indeed forgotten her actual name as soon as I'd heard it.

"And the woman you were dating for a few months last year. You introduced me to her on three different occasions, never using her real name. Instead you referred to her as—"

"T&A." I chuckled, remembering the tits and ass on that one. Couldn't remember her name either, although I did know it started with a C or a K.

"And then there were all the women in college and since you started fighting who got some kind of nickname, mainly based on some part of their anatomy, I might add."

"Yeah, yeah, I get it." I waved him off, turning back to my desk.

"Yeah well, so for you to refer to a woman by her actual name speaks volumes."

I dropped the pen I'd picked up and turned to Lenny. "It doesn't say shit except that I decided to give her a shot at being my trainer. That's it." I wouldn't go around calling anyone on my staff Legs or T&A or any bullshit like that.

"If you say so."

"I fucking say so."

"You really hired her?"

I rocked my head back at the same time Lenny stepped away from the door, allowing me to see Greyson standing behind him. My defenses alerted at the bass he had in his voice.

"What the hell is it to you?"

He raised his eyebrows and a contrite expression covered his face. "Nothing," he answered, shrugging. "I just don't think she has the experience you need."

"Kid, opinions are like assholes. Everybody's got one."

"I just meant—"

"Yeah, whatever. Don't you have a class to teach?" I turned my head, looking up at the clock.

"I'm going," he mumbled before walking off.

"The hell is that about?"

Lenny laughed. "You know he was angling for the head trainer position since you hired him."

"And he fucking knew that position wasn't available to him." I'd made that clear since the day he started. Greyson might've been able to take on some aspects of my training, but he lacked the overall skill I needed in a trainer. His performance against Syd minutes before proved it. I needed a grappler and Syd had swiftly taken down a man twice her size without breaking a sweat.

"Anyway, man, I got a call back from Rodriguez's people." Lenny began, changing the topic. "They're really interested in pursuing this fight. From the sponsor calls we're getting you could easily walk away from this fight banking at least two million. That's even if you don't win."

"Why the hell would you tell me the amount for losing?" I turned sharply toward Lenny, glaring at him.

He held up his hands. "I'm just saying, even if you don't win this fight that's still a nice number to walk away with."

"What the fuck ever," I said. Before I could say anything else my phone rang, and I lifted it from my desk.

PITA.

"Fuck off, very much," I grumbled, hitting the ignore button and tossing my phone, facedown onto the desk.

"You're going to have to buy another one of those soon if you keep tossing it around like that," Lenny warned, tilting his head in the direction of the phone.

"Hey, Lenny, the next time you want to warn me about something, remember I don't give a shit."

He laughed as he turned for the door taking my comments in stride.

"What are you thinking about this Rodriguez fight?" he questioned while standing in the doorway. "Should I give them the go ahead or not?"

I lifted my gaze and stared out at the rest of my gym. Some of the instructors for the day had already begun trickling in along with a few of our students. Parting my lips, I went to tell Lenny yes, to give them the green light but what came out was, "I need to discuss it with my trainer, first."

I ignored the shocked whistle he let out.

It'd been two years since I'd made that statement, but Syd's comments about me taking on too many fights lately replayed in my mind. I wasn't fully convinced she knew her stuff yet, but she might've been on the mark about me overextending myself.

"All right, I'll put Rodriguez's people off with a 'maybe' for now."

I nodded, not really giving a fuck either way. Rodriguez and his people could wait.

Len left and I was about to get started on the paperwork I needed to do when my phone buzzed again.

"For fuck's sake Pit," I groaned as I turned the phone over, but suddenly stopped. This wasn't Pit calling yet again.

"Shouldn't you be cutting some broad open and inserting saline balloons into her tits?"

Jacob chuckled on the other end. It was a sound I hadn't heard in… maybe ever.

"That's not quite how I'd describe my job."

"It's close enough," I retorted. Jacob, my older brother was a plastic surgeon. A very good one by all accounts. While he and I hadn't spoken at all since he'd left when I was around twelve years old, we'd recently reconnected. My hold on the phone tightened as I thought about how and where we'd done so.

"I'm opening up my practice."

I snorted. "No shit, first you go and lock yourself down with one woman for the rest of your life and now opening a business," I murmured, sounding bored.

"Sort of like I'm actually building a life or something."

I gritted my teeth for some reason. "Next, you'll be having kids."

"That's not happening." His tone was sharp.

"Hope your wife is okay with that," I mocked.

"She's more than okay with it."

"Good for you. When's the opening?"

"A few weeks. I'd like you to attend."

"I need to dust off my tux again?" Grace and Jacob had married a few months earlier. I was one of the only attendees, aside from Grace's sister and parents.

"Won't be that big. A few people from Grace's family and some co-workers, namely those who like Grace."

I let out a laugh. "What's the matter, bro? Co-workers can't handle your sparkling personality?"

He snorted. "Not so much."

"Tell me the time and place and I'll be there."

I didn't need him to explain why I was the only person he was related to that was invited to this opening. Saying our family dynamics were a little fucked up was like saying the effects of climate change were a minor inconvenience.

"The end of next month. Here in Williamsport at the office and we're making reservations for lunch at one of Grace's favorite restaurants on the Riverwalk afterwards. I'll have to call you with the exact date."

"Low key. I can respect it. Count me in."

He cleared his throat on the other end, and I got the feeling he was gearing up to say something.

"Just spit it out, Jacob."

"Thank you for coming."

I cleared my throat. "Yeah, don't mention it."

I smirked at the pause on the other end of the phone, knowing how uncomfortable my brother must've been feeling. Neither one of us had a sensitive bone in our bodies. At least, I hadn't thought so, but the more I found out about my brother, the more I reconsidered that notion.

Especially since I saw the look in his eyes whenever he spoke about his wife. I'd formally met her the day before their wedding, but that wasn't our first encounter. She was there the first time I'd seen my brother in person since I was a teenager. Unfortunately, she'd almost gotten in the middle of my swinging on him. It hadn't dawned on me until much later, Jacob hadn't even tried to fight back against my punches, until I called his lady a bitch. That was when his whole demeanor had changed.

I wasn't one for happily ever afters or sappy, bullshit endings, but if Jacob was happy, I wouldn't be the one to remind him that shit never lasted. Let him find out for himself.

CHAPTER FIVE

Pain in the Ass

Luke

As soon as I turned into the parking lot to my gym, I spotted her car, parked in the usual empty space. I took my time gathering my belongings, which consisted of my gym bag, gloves, pre-workout shake and an extra bottle of water from the passenger seat. Stuffing everything except the shake into the bag, I finally exited the car, slamming the door shut and locking it before strolling toward the gym's entrance. Once I rounded the corner, I found her leaning against the gym door, one leg crossed over the other as if she had no other place she'd rather be.

"You know I'm going to need a key, right?"

Pausing, I looked her over with a wrinkle in my brow. "For what?"

"To set up before you get here so we don't waste unnecessary time. That fight with Rodriguez is in six months."

"I haven't agreed to that fight," I reminded her as I entered the gym, leaving the door to close behind me as I always did. If Syd hadn't been hot on my heels it would've slammed in her face.

Moving around me, she stopped directly in front of me. "I've been watching video on him. You're doing the fight."

I raised an eyebrow.

"It's a great opportunity, worth a lot of money, and most importantly, you want the title. This is a title fight."

"How the hell do you know what I want?"

She didn't respond. Instead, she folded her arms over her chest, observing me with a half smile on those fucking full lips of hers, and that damn beauty mark. After thinking about it, longer than I should've, I realized that it wasn't one of those makeup beauty marks either. It was real.

If I were to give her a nickname as I did with most women, it would've been lips. Or maybe, eyes. I did my best every time I came face to face with her not to stare into them for too long. Better yet, her nickname would be Medusa.

"What'd you have for breakfast this morning?" she suddenly asked, jolting me back to the moment.

I held up the cup with my pre-workout in it. "This is my breakfast, darlin'."

She frowned.

"What did I tell you about those damn pet names?" Her eyes narrowed as she glared at me.

Medusa. Definitely Medusa.

"I wouldn't hold your breath."

Stunned, I spun on my heels to face the doorway.

"Aw hell," I cursed at the new intruder. "I need to start locking that fucking door behind me."

"Not before you give me a key," Syd commented. "And who's this?" She questioned moving to my side, staring at the man in front of us.

"Not sure that's any of your business. Who are you?"

"Syd. His new trainer." She grinned and stuck out her hand to shake.

Pit lifted his eyebrows in surprise as he let his eyes roam over to meet mine. A smirk played at his lips.

"Oh, this should be interesting. Name's Pit, but I'm not touching you. My woman gets one whiff of you on me and she'll cut us both. Not in the mood for that shit today, but I hope like hell you know what you're getting yourself into with this one."

Syd turned to me. "I hope so, too."

I cut my attention from her back to Pit without responding. "The hell are you doing here?"

"What the fuck did you think was going to happen? Your number hasn't changed and you're not dead, so here the fuck I am."

I grunted and then motioned with my head for Pit to follow me. I took exactly three steps before stopping abruptly and turning to look over my shoulder. "You, don't follow. Keep your ass right there."

Syd shrugged. "I need to set up out here anyway. Pit, I'm sure whatever you need to discuss with my fighter is important, but I need you to make it quick. We've got training to do."

Pit frowned before turning back to me. He folded his arms across his chest and grumbled to himself. "His trainer, not mine. Let's dial that down."

I started for my office, followed by Pit, shutting the door behind me once he entered. I took a seat in my chair, pushing to lean back with my hands crossed behind my head, staring at him.

"Thanks for the offer, but I'll stand."

I shrugged. "The floor's available."

"Sniffle my balls, you queef."

"Takes one to know one."

"You lose your damn phone?"

I plucked my phone from out of my bag and pulled up the missed call list, turning it to him.

"She's right here."

"Who the hell is PITA?"

I grinned. "Stands for Pain in the Ass."

He shook his head and gave me the finger.

"You hired a new trainer." He stared out the window, watching Syd as she moved mats around. I noticed how she'd kicked out of the four inch stilettos she'd worn. But when I cut my gaze back to Pit to see him still observing her, something in my stomach heated.

"You come here to stare at tits and ass all day or did you need something?" I snapped.

He turned back to me with surprise in his eyes, tilted his head and laughed. "Is that jealousy I detect?"

"I wouldn't know jealousy if that bitch ran up and kicked me in the ass. Damn sure not over a fucking woman. Especially not one I work with."

He snorted. "If you say so."

"I say so."

"Yeah, well then you might want to take her advice and watch those pet names like she said. Damn sexual harassment suit waiting to happen."

I grunted. "You sound like Len."

"What's he up to these days?"

"Still breathing. Still my lawyer and manager."

"Hm."

"Now what the hell are you here for?"

"I can't drop by to see an old friend?"

"We're friends?"

"I'm still questioning myself on this. Yeah, we're fucking friends. Speaking of friendships." He moved to pull something out of the back pocket of his jeans and stepped forward, tossing it on my desk.

"What's this?" I questioned, peering up at him from the paper that had a date written on it.

"That is the date you're to have your ass in Vegas for my bachelor party."

I lifted an eyebrow. "No shit," I stated, sitting back against my chair, again folding my hands at the back of my head. "Who's the lucky lady? Do I know her?"

His grin widened. "As if you don't know it's Skittles."

I laughed. "No shit. How is Taste the Rainbow these days?"

His eyes narrowed. "You know if you were anybody else, I'd kick your ass for calling her that."

"But I'm not anybody else and you wouldn't dream of threatening a professional NFA fighter, would you?" I squinted, giving him an I double dog dare you look.

"Fucking asshole."

"Got the tattoo to prove it." I patted my chest.

"Hm." He grunted and moved on as if I haven't spoken. "Speaking of fucked up career moves, what the hell is wrong with you lunging at that reporter?"

"Now, we finally come to the real point of this impromptu drop-in."

"First, your ass owes me for the flight. That's a round trip ticket. Ass face, next time answer your fucking phone. What the hell, Luke? You know your ass can get kicked out of the Association for shit like that."

"They're not about to kick me out." I dismissed his warning with a shake of my head.

"And what if they do? This isn't the first time you let that hot-headed temper get the best of you with a reporter."

"Suddenly I'm the only one with a hot head?"

"Nope, but it takes one to know one, remember? We don't let one another fuck up where it matters most."

I clenched my teeth because what the hell was I supposed to say to that? Pit was right, but I hated admitting it, so I shut the fuck up.

"Look, get your shit together, man. Hopefully, this new trainer…" He paused as his gaze slowly moved to the window staring again at Syd. "Will kick your ass back into shape."

"You've got a real fucking way with words, Pit." I stood, glaring at him.

He snorted and chuckled at the same time. "I do, don't I. You better be there. She wants it." He nodded at the paper on my desk.

I picked up the paper, along with one of the push pins I kept in a holder on my desk and pinned it to the corkboard that hung on the wall.

"If it's on the board, it's as good as done."

Pit nodded. "Keep your ass out of trouble and your nose clean in the meantime."

"The fuck is the fun in that?" I grunted. "Hey, you spoken to Kelex lately?"

He looked at me with that same forlorn look all of us got when that subject was brought up.

"I'll take that as a no. He showed up at a fight of mine last year. That was the last time I've seen him."

Pit nodded. "Skittles knows how to find his ass. I'll reel him in."

I nodded, knowing he would.

The pit in my stomach grew as I thought over how long it'd been since I'd been back to Vander City to hang with Pit and the rest of the crew. Maybe it was time to make a trip back to catch up with Pit, Skittles, Deacon, Tak, and maybe even Kelex. If his ass would quit acting like a bitch and show his damn face.

Pit headed out the door. I didn't bother following, but my eyes narrowed when I watched him saunter over to where Syd was still setting up, pausing to talk to her.

Something rose in my chest, causing me to glare at both of them. Typically, I could care less about most conversations that didn't concern me. Yet I found myself questioning what the hell he was saying to her.

Syd

I watched as both men strolled in the direction of Luke's office. They didn't look alike at all, but there was a certain type of similarity there. I couldn't put my finger on it, and I forced myself to not even think about it. This was my first day at this job and I needed to prove to myself I hadn't bitten off more than I could chew.

Stepping out of the heels I wore, I proceeded to size up the entire space of the gym, figuring out where to set up what I needed and how to do so. Once I heard the door shut to Luke's office, I padded across the floor to the crates that held the punching pads and mitts. Carrying those to the mats along with a speed jump rope and timer, I placed them down at the center.

Pulling out my phone, I busied myself by going over the workout I had designed for Luke that day along with sending a text message to a nutritionist I knew. I suspected Luke would need a new meal plan, and somehow, I also knew he'd be resistant when I told him as much.

I heard the door to Luke's office open but didn't pay much attention until I felt someone standing behind me. Turning, I was surprised to find not Luke, but the guy introduced as Pit standing over me. His expression was unreadable. I started to look toward Luke's office window, but I didn't want to break eye-contact with Pit. It seemed as if he was searching for some sort of weakness.

"You better know what you're doing."

I scowled in annoyance and confusion. "I wouldn't have taken on this job if I didn't know what I was doing."

He snorted. "Yeah, just make sure you didn't take it on for other reasons."

Slamming my hands on my hips, I questioned, "What other reason would that be?"

"I'm sure you know what I'm talking about."

Pit lowered his eyes to the fists I made at my sides before rising to meet mine again.

"Take care of him." He looked back over his shoulder toward Luke who stared at us through the window. Luke didn't bother trying to hide it either. Pit nodded at Luke before giving me a final look and then headed toward the exit. I watched him walk away before turning back to Luke who was, surprisingly, eyeing me. Unlike Pit, Luke's face was completely readable. His expression said annoyed as he lifted from his chair and came back out to the main area of the gym.

"For that interruption, you owe me an extra twenty minutes," I declared. His scowl deepened. "As I was trying to ask you earlier, what's your daily diet consist of?"

"Are we really doing this?"

"Yes. It's important to your training."

He rolled his eyes.

"Be careful before they get stuck like that," I teased, but Luke's entire body stilled.

"What did you just say?"

I shrugged. "Just something someone used to say to me. About the diet?" I looked at him, expectantly.

"Typically, I'll drink a pre-workout before my morning session, followed by a breakfast of eggs, bacon, and half an avocado if I feel like it."

"No doubt it's not low sodium bacon or at least the kind without nitrates and all the garbage in it."

"That other shit tastes horrible."

I shook my head. "Knew it." At the same time, I made that declaration my phone buzzed in my pocket. I smiled as I read the message. "That's your new nutritionist now."

"My new what?"

"Nutritionist. Don't tell me you haven't worked with one before."

He shook his head. "Never needed one."

"Or so you think. We have a meeting with him later this week. For now, let's get started."

"Whatever," Luke grumbled as he removed the V-neck T-shirt he'd been wearing, tossing it to the ground.

Briefly, I let my eyes graze over the many tattoos that covered his chest and arms. A shiver ran through my body, before I pulled my attention back to the timer in my hand. I shook off whatever that feeling had been and put Luke through a grueling workout. My goal was to see how far I could push him, what type of shape he was in, and whether or not he would actually take direction from me.

There was plenty grumbling on his part, but once he started, it was as if a light switch got turned on and he went on autopilot. The questioning, snark, and overall asshole comments from earlier dissipated as he worked up a sweat, going round after round with the jump rope, punching bag, speed bag, and all the other exercises I had him do.

He did, however, question it when I had him do some groundwork with me. Though, I suspected he knew that was his main weakness.

"Don't forget we've got an appointment with the nutritionist next week. I had to push it back to fit his schedule," I stated as I packed up my belongings and stepped back into my heels. I was going to have to rethink these shoes for our morning training sessions. "Once your diet is in place, we'll be going up to two-a-day workouts. In the meantime, instead of here, we're going to meet somewhere else for our morning training."

"Where?" He asked with squinted eyes.

"It's a local place. Perfect place to really begin your groundwork training. I'll shoot you a text later today with the address."

"How? You don't have my cell and I'm not giving it to you."

I laughed. "Are you certain I don't have it?"

He cocked his head to the side.

I widened my grin. "See you in the morning. Don't be late."

He didn't say anything, but his expression gave his thoughts away. He was beyond skeptical. That was fine with me. I was okay with proving myself to him and anyone else who doubted me.

CHAPTER SIX

Good to Great

Luke

"What does this broad have me doing?" I mumbled as I turned into the parking lot of the address she'd texted me the day before. It was that of a strip mall about thirty minutes from my gym.

"Denis's Dance Studio," I read the name of the business I'd parked in front of. I stared at the light pink doorway with an image of a couple dancing some silly ass dance from the last century.

I shook my head because this couldn't be the right place. Syd likely got her shit wrong and sent me the wrong address. We must've been meeting at the gym that was only a few doors down from the dance studio.

Getting out of my car, I headed in the direction of the gym. However, I only got a few steps when I heard her voice behind me.

"Wrong way."

"You're shitting me, right?" I asked, pointing toward the dance studio.

Her response was a slow smile and a shake of her head.

Glancing over my shoulder, I peered at the gym before looking back at Syd.

"Let's go. The owner's doing this as a favor for me."

"I'm not going in there," I said, squaring my shoulders and looking her in the eye.

"Luke, you have to. This is part of your training."

"Bullshit it is."

She sighed and moved toward the door of the dance studio, knocking on it. "You're going inside."

Before I could let her know that I most definitely wasn't going in there, the door flung open.

"Syd," a male voice yelled, too excited for it to be so early in the morning. "Greetings. Come in," he said in a thick accent.

"Denis, good morning. This is Luke McConnell. The fighter I told you about," she said, extending her hand to me.

That was when I watched as a balding dude dressed in black heeled shoes, dress pants, a vest with a white button up beneath it, stepped from behind the door.

"No fucking way," I said, folding my arms across my chest.

"You're coming," Syd said as she approached, moving behind me and pushing me in the direction of the studio's door.

Entering the space, I saw it really was a fucking dance studio. The kind with hardwood floors, open space in the middle, mirrors on each of the far walls type of deal.

"What are we doing here and what does this have to do with my training?" I turned, pinning Syd with my stare.

"Calm down. Denis has been kind enough to give us private dance lessons for this phase of your training."

I chuckled and shook my head. "You're trying to get my ass kicked."

"No, Luke. I'm helping you. Now pay attention."

I gave her a sideways glance at the same time some ballroom type of music started playing through the speakers mounted in the corners of the studio. Denis walked to the front of the room and smiled, nodding at Syd.

"Syd, tells me you are a fighter, no?"

Frowning, I held his stare with my arms folded across my chest.

"Yes, he is. One of the best," Syd answered on my behalf.

"Excellent. Here at my studio, we teach everything from ballet to the lindy hop to the waltz. I am one half of the Waltz Parisian Championship in 2010, 2012 and 2013. We have—"

"Yeah, yeah, whatever. You dance. I get it," I interrupted. "Can we go to a real gym now?" I turned, asking Syd. But before she could answer, I started for the door.

She caught up with me, moving in front of me right before I hit the door. "No. You're staying here and we're dancing. Let's go, Denis," she said, pushing me back to the center of the room. I let her, but my patience ran thin as the hair on Denis' head.

"Very well. We'll begin with the Waltz. It is the classiest of the dances, in my humblest of opinions, and perfect for what you're going for, Syd." He nodded at Syd as he approached us.

"You will be the lead," he told me.

I kept my gaze pointed straight ahead, frowning at myself in the mirror. Syd moved directly in front of me.

"Don't touch me. You tell me where to put my arms and I'll move 'em," I said to Denis when he tried to position my arms around Syd.

Denis nodded and directed me how to hold Syd. She placed her hand in mine and the other on my shoulder and at Denis' instruction we began to move. More like Syd moved and I stood there still as a fucking statue.

"This doesn't work if you don't take the lead."

"It's not going to work then because fuck that."

Syd sighed. "I know this is unconventional."

"You think?"

"But it's for your training. Believe me."

"I don't believe anyone."

She turned her head toward the ceiling before, glancing back at me. "Dancing is like fighting in a lot of ways. Especially, ballroom dancing, where you're dancing with a partner. There's a give and take that needs to happen in a fight, the use of body structure to leverage your partner or, in your case, opponent's weight. Dancing is going to teach you how to move against your opponent when they don't want to be moved. All the types of mechanics you need to improve on your locks, arm bar, and, once you get them to the mat, the ground and pound."

I gave her a side-eye.

"Go with the flow."

I shook my head but didn't say shit. As soon as this lesson or whatever it was, ended, I was out of there and never looking back. I remained silent as Denis continued with his instructions, having me spin Syd around the room. More times than I could count, we had to stop after I stepped on her toes, trying to follow the rhythm Denis clapped out in time with the music.

Even worse, I didn't know what had my head spinning more, the dancing or the scent of Syd's perfume. It wasn't overbearing, but with each twirl and movement I got a whiff of it. Every time Denis said something that made her laugh, she'd toss her head back, filling my nose with more of those floral notes.

"Waste of my damn time," I griped, pushing the door open and heading for my car, an hour after I arrived.

"You could've at least held the door open for me," Syd yelled, coming up behind me.

"I lost an hour of training over this shit," I said, turning to face her.

"That was training."

"Yeah, if I want to try out for the Nutcracker."

She frowned. "That's not the same dance from the Nutcracker."

I deepened my frown. "You're fired." I turned taking another step for my car.

She sucked her teeth and ran to get in between me and my vehicle. "You can't fire me. We have a contract, remember? Anyway, today's session went well."

"How the hell do you figure that?"

"It gave me more insight into the key areas you're lacking and what we need to work on. Your left leg's weaker than your right. Your right shoulder is more dominant than your left, which means when you go to the ground, you'll want to favor a particular side."

"You got all that from a one hour dance lesson or did you just read my fucking bio and find out I had a torn ACL in my left leg a few years back and a jammed shoulder two years ago?"

"Both, honestly. Dancing is going to teach you how to move with the confines of your body to fight better."

"I already know how to fight," I yelled, and ran my hand through my hair.

"You know how to fight but you've forgotten how to win."

I blinked.

Syd moved closer. "I didn't pluck this out of my ass, Luke. I've studied you and I've studied Rodriguez. He knows what he's doing and yeah, you can stand with the best of them, but you get sloppy. You rely too heavily on your old skill set. And I can promise you, as much as you might be watching and studying Rodriguez, he's doing the same to you. He'll know your game inside and out. You need something new. You've gotten stale."

I snorted and narrowed my eyes.

"You know it's true. It's why so many of your fights have gone to shit, lately. You're a good fighter. But don't rely on your past to get you to the next level. You're letting the fact that you're good get in the way of you being great. Get out of your own way, Luke."

Glancing up and around the parking lot, I pressed the button to unlock my car door.

My heart hammered in my chest and I refused to look her in the eyes. I didn't know what the hell she said that stirred something deep inside me, but I knew I didn't like it.

"Move," I said.

Syd stepped out of my way without another word. She stood there staring at me as I climbed in my car and pulled out of the parking lot.

CHAPTER SEVEN

The Peach Pit

Luke

"What are we doing here?" Lenny asked as I approached his seat at the bar.

We were at a local sports bar.

"I needed a drink after training," I said, waving the bartender over, taking my seat on the stool next to Lenny.

"You don't drink during training. And I thought you were only doing your early morning training with Syd still."

"I am." I went to say more but a feminine giggle behind me plucked at my last nerve. Glancing over my shoulder, I caught sight of a bleach blonde giving fuck me eyes to a dude seated two stools down from me.

She peered up and caught her gaze with mine. She winked at me over dude's shoulder. He turned around and leveled a look at me.

"Sean, I'm trying to tell you about my day," she whined, turning his face back to hers with her hand. Her high-pitched voice grated my insides, like nails on a chalkboard.

I shivered and turned back to Lenny. "What were you saying?" I quickly held up my hand to Lenny when the bartender approached. "Two beers and a Coke. With lemon."

"I asked about your training," Lenny continued once the bartender left. "And what are the two beers for if you're not drinking?"

"Training's whatever. And beers are for you." Smirking as the bartender placed my drink order on the bar, I pushed the bottles in Len's direction before taking a sip of my soda.

He looked at the beers and then back to me before shrugging. "Whatever. How is it working out with Syd? Is she holding up as your trainer?"

I snorted. "She's got me fucking dancing."

His eyebrows lifted. "What kind of dance?"

"I don't know. Waltz or some shit. I do my best to tune out when the instructor's talking. Twinkle Toes likes to go on and on about the history of the dance." I waved my hand in the air with flare in the way Denis does.

"Why are you dancing?"

"She says it's beneficial to my groundwork. Look, how tight is that contract I had you draw up for her?"

He pursed his lips. "It's airtight. She had her own attorney look it over before signing. She's no dummy."

I sighed and gulped down half of my drink in one swallow, wishing it were something stronger. My no drinking while training rule started to become a pain in my ass.

"Do you trust her?" Lenny asked.

Cocking my head to the side, I stared him in the eye. "Why would you ask me some bullshit like that?"

His question brought to mind the memory of holding her in my arms as we spun around that small ass dance studio that morning. If I thought too long, I could still capture the exact scent of the perfume she wore.

I cracked my knuckles and gritted my teeth at the memory. The uncomfortable burning in my gut, that appeared every morning we practiced together, started again.

"Isn't trust important between a trainer and trainee? You trusted Banks with your life," Lenny said, pulling me from thinking about Syd and that damn lesson.

"Don't mention Banks." I jutted my finger at him before grabbing my glass and finishing off my damn Coke. I definitely needed something stronger.

Waving the bartender over again, I ordered another Coke with lemon and a third beer.

"I haven't finished the first two," Lenny said.

I shrugged. "What's your point?"

He huffed and gave me confused and frustrated look before narrowing his eyes. "What are you doing?"

I grinned and shook my head. "Nothing. Anyway, never mind my new trainer. Aren't we here to discuss my contract for the Rodriguez fight?"

Len nodded. "About that." He paused and pulled out some papers from the black briefcase sitting on the bar in front of him.

At that same moment the patrons at the bar erupted in applause. Lifting my gaze, I watched one of the mounted screens over the bar as it replayed a hockey player making a goal. The annoying woman a few stools down from me laughed and cheered in that high-pitched voice, stomping all over my nerves again.

I lifted my finger and nodded at the bartender to order another beer.

"So far, we're still negotiating with Rodriguez's team and the higher ups at the NFA, but they won't budge on you doing at least one press conference."

I cracked my neck. "Why can't you get me out of it? Isn't that what I pay you for? To advocate on my behalf?"

Lenny pushed his glasses up his nose and glared at me. "You know how these things work, Luke. You're lucky I can get them down to just one press conference."

"They know I don't play nice at those damn things."

"Which is why they want it. Your attitude makes for good TV."

I sighed. "Make sure I get paid well for this."

"Let me do my job," he countered.

I chuckled. "Look who's grown a pair of balls." I waved at the bartender for another beer, unmindful of the previous three still sitting in front of Lenny, unfinished.

He frowned. "Here, take a few days to read these over and we'll discuss it next week before finalizing the terms."

"Keep 'em," I said when he tried to hand the papers to me. "Email them to me instead."

He frowned but nodded. "What about the realtor you had me contact out in Bridge Lake. He called this week and says he has a couple of houses you might be interested in."

I pulled a face, having forgotten all about the realtor.

"Are you still considering moving back to Bridge Lake?" Lenny asked when I didn't respond.

I didn't have an answer. I'd had him contact a realtor almost a year ago when I was at my lowest point after Banks' death. Something kept me from making a decision.

"Tell him to send some pictures," I said. Standing from the stool, I leaned over to the bartender and said, "You know what, I'm feeling generous tonight and our team is winning, why not get a round for the entire bar."

The bartender gave me an open-mouthed expression.

"Throw one in for yourself while you're at it." I tapped the bar with my palm and pointed at him like we were friends before picking up the still full bottles I'd ordered that Lenny never touched.

"Luke," Lenny called when I turned away. "Don't forget about the Rodriguez contract. There are a few things in it I'd like to go over with you."

"We'll discuss it as soon as you get with the twenty-first century and email it to me."

He huffed. "Yeah, I'll do that. Wait, where are you going? You haven't paid for all the beers you just ordered."

I stopped walking as I came up beside the dude, who grilled me earlier and his chick with the annoying voice. I placed the bottles of beer in front of him.

"The hell?" He griped when I threw my arm around his shoulders. "These are for you. Thanks, bud. Hey?" I called the bartender.

When he looked my way, I lifted my hand and pointed. "The beers are on him." Then I looked down at him. "Trust me, buddy, you're going to need all the alcohol you can get tonight if you plan on taking that hyena-voiced broad home."

I gestured toward blondie.

"The fuck?" He yelled as I sauntered off.

"Luke, what the?" Lenny questioned as I pushed through a few of the other patrons to get to the door.

I needed fresh air. More so, I needed some pussy.

***

"I ended up having to pay for that round of beers. He wanted to kick your ass," Lenny said a few minutes later as he exited the bar. "It's not funny, Luke."

"It is to me. Poor guy's going home with blondie. Did you hear her voice? I'd rather blow an eardrum than listen to that sound all night. The alcohol will at least help."

"You're a piece of work."

I shrugged. "I've been called worse."

"Yeah, by me."

"Quit belly aching about paying for a few drinks. You can afford to pay for a few rounds at the bar. You did that poor bastard a favor."

Lenny shook his head.

"I'll catch you in the morning. Send me that contract and the pictures from the realtor and we'll go over 'em tomorrow," I said.

"Constance is expecting me home soon anyway."

"How is the ol' ball and chain these days?"

"Well, she and I would both prefer if you didn't call her that."

"Not likely to happen but we can all dream."

Lenny sighed. "Marriage isn't as terrible as you make it out to be. Maybe you'll consider it one day."

An image of dancing with Syd that morning popped into my mind and I snorted. The same burning in my gut that overcame me in the bar, came over me at the thought of her. Yeah, I needed to get laid.

I visibly shuddered. "Bite your tongue." I rolled my eyes. "First, you find the love of your life in law school. Then, fucking Pit shows up with a date to his bachelor party. Hell, even Jacob went and got married. The world has lost its shit. At least Kelex, Deacon, and Tak are still single as a dollar bill," I mumbled, shaking my head.

"Maybe the universe is trying to tell you something."

"Don't start that weird The Universe shit with me, Lenny," I warned. My friend believed in that sort of mess.

"Fine, it doesn't have to be The Universe. Call it God or spir—"

"Stop right there. I don't want to hear this right now. As for marriage, save that argument for the assclowns who don't know any better. Get home to your wife."

Lenny looked like he wanted to say more. I could see it in his eyes. The same look he gave me when he wanted to continue his argument, but knew I was too fucking hardheaded to listen to his reasoning.

"You're not going to—"

"Get home to your wife, Len," I urged, knowing where his next line of questioning was headed. He didn't need me to answer where I was headed. He already knew, and I knew his feelings on the matter. Another thing which I didn't want to hear about.

I gave him a final toss of my head before turning in the opposite direction and starting for where I'd parked my car. The drive was only a few minutes from the bar. I opted to pull around back to the private garage parking lot of the stand-alone building.

"Welcome back to the Peach Pit, Mr. McConnell."

"Yeah, thanks," I told the parking lot attendant as I handed her my keys. I watched as she strutted toward my Maserati in the skintight, short black skirt and red crop top, climbing in behind the wheel to pull my car into a parking space.

"Here you go, Mr. McConnell. Enjoy your evening," the other chick behind the booth told me as she handed me a key tag for the night.

I nodded and moved past her booth to the elevator doors that would lead up to the second floor of the building. I was able to skip the first floor entrance since I was a member of the particular club.

As soon as the elevator doors parted the dark strobe lights and loud rhythmic music welcomed me in. There were lounge chairs and booths set up throughout the room. I counted at least five different chicks giving lap dances. I made a beeline for the bar.

"What's your flavor of the night, McConnell?" the red headed bartender questioned as she leaned over the counter, exposing her surgically enhanced boobs. I didn't bother hiding my stare as I dropped my gaze to scope out her merchandise.

"I'm looking for some brown sugar tonight, Bosom. Medium brown skin, about five-six, thick thighs and hips but small up top."

She rolled her eyes at the nickname I'd dubbed her with since the first time I stepped into Peach Pit over two years ago.

"One day you're going to remember my actual name."

"Don't count on it, sweetheart," I quickly shot back before giving her a smirk.

"Lookin' to get wasted tonight?" She turned her head and lifted her gaze to the selection behind her.

I shook my head. "Right now, I'm looking to get the snake drained."

She nodded. "We've got whatever you want on the menu."

"That's the only reason I come here, doll."

She motioned her head in the direction of the private rooms. "2D is all yours for the night."

I nodded and started down the hall, passing stripper after stripper winking at me, trying to convince me to pay them for a dance.

Not now, sweets. I thought.

That night, I had only one goal in mind. To get a certain woman out of my thoughts. Which, of course, was why I'd asked for a Black chick with the specifications I'd requested.

Entering the room, I tossed the jacket I'd worn onto the made up bed and undid the top few buttons of my shirt before taking a seat on the navy, velvet couch. The couch sat about only six feet from a pole that stood at the center of the room.

I began to regret my no drinks while training rule when the silence of the room started to get to me. I could still hear the music from out in the main area of the club, but it was reduced greatly with the door closed.

A heartbeat later the music grew louder as the door opened and then closed. I cut my eyes to the woman entering. Sizing her up, starting at her feet, I noticed the tall strappy stilettos she wore, frowning, because they looked cheap in comparison to the woman I was seeking to get off my mind.

Lifting my gaze up her medium length legs, I noted she didn't wear any stockings which was a plus. The warm brown tone of her skin was closely aligned with what I was looking for. And though her thighs and hips weren't as flared as another pair I couldn't forget, she would do.

"Mr. McConnell, I'm LaTasha. How're you doing?" She purred, moving closer. Her voice almost threw the entire fantasy off. It was too high-pitched.

"Don't speak," I ordered in a clipped tone.

She nodded.

"I'm not looking to hear your voice, maple." A nickname from the color of her skin. "I'm looking to get my cock drained. Can you do that?"

She nodded, silently.

Perfect.

"On your knees."

She moved, swiftly, strutting in front of me and seductively lowering to the floor, in between my legs.

I shifted my gaze from her face to my crotch, signaling she was to pull me out of my jeans. She moved her fingers quickly, undoing the buckle of my belt and the button. I was already semi-erect when she pulled my cock free. Visions of a woman I had no intentions of ever touching had been dancing through my head all fucking day. Finally, I was about to get some relief.

As Maple parted her lips and lowered her warm mouth over the tip of my cock, I dropped my head back against the couch. Closing my eyes, I tried to envision someone, anyone else besides the new woman I'd hired to be my trainer. But it was no use. Syd's perfectly rounded ass, thick thighs and hips kept coming to memory. Even as the stripper I'd dubbed Maple moaned around my dick, it was Syd's plump lips with the mole that rested above the right corner of her mouth that I pictured.

"Fuck," I groaned, the picture of Syd sliding her lips down my shaft over and over again, ran on a loop in my head.

This shit had been an ongoing problem for days. Ever since she'd appeared at my gym out of nowhere, begging for the job as my trainer. That first day I hadn't given her much thought, save for the fact I couldn't shake the look in her eyes or that beauty mark I'd sworn was fake at first look. But the second day she showed up, and almost gleefully took on my karate instructor— going toe-to-toe with him in business attire no less— it was as if my dick grew a mind of its own.

And then there was the dancing. What the hell was that about? I found it useless to my training, but she remained adamant it was for my good. I'll continue to show up to the lessons to prove to her what a waste of time they are.

Agreeing to hiring her as my trainer probably wasn't the smartest thing to do, but I got the impression she wasn't going anywhere and hell, I'd wanted to get Lenny, and everyone else who'd been asking for months, off my back.

Now here I was, in a private room at the Peach Pit, Maple sucking my cock for dear life, and still, all I could think about was how I wished it were Syd down on her knees in front of me, about to take my load in her mouth.

"Shit," I grunted, raising my hips off the couch, seeking more of what Maple delivered. She moved her hand to cup and massage my balls. I shoved one hand in her hair, gripping it tightly as I shot my load off, right into her mouth.

Straining under the weight of my orgasm's release, every muscle in my body tightened and flexed as stream after stream of my semen poured into the woman's mouth.

By the time my body relaxed, I felt no relief whatsoever. My cock still stood at attention as if nothing had happened. My mind was still assaulted with images of Syd and I spinning around that dance studio or her, bent over as she hauled pads and equipment around the gym for my workouts.

"We're not done," I growled to the woman in front of me, lifting her from her kneeling position to stand. Quickly, I pulled out a condom from my wallet and sheathed myself, before pulling her onto my lap.

She lifted the short dress she wore, exposing the fact she wasn't wearing panties, and she was all bare down there. Though I preferred my women with a little hair, I yanked her hips downward, piercing her with my cock. A loud moan ripped from her throat and I pretended it was Syd bouncing up and down on my dick, and not the chick I'd hired to take the edge off.

The Peach Pit was one of my many vices. The place I went to when I didn't want to be bothered with being nice to a chick, even for a few hours. The women here were looking for a payout, and if they were lucky, an orgasm in the process. I didn't mind supplying both. There were no thoughts of a possible future, no awkward conversations of trying to get to know one another. None of the bullshit I'd given up on a long time ago. Every time I'd shown up before, it worked. I got what I needed.

Except that night.

Even as I came a second time, Maple's hips wildly gyrating on my lap, it still wasn't enough. I found myself wanting.

"How was that?" Maple questioned breathlessly, both her hands coming down on the back of the couch, bracketing me in. She hovered a few inches from my face.

I pushed the top half of her body away from me. She was too fucking close to my lips.

"I told you not to speak," I demanded, lifting her by the hips off of me and quickly spinning her around as I stood. Guiding both of our bodies over to the bed, I bent her over, taking her by the hips before thrusting my cock into her once more.

Third time had to be a charm.

But even after coming for the third and final time that night, I was still left feeling empty and wanting. Not necessarily two feelings I was unfamiliar with, but I'd sure as fuck never experienced this shit over a woman. Especially over a woman I couldn't have.

CHAPTER EIGHT

Changing Your Diet

Luke

"You're late."

I blinked and stared down at the five-foot-six woman standing in front of me with her hands firmly planted on her hips. A deep frown marring her face and eyes that... nah, I didn't bother looking into her eyes. That shit would have me with half a boner throughout the remainder of this fucking workout.

She'd finally decided to take the dancing down to only twice a week. That morning we started my training in the gym.

I peered up at the clock overhead. "It's seven-oh-three." Our session started at seven in the morning.

"Which means, you're three minutes late. Which means, you owe me an additional thirty minute session this afternoon."

"How in the fuck does three minutes turn into thirty? And since when are we doing afternoon training?"

"Since today's your first consult with the new nutritionist."

I frowned but didn't say anything.

She spun on those heels, reminding me of her moving across the hardwood at the dance studio.

Pull it together, McConnell.

"Let's go, today's a conditioning session and this afternoon is where we start taking what you've learned in our dance training to the mat. I've got some fun stuff planned. Plus, the nutritionist I've hired for you will be coming in at nine."

I squinted. "You're usually out of here by nine."

"Not today."

I didn't ask questions even though I wanted to. I found the best way not to get attached to someone is to mind my business, and not ask questions. Nothing good ever happened from asking questions.

"What is this douche-canoe gonna tell me that I don't already know? I know how to eat," I said, pulling my T-shirt over my head and tossing it onto the duffel bag I'd dropped in the corner of the room.

Syd's gaze trailed over the many tats that covered my chest before she blinked and peered up at me. The movement was so quick, I started to question whether or not it really even happened, but this hadn't been the first day I'd caught that same reaction whenever I pulled my shirt off to begin a training session.

"You eat too much processed food and way too much meat."

"Muscles need protein to rebuild. Ask any two-bit trainer off the street. Hell, you could throw a rock on the corner of any block in SoCal and hit one. They'd tell you how essential protein is."

Syd rolled her eyes as she folded her arms. "Yeah, and I'd tell them to shove their advice up their ass. Trainers aren't the same as nutritionists. Which is why I've hired one specifically for you. I'm your head trainer," she responded, pressing her palm against her chest. "Rick will be your nutritionist. He's got a Master's in nutrition and dietetics, as well as a number of other continuing education credentials. He's big on holistic and alternative medicine and treatments as well. You'll like him."

"Don't hold your breath on that score."

A faint smile crossed her lips. "I won't. All right let's go. Warm up time," she called, clapping her hands signaling it was go time.

I endured a few rounds of jump roping, shadow boxing in the ring, and burpee drills to get my body warmed up before heading over to the weights section of the gym. Syd's workout consisted of rounds of heavy ropes, squats, deadlifts, upper back conditioning, and core strengthening exercises. All of that was before we got down to grappling drills. Finally, we finished off with about twenty minutes of mobility work.

I felt good when all was said and done. While toweling off, I watched as Syd pulled out her phone, her thumbs typing furiously. The look on her face was serious as her brow wrinkled in concentration and she bit her bottom lip.

"What're you typing?" I asked in spite of my earlier protestations about not asking questions.

"Notes from your workout. We need to work more on your flexibility and mobility. We're definitely going to need to up your afternoon sessions to strictly focusing on grappling. We'll probably have to go longer in the mornings and add on an extra thirty minutes in your evening workouts. You have almost twenty-four weeks until your fight with Rodriguez."

I nodded as I toweled the sweat off the back of my neck. The contract for the fight had been finalized a day earlier, solidifying the date of the fight. I had exactly six months to train.

"He's here. Good." Syd looked up and rushed to the door as some guy entered.

"Rick, you made it. You didn't have trouble finding the building, did you?"

"Not at all. Hey, Syd," Rick greeted.

My top lip curled into a snarl when I silently watched him pull her into a hug. She willingly returned the embrace, which pissed me off even more.

"Rick, this is Luke McConnell. Luke, this is Rick Estrada, the nutritionist I was telling you about."

"Nice to meet you, Luke. I'm a big fan." He stuck out his hand with a stupid fucking grin on his face.

I dropped my eyes to his hand as I continued to wipe the sweat from my body, before raising my gaze to meet his. When I made no further movement after a while his hand fell to his side. He turned confused eyes onto Syd. I curled my top lip and cracked my knuckles staring at the douche-canoe in front of me.

"Strange for a nutritionist to be making house calls, ain't it? You hard up for money or something?"

I didn't bother waiting for his response as I strolled over to my office, leaving both of them in my wake.

"Luke, don't be an ass," Syd snarled from behind me and for the first time that day I cracked a smile.

Turning back to the both of them, I folded my arms and leaned against the doorframe of my office.

"I wouldn't be me if I wasn't."

"Now that's something we can agree on."

My smile widened as I caught the wrinkle of annoyance in her face.

"Rick, unfortunately Luke isn't all that convinced he needs a nutritionist. Please don't take his sourpuss attitude personally." She cut her gaze to me before turning back to Rick. "But as you and I have discussed there is some incredible research coming out recently in the field of nutrition that counters what we, in the athletic world, have come to believe about food, protein, and the building blocks of good recovery."

Syd brushed past me, effectively pushing me out of the way of my own office to make her way inside. It was as if I watched the scene in slow motion, Syd taking the seat that belonged to me, as if it were her own. A whiff of her scent filled my nose as she did, and I couldn't find the words to kick her ass out of my damn chair.

Rick, on the other hand, hesitated, giving me a cautious look before stepping inside my office. I leaned against my desk arms folded, legs crossed at the ankles as I stared at Rick while he set up his laptop from the chair in the corner of the room.

"Since you're here. Might as well tell me what bullshit nutrition plan you've worked out already. I'm sure you'll charge me for it anyway."

"Ignore him," Syd insisted. "What were you thinking, Rick?"

"As you said, Syd, I've done tons of research over the past two years, mostly with high performance athletes and I've found many of them have a great deal of success with a whole foods, plant-based diet." Rick paused, looking toward me.

"A what?"

"Vegan," Syd answered.

"Fuck no!" I shook my head adamantly.

She sighed, her shoulders deflating. "I knew you'd respond like this. Can you just hear him out?" She pleaded.

"I could but my answer's still going to be the same, so what would be the point? You're wasting your time," I said to douche-canoe.

"Just listen to what the man has to say."

Refolding my arms, I pierced him with a hard glare. "Talk."

"As I've said, many of the athletes I've researched have had a great deal of success with this type of diet. I'm talking about quicker recovery times, less fatigue and in some case, less injury altogether. And I think it would benefit you immensely. I can easily design a meal plan, based on your needs. I'll need to know information such as…"

I started to drown the douche out. Syd had to answer his questions when he asked for specifics like my height, weight, number of hours spent training per day and on and on.

"It's not fucking happening," I told Syd as soon as the door shut behind Rick once he left. "And get the hell out of my chair," I barked, feeling irritated.

Instead of rising, Syd uncrossed and then recrossed her legs in the opposite direction. My eyes were glued to the movement, appreciating the high-waisted, plum colored pants she wore. Why the hell she dressed as if she were going to a day at the office for our morning sessions was always on the tip of my tongue to ask, but again, my no questions rule stopped me. Honestly, it'd started off as a no questions rule, but had somehow worked its way down to ask as few questions as possible.

"Why are you so resistant to even considering changing your diet?"

"Because I'm a man who likes food. And I don't trust this new age bullshit all these vegans are spouting."

"It's not new age. Did you even hear what Rick said?"

"I tried not to."

She sucked her teeth and the muscles in my stomach clenched. *That fucking mouth.*

"A plant-based diet isn't new. According to Rick, research is showing Greek gladiators literally survived on this type of diet."

I snorted. "You want me to believe gladiators survived eating rabbit food?" I shook my head in disgust.

"It's not rabbit food. How about we watch that documentary Rick mentioned."

"What documentary?"

"You know what, I'm going to ignore that question." She stood, smoothing out the wrinkles in her pants, brushing herself off. "You and me have a date with that documentary tonight." She waved her finger between the two of us as if I didn't already know who she meant by you and me.

"The hell we do."

"Yup, right after your evening workout. It's on Netflix. So, here's the plan, we'll do your two-hour session here. Then I'll stop by that popular vegan place across the street to pick up dinner and bring it over to your place so we can watch the documentary together."

"Wait, what the hell?"

"Yeah, it'll be perfect." As soon as those words fell from her lips, her phone buzzed.

"Forget that plan, I'm not doing it." I waited as she held up a finger to answer her phone.

"Tanisha? What's up?"

I seriously waited there like a jackhole as she stood in my office, taking calls from who the fuck knows, silently wondering what the hell I'd gotten myself into by agreeing to let her train me.

"Yeah, I'm on my way now. We'll work it out when I get in. All right, bye."

"Syd, I'm not going vegan."

"I gotta go, Luke. I'll see you tonight. Be ready to practice those grappling skills."

She skirted past me and I was left standing there, speechless again. My eyes had an uncanny way of—in spite of my pissed off mood and confusion as to how the hell I'd let this woman bum-rush me again—falling to her ass as she sashayed out of the gym, waving at a few of the instructors and students who'd entered for their morning workout sessions. I shook my head, wondering what the fuck I was going to do now.

Syd

"Damn," I commented as I stepped out of my car with the bag of food in one hand and my handbag in the other. I knew Luke's home would be pretty sizeable by the address and neighborhood he'd told me earlier. Which was like pulling teeth to get out of him.

Truth be told, the home was relatively smaller than the other homes in this neighborhood, looking as if it fell a little under four thousand square feet. But the modern style build with granite colored brick and dark wood siding, complete with a plethora of windows, gave the home an appeal the other homes on the block didn't have. In the distance, the sound of the waves crashing was an even larger draw. I stood there for a moment sizing up his house, until I heard the front door open.

"Are you gonna' stand there staring at shit or bring your ass inside? I'm hungry as hell after that workout you put me through," he grumbled.

Shaking my head, I made my way up the brick lined walkway to his front door.

"The food better not be terrible either. Otherwise, I'm going out and getting a porterhouse."

"It'll be delicious. I've eaten at this place many times before and have never been disappointed.

Luke grunted and grabbed the bag of food out of my hand, peering inside. He turned and headed inside, leaving me to scurry and catch the door before it shut in my face. "What'd you get me?"

"A black bean burger with the works and a side of hand cut sweet potato fries. All vegan and guaranteed to change your mind about sticking to a plant-based diet."

He stopped and turned, looking back at me with a frown.

"Just try it."

He rolled his dark brown eyes and not for the first time, my stomach clenched. I closed the door fully and followed behind him, looking over the light-colored hardwood floors that ran throughout the entirety of the first floor, from what I could see. The kitchen was plenty spacious with its black cabinetry. Unsurprisingly, everything looked pristine, as if it hadn't been touched since it was installed.

"I guess I'm not going to get a tour of the place."

Luke's frown deepened. "Did you come here to conduct an inspection or to watch this documentary?"

"I can't do both?" I quipped.

Luke mumbled something under his breath and turned from me, moving to the cabinets over the sink, opening it and pulling out two plates.

"Oh, so you don't eat like a barbarian? Good to know," I joked.

"You know you can easily get put out on your ass."

I chortled. "You wouldn't."

I expected a smartass retort, but one never came. In fact, I watched his eyes narrow and his lips thin as if he was biting his tongue to hold back whatever he'd been about to say. I didn't give it much thought, not wanting to press my luck too much.

I always felt like I was skating on thin ice with Luke. Like he'd only take so much of my trying to bulldoze him before he really did kick me out on my ass. While I'd often gotten that impression from most people and didn't care one way or the other, with Luke, I did.

"You do have Netflix, right?" I questioned as he led me into his living room with our plates of food and cans of flavored seltzer water in hand.

"You wouldn't be here if I didn't," he answered, lifting the remote and turning on the flat screen mounted to the wall, opposite his dark grey, leather couch. Above the couch, on the wall, hung a sectioned painting of an older man smoking and the smoke creating these beautiful dark blue clouds above his head.

"That's a beautiful painting. You had someone in here to decorate?"

"I'm a fighter not an interior decorator," he said before sitting down unceremoniously.

"I'll take that as a yes."

I stood there silent for a moment when he didn't say anything. He barely acknowledged my presence as he set his plate and seltzer down on the coffee table.

"You're a real charmer, you know that?"

He looked over at me, before taking his first bite of his burger. "Are we on a date? Am I supposed to be wining and dining you?"

Rolling my eyes, I responded with, "I would never dream of it."

"Good." Was all he said before taking another bite of the burger made out of black beans and quinoa, topped with mushrooms, red onions, lettuce and a chipotle vegenaise sauce.

Sitting with my own plate, I anxiously waited to see what Luke's verdict on the food would be.

"Well?" I questioned when I couldn't wait any longer, before he moved to take his third bite.

"Well, what?"

"How is it?"

"I'm still eating it, right? Haven't tossed it across the room and shoved you out the door, have I?"

"I suppose you haven't."

"Then we can assume I like it."

I shrugged. That was good enough. Grabbing the remote, I used the arrow buttons to search out the documentary Rick had told Luke and I about earlier.

"Plant Eaters. The hell kind of name is that?" Luke grunted, taking another huge bite of his burger.

"Just give it a chance."

He didn't respond, but instead, sat back against the couch, eating the rest of his food and nodding his head in the direction of the TV, urging me to start the movie. I did so, anticipating what kind of information this film would reveal to us and hoping it would convince Luke to give it a chance. I knew he had the potential to become an even greater fighter than he already was, and to win another title.

While he wouldn't admit it, the loss of his last trainer had hit him hard. He'd only interacted with Lenny and that guy Pit in the few days I'd been working with him. Even when he worked out or grappled with the other guys in his gym, it was focused, with little banter or friendly side conversations. He was closed off to most of the people around him. Only a select few gained access to the real Luke McConnell.

"I know him," Luke said out of nowhere. At least, I thought it'd been out of nowhere. Turns out, I was the one who wasn't fully paying attention to the film because I'd gotten lost down a rabbit hole, thinking about Luke and his lack of an inner circle.

I peered up at the screen, my eyebrows raising. "That's Phillip DeLuca, right?"

"Yep."

DeLuca was a famed fighter about twenty years ago. He was largely held responsible for the rise in the popularity of MMA fighting here in the U.S.

"You ever train with him?"

Luke shook his head. "Was before my time. Would've loved to though," he said peering at the screen, before finishing off the last of his sweet potato fries.

We watched in silence as DeLuca discussed how in the latter years of his fighting he'd dealt with injury after injury, and while looking for the best recovery methods he'd stumbled upon the benefits of a plant-based diet. Glancing from the television screen to Luke, I believed I saw his intrigue. His face was set in a hard mask of indifference, but his eyes held firmly on the screen, taking in everything DeLuca, the researchers, and doctors he spoke with had to say.

Even I was a little surprised to learn some of the benefits DeLuca spoke about in his recovery and healing time. Not only that but his performance increased greatly in those latter years.

"Banks used to remind me that because I was getting older, didn't mean my performance had to suffer. He always talked about DeLuca winning that championship title in his final year as a pro. Never said it was because he was a fucking vegan. Probably didn't know." His last few words were said low as if filled with remorse.

"Banks, your former trainer." I said.

Luke turned to me with raised eyebrows, as if just realizing he'd spoken out loud. He gave me a curt nod. "Yeah."

I nodded. He may not have wanted to reveal it, but the tone of his voice spoke volumes. There was a deep affection there for the man who'd trained him from early on in his career.

"Well, now you know his secret," I spoke into the silence.

Luke's gaze held mine for a heartbeat before he nodded and turned back to the screen, setting his plate down before folding his arms over his broad chest, sitting back. The rest of the movie was watched in silence. I finished the Mediterranean bowl I'd picked up for myself, also appreciating the benefits of a whole foods plant-based diet.

Though I kept straying back to wondering what Luke was thinking. Was he buying into it? This, along with increased training in the areas he was weak in, and somehow trying to control that temper of his, could be the secret to his winning another championship title.

"You done with that?"

Blinking I peered up to see Luke standing over me, his arm stretched out to take the plate I still held in my lap.

"Yeah." I rose to follow him into the kitchen as he carried both of our dishes. "What'd you think?"

He didn't respond until he placed both of our plates into the sink. Spinning around and leaning against the sink, folding his arms, he said, "You're trying to make me into a pansy ass. First dancing and now taking away meat."

I inhaled deeply and pinched the bridge of my nose. "I've told you the relevance of dance to your training. And with quicker recovery time from a plant-based diet, you're going to see major improvements in half the time you'd expect."

He eyed me, his gaze darkening.

"How do I know I'll get enough calories to sustain my training?"

I nodded, anticipating he'd give me a little quiz on this. "Rick's already mapped out a daily meal plan for you. Completely plant-based and given we'll be doing four hours of training, five days a week, it allows for 2,500 calories per day. More than enough."

"I need to maintain my weight class to fight Rodriguez."

"The caloric intake won't create a deficit and you can increase the calories if you need to. You will not starve on a plant-based diet. I've already worked it out, Luke. All you need to do is follow my lead."

His eyes narrowed and my stomach flip-flopped.

For the smallest instant my thoughts wavered from the topic of the conversation at hand, when I caught sight of the tattoo peeking out from underneath his V-neck. From memory, I knew the rest of the tattoo was of a dragon breathing fire out of its mouth. That reminded me of all his other tattoos. The ones that only when I was alone at night before falling asleep, I'd admit to memorizing their exact location on his body.

The dragon on the left side of his chest was interesting. However, it was the tattoo of a wrecked car that spelled out the words 'Asshole 4 Lyfe' I found most compelling. There was also a particular tattoo on his back that ran down the length and got lost underneath the waistband of whatever pants or shorts he wore. I often wondered if that tattoo extended as far down the length of the backside of his body as my imagination carried it.

Slowly, I let my eyes drift upward to connect with his dark brown orbs. This time, unlike so many others, Luke didn't cut off eye contact with me. Since I'd been training him, it seemed like he went out of his way to ensure we never stared eye to eye for too long.

As I wondered why that was, I felt my breathing hitch. Blinking, I realized Luke was no longer standing across the kitchen, leaning against the sink. Instead, he was standing over me. He lifted his hand to the sterling silver boxing glove pendant I always wore. My heart thumped against my chest as he eyed the glove, as if searching for its meaning.

After a few heartbeats of silence, he raised those dark brown orbs to meet mine again. He hovered over me wordlessly. It felt like we stood there for minutes, possibly hours, trapped inside something that was beyond my vocabulary.

"You need to leave," he said in a husky voice. He dropped his hand, took a step back and blinked before turning his head. "It's late and I have a pain in the ass trainer who gets on my case whenever I show up even a few minutes late."

The comment was meant to insert some sort of levity into the moment. To wash away the electric current that'd sparked between the two of us. I knew it and so did he. Though, I was too much of a coward to say it.

I nodded. "Wouldn't want to get on your trainer's bad side."

He dipped his head and turned, exiting the kitchen without another word. He was such a strange man. As much as I hated it, I found it intriguing nonetheless.

CHAPTER NINE

Green Juice

Syd

As I walked around the gym, the only sound that could be heard was the sound of my high heels against the linoleum floor. While lining up the pads I would have Luke working on that morning, a buzzing from the pocket of my pants interrupted me.

Pulling out my phone, I noticed it was a call from the office. "Vince?"

"No, sorry, Ms. Quinn, it's not Vince. It's Melody."

I wrinkled my face, confused. "Melody, is everything okay?" Melody was one of our part-time 'medics at ParaSquad. She'd been with the company for a little over a year now.

"Yes, fine but I came in early to see if I could have my shift rescheduled but you weren't in, so I'm calling from the office. I'm supposed to be working the half-marathon tomorrow, but I just got a call from my sister. She fell and severely sprained her ankle and she's going to need some help over the next couple of weeks. I have to go out of town."

"Of course, Mel. Go help your sister. I'll find someone to cover the half-marathon. Even if I have to do it myself." I bit my lip as soon as the words were out of my mouth. I began wracking my brain for who I could call on, on such short notice. Tanisha was out of town with a few of our other paramedics working a three-day biking race. That left us short-staffed already. Surely, with Melody out of the picture, I was going to have to don my ParaSquad shirt and get to work in the trenches.

"Are you sure? I know Tanisha and the others are out of town."

"Don't worry about it, Mel. Go take care of your family. We'll be fine, and right here when you get back."

She let out a sigh of relief. "Thanks, Syd. You're the best."

"I am," I teased before hanging up the phone, already reworking my schedule in my head.

"Taking personal calls on my dime?"

Startled, I turned to find Luke staring me down with pinched eyebrows.

"That was work."

He spread his arms out wide, glancing around. "This is work."

I tutted, shaking my head. "I also have another job. A business, actually."

"Doing what?" He crossed his arms, almost defensively.

I titled my head to the side and laughed.

"Am I Eddie Murphy all of a sudden? The hell is so funny?"

I shook my head. "You. Asking questions. You never seemed interested before."

"You make it seem like we've been working together for years and this is the first time I've asked you about your life. You've been my trainer for all of, what? Two weeks?"

Rolling my eyes, I nodded. "You're right. Anyway, yeah, I own a business. Or co-own, I should say, with my best friend, Tanisha. It's called ParaSquad."

"Sounds like a group for a bunch of Navy Seal rejects."

"Up yours," I replied.

Shaking his head, he said, "I'm not in to butt stuff. Not my own, anyway."

I rolled my eyes. "We hire part-time EMTs and paramedics to work events, mostly sporting events but we also do concerts, festivals, things like that. To keep everyone safe and ensure they have access to first aid personnel when needed."

He looked at me and nodded. "You've got your sixty second elevator pitch down," he condescended, raising a cup to his lips, taking a pull from the straw.

That was when I noticed the mid-sized clear plastic cup was filled with a green liquid.

"Are you drinking a green juice?"

He nodded.

"Did you make that?"

"Nah. Stopped by one of those juice bars or whatever they're called that are all over Los Angeles."

I grinned as I folded my arms. "Decided to skip that crappy pre-workout you've been drinking."

He shrugged. As if it were no big deal. "I watched another one of those documentaries about being vegan after you left."

"Thought you were going to sleep," I called from behind him as he started for his office door.

"I tried. Had some trouble so I turned to Netflix and clicked through their recommended films. My queue is full of veganism shit now thanks to you and that damn movie."

"You watched. And?"

Another shrug. "Some of it made sense. So, I thought why not. I got up and went out to an all-night grocer and stocked up on vegan food, vegetables, tofu, seitan, all that shit I said I'd never eat. I'll give it a try, for the next ninety days. Beyond that, I'm not making any promises," he stated sternly, pointing at me.

I clapped, feeling giddy. "That's great news, Luke. There are so many great vegan recipes and options. I don't think you're even going to miss all that red meat you're used to eating."

He frowned. "Don't bet on it, Syd. But I'm up for trying just about anything once."

A chill ran down my spine, the way it always did when he said my name.

"I just need to figure out how I'm going to work out this vegan deal when I go out of town next week."

"Wait. What?" I held up my hand to keep him from barreling past me out the office door.

He paused, as if confused. "What, *what?*"

"Since when are you going out of town?"

"Since my fucking brother and his ball and chain decided to open their own medical practice."

I gave him a confused look.

"He's opening the practice and having friends and family there to celebrate." His expression was deadpan.

"Okay, number one, I wouldn't describe his wife as a ball and chain in front of him. Number two, you have a brother?" My research on Luke hadn't indicated he'd had any siblings. In fact, the number of articles I read about Luke McConnell hadn't brought up much on his past. All I knew was that he grew up somewhere in the Northwest.

"Yeah." He brushed past me.

"What do you mean, yeah? And why isn't that in your bio?"

"'Cause it's no one's business, got it?" He roared, spinning around to face me.

It was enough anger to stop me in my tracks, but not nearly enough to stop me from wondering what was going on. I'd found it strange it was so difficult to find out information about Luke's past from write ups and articles on him. Anything having to do with his life before joining the NFA was vague and nebulous.

"How did you meet your old trainer?" I questioned.

Luke's lips pinched. "Didn't I tell you conversations about Banks were off-limits?"

"You did, but that's obviously not stopping me from asking."

He grunted. "You're a bigger pain in my ass than he was."

"Thank you."

He shook his head, lowering it and for the first time, ever, I think, I caught a glimpse of a genuine smile on his lips. Not one of those cocky smiles he often gave right after saying something totally uncalled for, but a smile that wasn't forced. Unfortunately, before I could get a full look at it, it was gone. Like it never even happened.

"Let me finish this green shit and then you can tell me what the workout for today is."

"You're going to enjoy today's workout and I'm sure that green shit, as you put it, is going to give you more energy than you think. Also, what day are we leaving next week to head to the opening?"

Again, his look was poignant as he stared at me as if I had three heads.

"We aren't going anywhere, sweetheart. I am going to Williamsport by myself to meet my brother and his wife at their office. Eat a meal and then bring my ass back out to the West Coast."

I nodded. "Right. All of that sounds great except for the part where you're going alone."

"I don't need a date."

"Great because I'm not offering to be your date. I am your trainer and you're training for a very serious fight. Which means, you don't get to take any days off except the ones I've already scheduled for you."

"Fine. Give me the workout and I'll do it while I'm away."

I shook my head. "That's not how this is going to work. As your trainer, especially as your new trainer it would be detrimental to the development of our relationship for me not to be present at your workouts… our trainer-trainee relationship." I emphasized the last part, more for my benefit than for Luke's. I hadn't missed the shiver that ran through my belly when I said the words 'our relationship.'

"You're not coming with me to Williamsport."

"I am."

"Don't you have a job? Besides this one? How are you going to take days off?"

"I own the company. I'm not scheduled to work any events next week. My business partner will be back, and she's more than capable of handling any last minute events that come up. Paperwork and meetings can be handled through email and videoconferencing, if necessary. So, it looks like I'm all yours."

Luke's eyes darkened when I said those words and I quickly stepped around him, moving toward the floor mat where I was going to begin his workout session, so he wouldn't see the way my nipples reacted to that look in his eyes.

"You're not bringing your ass to Williamsport," he insisted, following me.

"This morning's session is going to focus on arm locks and takedowns," I responded, ignoring his comment.

My mind was already made up. If he was going to Williamsport, so was I. I didn't need to attend his brother's opening.

Obviously, that was a family affair and I wouldn't intrude. I was certain there was a very important reason why he kept his family life a mystery to the public. Lord knows, I didn't need him finding out about my own family history. He'd likely throw me out on my backside if he did.

However, I was going to Williamsport with him.

CHAPTER TEN

Half-Marathon

Luke

It was a Saturday. I'd already done my scheduled workout for the morning. It was the perfect time for me to climb my ass back into bed, or better yet, go find some pussy I could crawl into for the day. Paid or unpaid, it never mattered to me in the past.

Yet, instead of conducting one of my usual past times on a Saturday afternoon, I found myself downtown, wandering the sidewalks, amongst people cheering for their husbands or wives, or kid, or friend who were running the city's annual half-marathon. The main streets of downtown had been blocked off to cars to make space for runners. All up and down the street people were running, trying to prove to themselves or someone else that running thirteen point two miles meant something.

Dumb fucks.

I cursed as I pushed past the cheerers, searching out someone who wasn't there to run. What drove me to be out there, amongst the crowds of people, seeking out one person, I didn't know but I couldn't sit my ass at home either. So there I was.

"Hey, you're Luke McConnell, aren't you?"

Shit.

Most of the time, I could put on an old baseball cap and go out in public and not get noticed. I wasn't that famous an athlete who needed security and all that bullshit to go unnoticed, but every now and again, I'd run into someone who recognized me and wanted to fucking chitchat.

"No, and I can't stand that fucker," I growled at the guy.

His face quickly morphed from excitement to confused, but I didn't bother with sticking around for him to figure out the truth. I never got into fighting to be recognized. I hated the shit and avoided public locations whenever possible.

Pushing past the douchebag and all the other onlookers, I continued scouting the area for the one person I was looking for. Along the sides of the street, just off of the sidewalk were volunteers handing out paper cups full of water and electrolyte drinks, and power bars for the runners. None of them were her.

After about twenty minutes of searching, frustration began to mount, and I started to call myself all kinds of fools for even bothering to go out there and search. Right when I'd begun talking myself into carrying my sorry ass home, I spotted her silhouette. Somehow my mind committed her body's shape and size to memory without my damn consent.

I just knew. Even with her back to me. A pair of dark denim pants and a navy blue shirt—pretty nondescript, especially from behind. Nothing like the high-waist pants and silk blouses she wore in the mornings to our workout sessions. Yet, I still knew it was her.

"Did you have anything to drink or eat during the first ten miles, Mr. McCaffrey?" She questioned someone as I walked up behind her.

Not for the first time, I realized the sexy, breathy nature of her voice. It wasn't done on purpose. Not like most females I came across. She wasn't intentionally adding sexiness or an alluring element to her voice. That made it even sexier.

"No." The older man shook his head as I peered at him over Syd's shoulder. "Don't need it. I'm as healthy as an ox."

"Well, your blood pressure is pretty low and considering you almost fainted out there on the course, I wouldn't advise you try to finish these final three miles."

"I'm gonna' finish, dammit," the old man grumbled, standing from the folding chair nearly falling over as he did so.

"Calm down, old man. She's just trying to help your decrepit ass," I grunted, pushing past Syd to get in between her and the geezer.

His eyes widened in shock as his legs gave out and he fell back into the chair.

"Luke," Syd called from behind me, but I ignored her.

"You want to die, that's on you but seeing as how you probably didn't come here to be carried out on a stretcher but to finish the race, it'd make so much more sense if you took the woman's advice. Drink the Powerade or whatever the hell she's serving you, eat that nasty ass Gu and walk to the finish line. It won't be pretty even with all that, but at least you'll be on two legs instead of a stretcher."

I glared at the man, daring him to contest anything I'd said. He grumbled a bit, but took the packet of the electrolyte gooey, fruit flavored substance I offered and stubbornly opened it. Not until he was finished did I step out from between Syd and him. That was when I spun around to face a pissed off looking Syd.

"How're you feeling now, Mr. McCaffrey?"

"Better."

"Watch your tone." *Jerk off.*

That was all I said as I stood by and watched Syd accommodate this selfish old man, who probably had more days behind him than he had ahead. The ungrateful bastard didn't even thank her, once she removed the blood pressure cuff from his arm and allowed him to stand and continue in the direction of the finish line.

"What the hell are you doing here? And why are you being rude?"

"Me?" I pointed at the fossil who'd barely made it two yards from us. "Don't you mean him?"

Syd shook her head. "I'm talking to you. You didn't have to talk to him like that."

"He didn't have to speak to you that way."

Syd snapped her head back in obvious surprise. Hell, internally, I had the same damn reaction. Why anyone speaking to her in such a condescending and abrupt tone bothered me was a fucking mystery. One I didn't have a particular interest in delving into at the moment.

Syd folded her arms. "He's not the only one who's spoken to me like that lately."

"Yeah, well, he isn't me."

She lifted an arched eyebrow and my fingers itched to grab both sides of her face to pull her to me. That particular urge had been occurring more and more lately. No matter how many times I visited the Peach Pit to get sucked off or to fuck one of the chicks who looked just like Syd, it did fuck all to curb my mounting desire for her. My damn trainer, nonetheless.

"No, he's not you. He had a certain charm."

My frown deepened, but Syd laughed as if her joke was hilarious. My fingers itched again, but this time it was to paddle her ass. I really was losing my shit over this woman, and I doubted she had any idea.

"But what are you doing here?"

"Looking for you."

What the hell did you go and say the truth for, idiot? I lambasted myself. It was the truth. The only reason I was anywhere in the vicinity of this damn race was because she was there.

"Why? Did you have an issue with your workout this morning? Did Daniel show up for the sparring match?"

"Yeah, he was there, and it was fine."

"How did it go?"

"I kicked his ass. He's a pansy. I'm gonna need stronger sparring partners if we're getting me ready for the Rodriguez fight."

She appeared relieved. "Oh, so you're here because you don't think I'm holding my weight as a trainer. I thought you might be thinking that." She nodded as she fixed the chairs and the medical supplies that sat on a small folding table for the racegoers. "But right now, we're still in the figuring out one another phase. Besides, with the recent changes to your diet, I'm letting your body adjust. We'll start taking it up a few notches in the next couple of weeks."

I nodded, not really caring about the particulars of the training regimen she was putting me through. I knew my body and fighting well enough to know it wasn't the time to up my training. For her part, Syd kept up on latest research, constantly checked in on my diet plan and introduced me to a new physical therapist to aid with recovery. I wasn't a hundred percent certain she knew what the hell she was doing, but at least, she put on a good show.

"Yeah, whatever," I responded because I had no other words.

She shook her head. "You don't like to say much but there's a whole world of thoughts happening in your eyes."

Peering down at her, I wrinkled my forehead. For the second time, I allowed myself to stare at her in the eyes, not to look away. Yup, that same feeling that caught me off guard the first time we met was still there.

This time it was accompanied by a feeling of drowning. A feeling I wasn't unfamiliar with. Shaking my head to remove that memory, I lifted my gaze to look at the people around us.

"So, this is your day job, huh? What, I'm not paying you enough?"

She shrugged. "I didn't start training you for a paycheck."

"Then give me my money back." As per the contract she signed, she received twenty-five percent of her stated total so far.

She laughed and shook her head. "Where do you think your nutritionist, physical therapist, and new equipment is coming from?"

I cocked my head to the side. "You're paying them? Out of your salary?"

She shrugged. "No biggie." She started to say something else, but one of the racegoers came up to her needing help after they'd fallen. There was a golf ball sized gash on the woman's knee.

I silently stood back and watched as she cleaned out the minor wound, assessing the person likely didn't need stitches before bandaging it up to allow the woman to finish the race.

"Cut was pretty superficial."

She lifted her eyebrow. "You're familiar with wounds, considering your career choice, huh?"

"That and the 'medic training," I answered before thinking better of it.

"What training?"

"In high school and first few years of college. I began training as an EMT and became a 'medic once I went away to school."

"Wait. A paramedic and college?"

I sighed and again called myself a dumbass for revealing that little bit of information about myself. Very few people knew my history and I liked it that way. Before Syd could question me any further, another runner came up to the table in need of assistance. Moments later, two spectators that'd gotten into a fist fight with one another needed Syd's help. One of the dumb fucks actually did need stitches, which Syd had to triage and pass the fucker onto an EMT on the scene to be taken to the hospital.

"How long were you a 'medic?" I questioned when she had some downtime.

"All together? About ten years before starting my company."

She spent the next twenty minutes, between helping runners and spectators alike, telling me about her business, ParaSquad. While my face remained neutral, I grew more and more impressed with the company she'd started with a friend of hers.

Before I knew it, I'd been there for about two hours, watching Syd help people, admiring her first aid expertise and being thrown back to the time in my life when I was certain I was on my way to medical school. My jaw began to ache from the pressure I'd put on it as I grounded my teeth together just thinking about that period in my life.

"Hey, Luke? You still with me?"

"What?" I questioned, shaking my head.

"I said, we're about done here. I have to go drop off my equipment at the office."

"Oh." I glanced around, seeing that aside from a few stragglers, the race was nearly over. Where the time had gone, I didn't know.

"Are you hungry?"

I frowned, giving Syd a confused expression.

"It's almost five o'clock and I haven't eaten any real food since this morning. I'm not about to eat runner's Gu for dinner."

"Yeah, I could eat. But it has to be plant-based. My pain in the ass trainer has me on a new meal plan."

Syd laughed and my body tensed. Not in the way it does when I'm pissed off or annoyed. Something entirely different.

"There's a place with pretty good vegan options not too far from my work."

I nodded. "Give me the address and I'll meet you there. My car's parked about a mile from here and I'm betting it'll take a while before either one of us are able to get out of here with all of these people around."

Syd agreed, giving me the address of the restaurant. According to the GPS it would take me about thirty minutes to get there, given the extra traffic due to the race.

At least you're not eating at your place again.

That thought alone had me pushing out a breath of relief. The night she'd brought dinner over to my place and we'd watched that documentary, it'd taken every ounce of my being to overcome the animalistic instinct I had to rip her clothes from her body. She had no idea of how dangerously close she'd come to being thoroughly fucked on my kitchen counter.

We wouldn't be alone in a restaurant. All I needed to do was get through the next few months of training, beat Rodriguez's ass and kick Syd the hell out of my life for good.

CHAPTER ELEVEN

Skullcrusher

Syd

I had no idea why Luke had shown up out of the blue at the half-marathon. But when I spun around and saw him glaring at the old man who had been kind of rude toward me, I couldn't contain the excitement that filled my body. I'd had to remind myself over and over that, technically, I was Luke's employee. My job was to train him, not become attracted to him.

Those were the reminders I gave myself repeatedly as I entered the American style restaurant that was only about a five-minute drive from ParaSquad's business offices. I'd eaten at this place plenty of times, and even though it was a Saturday, early evening, I had no trouble getting a reservation for a table of two when I called after leaving the race.

"Syd Quinn," I told the hostess as I entered the restaurant.

"Oh, your date's already here," she told me, smiling.

"He's not my—" the words fell from my mouth as I saw Luke's large and looming frame rise from the wooden chair he'd sat in.

He was dressed in a dark V-neck and dark denim pants. His usual outfit outside of workout clothes in the gym. Yet, even though the muscles of his chest and abdomen were covered by the shirt, the muscles of his biceps and triceps bulged, drawing even closer attention to the colorful tattoos that resided there. The ones peaking above the collar of his V-neck also drew my attention to his upper body. Finally, I let my eyes lift to meet his handsome, yet grim face.

There were so many things I found intriguing and yet difficult about this man. As I approached the table, the fact that he'd had manners enough to stand and wait for me to be seated before he sat again was one of the many things I found drew me to him. His eyes were another.

Those dark brown orbs carried ghosts of a past he let few people in on. They spoke volumes, but the main command they gave was fuck off. Like a freaking moth to a candle, I found that look irresistible. Then there was the beard that surrounded his pink lips. Thick, shiny and perfect for—

"I'm hungry as a fat chick at an all you can eat buffet. I took the liberty of ordering hummus and pita chips before I pass the hell out," he said, pulling me from my reflections.

Rolling my eyes, I shook my head. Leave it to Luke to open his mouth and make me forget all the nice stuff I had been thinking about him.

"There're better ways you can relate your hunger."

He snorted. "What? I don't have anything against fat chicks. Some of the best one nighters I've had have been with the pleasantly plump."

Glaring at him across the table, I parted my lips and said, "You'd be so much more appealing if you just didn't open your damn mouth."

He chuckled. "Believe me that's not the first time someone has told me those exact words."

Rolling my eyes, I lifted the menu the hostess had placed on the wooden table in front of me. "Whatever, hummus and chips sound good. I'm pretty hungry myself."

There was silence as I stared down at my menu, but I could feel Luke's eyes on me. He did that from time to time. Silently watching, observing me. For what, I didn't know. I got the sense my presence in his world confused him. Truthfully, the space he'd begun taking up in my thoughts confused me. I'd started this job to get my foot in the door as a trainer and to seek a part of my history that'd been taken from me.

"Thought you've been here before."

That was when I lifted my gaze to meet his. He didn't look away as he usually did.

"I have."

"The way you were eye fucking the menu, I would've thought you didn't know what the hell they served."

I tilted my head to the side. "You say the craziest things." I shook my head, smirking.

He lifted one broad shoulder and dropped it, so casually, it too, was a turn on.

"What're you getting?" I asked when I realized he'd pushed his menu to the side.

"Portabella burger with the fixings and sweet potato fries."

"I've had that before. Their fries are delicious. I think I'm going to go with the steak and potatoes with a side of string beans."

Luke's face crumbled into a frown. "How the hell are you going to sit there and eat steak in my face while I eat a damn mushroom and pretend it's a burger?"

Laughter burst out from my mouth at the incredulity I heard in his voice.

"Quite easily, actually," I responded in between bursts of laughter.

He groaned. "This shit better be worth it."

"Aw c'mon. You haven't even complained once about the new diet. You come in every morning with one of your green drinks like you used to do with your pre workouts. I thought you were adjusting well to it."

"I am. Don't mean I want to sit across from you eating steak while I'm eating a damn mushroom."

I laughed again because I couldn't help myself. "You'll survive."

Something sparked in his eyes and they narrowed. "We'll see."

A shiver ran down my back. Not from the words alone, but the look in his eyes as he said them. It was as if there was a deeper meaning to the words. One I couldn't easily discern, but my body registered efficiently.

The waitress appeared a minute later, delivering the roasted pepper and garlic hummus with pita chips. She quickly took our drink and food orders when Luke told her we were ready for both to be taken.

"They make everything right here in the restaurant. Fresh," I informed him before taking my first bite of the hummus and chip in my hand. "Mmm," I moaned at the first bite. "You know, I hated hummus growing up. It's only been the last few years that I've come to appreciate it."

"Is that right?"

Something about the way he asked the question had my gaze moving to his stare. My body instantly stiffened at the way his eyes intently followed the movement of my lips. He wasn't even trying to be sly about it either. It was at that moment I knew that something between us had changed. Maybe not changed. Perhaps it had been there from the very beginning and was in the process of being exposed.

"What made you become a paramedic?" I blurted the question out, wanting to know so much more about this man who was such an enigma to me.

He continued to stare at me across the table. "You a cop or something?"

I frowned at the odd question. "Why would you ask me that?"

He paused before responding. "Just asking."

He was so defensive. Obviously, asking about his background made him uncomfortable, but that wouldn't perturb me from doing so.

"What made you become a 'medic?"

"Life."

"That's not an answer, Luke."

"It's the one you're gonna get, Syd," he condescended, leaning against the table, staring me in the eyes.

It was a dare. A challenge to press him for more information at my own risk. What Luke didn't know—or maybe he did know—was that I was never one to turn down a dare. It was one of my greatest strengths and my most detrimental weakness.

Placing my arms on the table, I leaned forward also. "Let me guess, you thought the training would look good on your college resumé? Needed the extra money for school? Considered going to medical school?"

With a lifted eyebrow, he leaned closer. "All of the above, except for the needing money part," he answered before pulling back.

I weighed his answer over in my mind, searching for the next logical question that would lead me down the road to knowing more about this man. But he beat me to the punch.

"And you? What brought you from being a 'medic to an MMA trainer?"

"Fighting's in my blood," I blurted out before I could stop myself.

He gave me an inquiring look.

Shit.

I'd gotten too comfortable. Revealed too much, too fast.

Luke's gaze dropped to the silver pendant I always wore around my neck.

"My uncle was a boxer and mixed martial artist in his youth, and he convinced my mom to put me in some sort of self-defense and martial arts when I was still young. He said all girls and women should know how to fight."

Luke slowly nodded his head, absorbing the information but not saying much in response. Then he asked, "So where did becoming a 'medic and eventual business owner come in?"

"My mom. In spite of her putting me in martial arts early on, she actually loathed the idea. Especially after she married my stepfather. Neither one of them saw the need for it, so she started to put me in other extracurriculars.

"She wanted me to become a nurse or a doctor. In high school, I started taking EMT classes. When I turned eighteen and went away to college, I majored in biology and worked part-time as an EMT, eventually earning my credentials as a 'medic.

I paused as Luke moved in closer resting his arms on the table, listening intently.

"Go on," he insisted when I stopped talking for too long.

"It only took me until my sophomore year to realize med school wasn't for me. I didn't want to spend the next decade of my life in school and working as an intern and residency in a hospital. So, I opted to get my MBA instead.

"And your friend? The one who runs the company with you?"

"Tanisha and I became friends in college. One night, we started talking. She complained about her job at the city's health department, per usual. I loathed the idea of going into hospital administration. That night, we put our heads together and the concept for ParaSquad came up."

I shrugged at the same time the waitress brought our food to the table. My stomach growled as soon as I smelled my dish. I'd hardly eaten any of the hummus and chips, since I'd gotten so wrapped up in the conversation with Luke.

"How long have you been in business?"

"Almost five years now."

He nodded, taking a bite of his burger, which had been cut in half.

"How is it?" I questioned.

He nodded, staring at the burger. Thankfully, he swallowed and wiped his mouth before answering. "Not bad."

"In Luke speak, that means it's damn good."

He hesitated on the bite he was about to take, staring across the table at me.

Damn, he's sexy as hell.

I squirmed in my chair.

"Luke speak," he repeated before snorting and then parting his lips to take another bite. It was my turn to watch the movement of his lips as he chewed.

"You're not hungry?" He nudged his head in the direction of my uneaten plate.

Shit! I'd done it again, forgetting I was actually very hungry. Picking up my knife and fork, I cut into my medium-well done steak, taking a small piece into my mouth. Admittedly, the steak was good, great even, but it still didn't compare to the previous thoughts I had about the man sitting across from me.

"You know, you still haven't answered my question," I finally said after a few minutes of eating in silence.

"I wouldn't plan on waiting for me to answer it, either," he quickly retorted.

I sagged my shoulders. It was on the tip of my tongue to beg him to tell me something, anything about his past. Something that I couldn't find in any of the articles or write ups online about him.

"Where'd you go to college?"

"You don't give up, do you?"

"These are simple questions. It's not like I'm asking for your social security or credit card numbers."

"You'd have a better shot at getting those."

"Come on, Luke."

He rolled his eyes, huffing. "Vander University."

"Really? That's a great school."

"You sound surprised."

"I am," I responded honestly.

"Why? A meathead NFA fighter can't go to a good school?" he questioned, defensively.

I shook my head. "You don't seem like the type."

He pulled a face before chuckling and pushing back a little from the table. "You're right. I'm not, which is why I dropped out before graduating."

"And then you became Skullcrusher." I grinned.

He gave a one shoulder shrug. "Technically, I was Skullcrusher before dropping out, but that's when it became my pro name."

"How'd you get the nickname?"

"Banks. He came to a gym I used to train at in Bridge Lake. He watched me throughout practice, noticing I always went for the headshot. After that, I became known around the gym as Skullcrusher.

"A year later, once I finally ditched school, I moved out here to train directly under him. He had to teach me the discipline of fighting. Of not always going for the head when a punch or knee to the ribs would do. But it's still my first instinct. To go for the head. Earned more than one knockout because of it."

I tightened my hold on the pendant, not even aware that I'd latched on to it. Clearing my throat, I asked. "You dropped out of college and then began your career as a fighter. What made you go in the first place?" I couldn't imagine Luke was ever the type to go the straight and narrow path.

His face immediately switched to a hard glare. He placed his elbows on the table and allowed his eyes to drop to my plate. "You finished with that?"

Startled, I looked down to my half-eaten plate, before I looked up again to see Luke waving our waitress over.

"Check," he snapped as soon as she arrived. Obviously, a nerve had been struck.

"You have an appointment tomorrow with the physical therapist for a massage," I informed him as we exited the restaurant's front door, me with a box in my hand to take home the rest of my meal.

"I don't need a massage."

"Need it or not, you're getting one. Also, when does our flight leave for Williamsport?"

He looked startled by the question, but he quickly slanted his eyebrows, giving me a frustrated look.

"Our flight doesn't leave because your ass isn't going anywhere."

"Wrong again." I shook my head. "If you're going to Williamsport, so am I."

He rolled his eyes. "Fucking pain in my ass."

"Thank you."

"I'm leaving Thursday and will be back on Saturday. Me. I'm going… alone."

I shrugged. "Okay. Fine."

His forehead wrinkled as his eyebrows lifted and he cocked his head to the side, eyeing me. He remained silent for a heartbeat, as if trying to figure out my angle. He didn't ask another question.

"I'll have a workout drawn up for you for the days you're away."

Something crossed his eyes, but it happened so quickly it was unreadable. Luke was silent as he traced his eyes over my face. We both stood there, eye to eye, toe to toe.

He moved closer somehow. Or maybe I had. Either way, we were only a hair's breadth away from touching. Luke reached a hand up toward the side of my face, just barely grazing it.

Everything in my body told me this was the moment before a first kiss and right when I started to turn my face up, allowing him better access to my mouth, he dropped his hand to his side as he pushed out a heavy breath. Shaking his head, he took a step backwards.

"Where're you parked?"

Blinking, I gave my brain a moment to restart to even understand his question. "Around the corner."

"Let's go."

He didn't wait for me to follow. Just assumed I did as he started in the direction of my parked car. That was classic Luke.

I picked up my pace to get even with him and his long strides.

He made sure to put enough space between us so that our bodies didn't touch as we walked. He kept his hands in his pockets and gaze straight ahead. It might've even appeared as if we were two strangers who so happened to be walking in the same direction. The energy we'd shared sitting across from one another during dinner, Luke staring me directly in the eyes, had shifted. He closed himself off again.

I fought hard not to analyze too closely what made him shutdown. Though it was probably in both of our interests to keep things as professional as possible. Everything in my mind told me not to go down the road my body was pulling me down. I had my own reasons for wanting to become Luke's trainer. Interests he probably wouldn't like. It was likely best I stopped right where I was and dropped my wandering imagination.

"What made you so closed off?" I blurted out as we came to my car, obviously going against my better judgment. Because no matter how smart I might be in school or business, I could never stop myself from reaching over to the dark side for a little taste.

However, as Luke moved in close, placing his arm on the roof of my car, trapping my body between the car and his, staring down over me, I knew I was asking for more than a little taste. I wanted him to lean down a few inches more, pressing his lips to mine, so I could find out whether or not I imagined the chemistry between us.

"You ask too many questions. Are you sure you're not a cop?"," he growled. While his face looked angry, I wasn't scared or put off, which I do believe was his intention.

"My mother used to tell me I asked too many questions also."

"It obviously hasn't stopped you."

I flashed a smile. "No, it didn't."

His teeth clenched, causing his jaw to flex and I wanted to run my fingers through his beard so badly, but I kept my restraint.

"Be careful of the questions you keep asking, darlin'. You might get some answers." With that, he pushed away from me, putting more space between us.

My body instantly deflated at his withdrawal. His nearness had caused my body temperature to rise and I started to feel cold the instant he pulled away.

"Get in your car," he demanded.

I clicked the lock to the driver's side door and slid into the front seat. As I started the car, I could feel Luke's eyes on me, as if searing my profile through the window. Taking one final look in his direction, I watched him as he watched me, sizing me up.

Yeah, he definitely wasn't going to Williamsport alone, whether he knew it or not.

CHAPTER TWELVE

Surprise

Luke

She hadn't asked about my going to Williamsport for the four days we trained together since the weekend of the half-marathon. I'd gotten dangerously close to saying fuck it and buying her a ticket on the same flight as me to the city where my brother lived. I stopped myself with the reminder that she was my trainer.

There were lines there that shouldn't be crossed. That reminder was my last defense against all the nasty shit I wanted to do to Syd.

My typical not giving a fuck attitude when it came to broads wasn't working this time around. It was the proximity. It had to be.

With most chicks, I could uphold enough conversation to land them in my bed for a night, if they were lucky, two, and that was it. No talking about my past, asking about careers and bullshit like that. With Syd it was different.

We worked together five out of seven days a week. As my trainer she had to ask questions like what I ate, how well I slept, how I felt physically. Naturally, that lent itself to deeper conversations. That coupled with those damn dancing lessons. I could still hear her laughter at one of Twinkle Toes' ridiculous jokes. It was like the sound burrowed itself deep inside my chest and refused to let me ignore it.

They say absence makes the heart grow fonder. What they don't tell you is that proximity makes the dick grow enamored. That's what had to be going on between Syd and me. This was the reason I didn't want to hire a woman as my trainer in the first place.

At least, that was what I told myself.

"The hell?" I grunted, sitting up from the bed I'd just laid down on after getting into my room. I'd landed over two hours ago but being hungry, I'd stopped by a restaurant for food before checking in. I hadn't even let Jacob know I was in town yet, so it obviously wasn't him knocking on my door.

"Keep your panties on. I'm coming," I yelled to the insistent knocker, assuming it was one of the hotel staff coming to let me know something I probably didn't care about. When I pulled the door open, it wasn't a hotel worker wearing a short-sleeved polo shirt with the words Renaissance Hotel across the left breast. No, that would've been a more welcomed inconvenience.

This disruption came in the form of a five-foot-six, brown skinned, mole at the top right corner of her mouth, pain in the ass. The very same one I'd just been silently thanking myself for leaving back in Southern California.

"What. The. Hell?" I managed to get out through gritted teeth.

"Surprise," she announced, pushing right through me and entering my hotel room.

"I don't do surprises," I blurted out, seething and turning to her after slamming the door shut.

"You look pissed," Syd surmised.

"Do I?"

"Let me explain," she insisted, holding her hands up in front of her.

I growled at the image in my mind of taking both of those hands in one of mine and slamming them up against the door as I pressed my body against hers.

"I know you didn't want me to come. I promise, I won't intrude on your time with your family. But I—"

"Brother."

"What?"

"Time with my brother. Not my family. There's a difference."

Her forehead wrinkled in confusion and son of a bitch, I found that attractive too.

"Okay... well, either way, I won't butt in on your time with your brother. You have my word. But I think it's important that I be here. The training phase you're entering is getting more complicated and not having anyone with you, even for the next few days, to make sure you're doing everything correctly, could be detrimental."

I listened as she went on about how vital her presence was to my training. I held off on telling her that in Williamsport, I had access to one of the top MMA fighters the last decade had ever seen. That also included his trainer. Why I held back was the ultimate question.

Because you want her here.

My brain shouted at me, daring me to deny it.

"You're not staying in here," I demanded, the only thing I could think of to say.

"No." She shook her head. "Of course not. My room is actually down the hall. Again, like I said, I'm not here to crowd your style or anything. Your brother's opening his business and I respect that. I'm just here to help guide your training. That's it."

I squinted at her, trying to figure out her angle. As I did, my phone buzzed with a text message.

Are you here yet?

It was from Jacob. I quickly typed out a response, letting him know I was at the hotel and what my room number was.

"That must be your brother. I'll leave you to it."

I didn't say anything as I glanced up from my phone to watch Syd roll her suitcase in the direction of my door, opening it, and seeing herself out. As soon as the door closed behind her the entire room felt bereft. As if, in the short three minutes she'd been in here, she'd breathed life into it. Into me. That was the bullshit I couldn't stand the most about being around her.

The emptiness in the pit of my stomach when she wasn't around.

That heady spark of energy I only felt while fighting, jumping out of a plane, racing down a long stretch of highway or, on occasion, fucking, Syd brought on by her mere presence. How the hell was I supposed to counter that?

"Fuck," I cursed before moving to the bedroom to unpack the few items of clothing I'd brought. I'd also brought with me a jump rope and a few bands to do some muscle activation as a way to loosen up after my flight.

Minutes after I changed into a pair of shorts to workout in, Jacob sent me a text informing me he'd be over around six to pick me up for dinner at his home. The house he'd moved into with his wife a few months ago. I'd started to decline the invitation because that was always my inclination, but I reminded myself I was there to watch my brother open his business. It was my job to be there and celebrate him and Grace. I'd showed up to watch him get married months ago, and now to the opening of their business.

Shaking my head, I began jumping rope out on the balcony of the spacious hotel room I'd made sure to reserve.

Although there was a gym on the fifth floor, I chose not to utilize it yet. This was a shakeout workout. Something to get the blood circulating. Not really a training session. And of fucking course, when my thoughts went to training, they strayed to the woman who'd had the unmitigated gall to follow me to Williamsport and reserve a room a few doors down from mine.

Remembering Syd was so close by pissed me off so much I was good and hot after my workout. Not hot in the traditional sense.

By the time I tossed my rope to the floor and made my way to the bathroom, turning the shower on, my cock was as hard as a rock.

I made the water as cold as possible, willing my body to calm the down. Even after stroking my cock—making myself come in the shower—thoughts of thrusting my concrete hard shaft inside Syd—instead of giving myself a hand job—assaulted me.

Only my second release left me calm enough to turn the water off and get my ass out of the shower. As I started to redress in a pair of jeans and a Polo shirt, a knock at my door interrupted me. Seeing the time, I assumed it was none other than Jacob, but once again, I came face-to-face with Syd.

"Oh, you're still here," she sounded breathless.

My eyes trailed her up and down to see that she too, had changed from what she wore earlier. She was now dressed in a pair of form fitting blue jeans, a light tan short-sleeved sweater, and black high heels. It was a more relaxed look than she wore to the gym most days, but I could tell she'd still put effort into her look.

I got the sense it wasn't for my benefit. Even when she'd been working the half-marathon, she'd donned makeup and styled her hair in a high curly puff. She wore it the same way in the hotel room.

"I'm about to head to get something to eat and I was wondering if you had plans... you probably have plans with your brother." She shook her head.

I started to respond to her inquiry but was cut off by another male voice.

"He does have plans," Jacob interrupted.

Syd's eyes widened as she turned, staring at my brother.

"You must be the brother in question." I caught her smile as I stared at her profile.

Jacob didn't smile back. He wasn't the smiling type, but that didn't seem to throw Syd off.

"I'm Luke's new trainer, Syd."

Jacob's gaze moved from Syd to mine, questioning.

I nodded, and he took the hand she offered, shaking it.

"Jacob," he replied.

Something bounced through my chest at the sight of his hand wrapping around hers, however brief the encounter was.

"I won't bother you two. Enjoy your evening."

"You can join us," Jacob suddenly invited.

I glared at him, wordlessly.

Syd looked between the two of us, her lips ajar. That fucking mole at the top of her lip caused my stomach muscles to tense.

"You might as well. You gotta eat, don't you?" I insisted.

Her mouth snapped shut and I cocked my head to the side as Jacob tossed me a stunned look. I shrugged, not giving anyone an answer. Instead, I re-entered my room, grabbing my hotel key off the nightstand along with my wallet, put on my shoes and headed toward the front door.

"If it's an inconvenience, I don't have to tag along. I hear there's some really great shopping in Williamsport that I could get into."

"It's not an inconvenience," Jacob said, before turning to me. "Is it, Luke?"

Fine time to ask me. After he'd already invited her. Now, I'd look like the asshole for saying fuck no it wasn't convenient. I couldn't exactly blurt out the real issue was I'd have a boner at my brother's dinner table, sitting across from my trainer the whole time. Usually, I didn't give a shit about hurting someone's feelings by rejecting them, but oddly, I started to care.

"It's fine. I'm hungry," I grunted.

"He gets hangry when he hasn't eaten in a while," Syd quipped.

Jacob snorted.

"I'm starting to see the family resemblance."

There was little conversation from Jacob and I as he drove us the fifteen minute drive from our hotel to his new home, on the outskirts of the city of Williamsport. As soon as we pulled into the driveway, Jacob's wife, Grace stood outside the door, waving at us.

The woman who'd stolen his heart after he'd believed for most of his life he hadn't had one. That was how he'd put it, anyway. I knew the feeling of not believing you had a heart.

My gaze moved across the car to Syd as she looked between Grace and my brother. I couldn't tell if she was shocked to see, like her, Grace was Black, or if she was trying to figure them out. Jacob's demeanor noticeably changed from reticent and borderline hostile to a touch below giddy as he took barely three strides from the car to the front door, wrapping Grace up in his arms.

Her laughter was effusive.

I rounded the car, moving to Syd's side, more so she wouldn't feel awkward standing by herself meeting another person she didn't know.

"Luke," Grace called. "Thanks for coming," she said excitedly. "We're so happy you get to see the finished product."

I nodded. "I came to ensure I got a place to get some work done if I ever need it," I commented, my eyes glancing over at my brother.

Grace laughed. "You'll always have a place here."

I shook my head. As much as I despised the idea of marriage or being tied to one pussy for life, I could silently admit the bastard had lucked out with this one.

"And this is?" Grace questioned, turning her attention to Syd.

"Syd, I'm Luke's trainer."

The women shook hands.

"Please, come in," Grace welcomed, stepping inside, leaving us to follow.

I let Syd walk ahead of me while Jacob followed.

"Your home is beautiful," Syd commented, taking in the modern style decor.

"Thank you. We're making some changes since Jacob moved in."

Syd, turned with a lifted eyebrow as we passed through the entranceway toward the living room.

"You've had this place awhile?"

Grace nodded. "Lived here for about five years."

"Nice."

"I hope no one's allergic to shellfish. Luke, Jacob said you weren't, but I didn't know you would be joining us, Syd."

"Yes, I guess I was kind of a last-minute addition. Jacob said it would be okay."

"It's fine," Grace quickly responded.

"Good. I usually would bring something, but this was short notice. And no, by the way, I'm not allergic to shellfish. But Luke is on a new plant-based diet as part of his training."

Grace looked at me with lifted brows. "I didn't know. Jacob you didn't tell me that."

"I didn't know either." My brother turned to glare at me.

I shrugged. "I forgot to mention it."

"It's a good thing your trainer is here," Grace commented.

"Yeah, fucking grateful, I am," I snarked.

"Watch your tone," Jacob snapped.

Blinking I looked to him and smirked, realizing he was protecting his woman. My gaze suddenly glided toward Syd and I wondered if I could ever be defensive over a woman.

Yes.

"My bad," I grunted out loud, ignoring the voice in my head that answered without hesitation.

"Luke can't help it. It's probably been at least two hours since he's eaten. He's hangry."

Grace giggled at Syd's joke.

"I can actually agree with Luke on that account. I can get quite hangry myself. Luke, if you don't mind waiting a bit, I can make up a roasted veggie pizza for you, without the cheese of course."

I looked toward my brother whose face was unreadable. "I don't mind waiting. Thanks," I added.

"I'll help," Syd added, surprising me.

"She cooks?" Jacob questioned as he moved to me but peered across the open living room space to where the women talked in the kitchen.

I shrugged. "Have no idea."

I regretted those words as soon as they parted with my lips. I prided myself on not asking too many questions of the women around me. It helped in not getting attached, but with Syd, I found that pride waning more and more. I suddenly wanted to be able to answer Jacob's questions about this woman.

"How long has she been your trainer?"

I pushed my hand through my hair, feeling uncomfortable. I couldn't discern if it was the fact that I was actually having a conversation with my brother or if it was the particular topic of the discussion. Or both.

"Almost two months."

"And she's got you eating plant-based?" He asked.

"That was my choice," I countered.

"Was it?"

"I just said it was, didn't I?"

He chuckled which is a reaction I wasn't expecting, but probably should've been. My brother and I had a complicated relationship. One that was mostly forged in an extremely hostile environment growing up.

Then followed by years of my resentment for his abandonment. At least, what I'd believed had been his abandonment. Turns out, he was actually looking out for me even when he wasn't around.

There'd been shit he'd endured I didn't even know about, that he did his best to make sure I didn't suffer. It took years for me to find all of this out. Now, we were working to rebuild a relationship that wasn't based on aggression or whatever. Jacob was further ahead at this shit than I was.

"How's it working out?"

I sighed. "Truthfully, it's not as bad as I thought it would be. I switched to these green juices in the morning, instead of the bullshit I was drinking, and I wake up with more energy. It's only been a few weeks, but I notice it takes me less time to recover in between tough workouts. There might be something to this nonsense."

Jacob made a contemplative expression before nodding. "Sounds like it might be doing what you need it to."

"We'll see."

"Are you training for that fight with Rodriguez?" he questioned as we took a seat on the couch in the living room.

"Yeah. I'm giving Syd the next five months to prove herself as a trainer and then we'll see where it goes from there."

"You're still going to fight after you win the title?"

"If I win the title," I grunted. "The way my fucking fights have been shaking out lately…" I trailed off feeling disappointed remembering the Caldwell fight.

"Yeah, that was a tough loss," Jacob added.

I pursed my lips as I nodded in agreement.

"Syd helping you with your ground defense?"

"Yep. Hey, O'Brien in town?" I questioned in a lowered voice.

"Seriously?" Jacob asked, angrily.

"Yeah, seriously. I need something to take the edge off." I glanced over my brother's shoulder to the kitchen where Syd and Grace were laughing and cooking.

"She doesn't seem like the type to put up with bullshit. Not nearly as firm and hard assed as Banks, I'd guess, but not to be toyed with either."

I gritted my teeth, hating when anyone brought up my former trainer. Especially those who didn't know him. Jacob had never met Banks. My brother hadn't been a part of my life when Banks was alive.

"She's not. She also doesn't have me by the balls, either."

Jacob turned to peer over his shoulder. It was only when I caught the movement of him turning back to face me, I realized I'd been watching Syd the entire time. My attention barely on my brother.

"Yeah, we'll see. Here's O'Brien's number. There's a fight happening tonight."

"I'll need that address."

"You'll need more than that."

My eye shot to meet my brother's. There was a warning look in his gaze.

"You got something to say, just say it."

He shrugged. "What's the point? I had to screw up everything myself, nearly lose my job in order to get out of my own way." He turned to look over at Grace who carried the food to the dining table. "Luckily, I had a woman in my corner who convinced me to stop being my own worst enemy."

I stood, rolling my head on my shoulders. "Yeah, good for the both of you."

Instead of getting defensive at my snide comment, Jacob merely stood, chuckling and shaking his head, and ensured I'd gotten the number and address he'd texted me.

"Dinner's ready," Grace called from the dining room.

I followed behind my brother in the direction of the smell of the food, but staring over his shoulder at a smiling Syd. Yeah, I was definitely going out tonight. I needed to blow off some steam.

CHAPTER THIRTEEN

Time's Up

Luke

"Are you sure this is the right place, buddy?"

I rolled my eyes at the Uber driver who sat behind the wheel. Pushing the back door of his Camry open, I stepped one foot out.

"Yeah, I'm sure. Don't call me buddy," I demanded, before getting all the way out and slamming the door behind me. I barely noticed as he speedily pulled off. Obviously, he didn't care too much whether or not this was the right location.

To someone who didn't know any better, this wouldn't look like the right place. The brick building from the outside appeared abandoned with its broken windows and padlocks on most of the steel doors. But there was one door that didn't have a padlock.

I'd been waiting to walk through that fucking door for hours, ever since Syd first showed up at my hotel room. The coiled tension that snaked its way through my limbs at seeing her, needed to be relieved somehow. I'd thought a few days away from her would do the trick, but then she showed up in Williamsport.

I couldn't keep my own eyes from continuously straying in her direction throughout dinner with my brother and his wife. I'd long since given up trying to avoid staring her directly in the eyes. Now, my body did it on its own volition. Seeking out that drowning feeling as if it needed its next breath.

Fuck!

I was losing my shit, over a fucking broad, no less. The only thing I knew to do to handle the stress was what drove me here to this building.

Raising my right hand, I gave two hard knocks on the door, paused, and then followed up with three hard knocks. This was the signature knock, according to Jacob and Connor O'Brien. The very same Connor O'Brien who had once been a title fighter in the NFA. In addition to other businesses, he now ran this underground fighting group, simply known to those in the know as The Underground.

"Who the hell is it?" Came a gruff voice through the hole made visible when he slid open the metal cutout at the center of the door.

"Your fucking mother. Open the damn door," I demanded.

A deep, unfriendly, chuckle moved through the hole before it slammed shut again. A few heartbeats later, I heard the unlatching of the door's lock right before it cracked open a few inches.

"You must be Luke. The pain in the ass. Your brother and O'Brien both said you'd be stopping by tonight."

"Then open the damn door."

"Watch your cock sucking mouth. I don't give a shit who you are."

"Let him in, Gunnar," A male's voice instructed behind him.

The behemoth standing guard at the door gave me a once over before stepping back, allowing me to pass through. I, too, gave him a look up and down, sizing up all of his weak points in case he decided to act stupid and make a move. Yeah, my attitude could rub a lot of people the wrong way, but that didn't mean I gave a shit. Especially since most of them couldn't beat my ass even on my worst day. Not even a guy his size.

I looked past the watchman or whatever the hell he was supposed to be, to find a shorter, older man with dark brown eyes and a hard glare.

A smirk slid across my lips. "You must be Buddy."

He inclined his head. "I must be."

"O'Brien's not around?" I looked around the room, staring over his shoulder to see the rectangle boxing ring at the other side, surrounded by folding chairs, and guys taking their seats in them.

"He's at home with his woman."

I frowned because that was another reminder of why I was here at The Underground, in spite of the possible negative repercussions it could have.

"Poor sap."

Buddy shook his head, chuckling. "You haven't seen his woman. He got lucky. Your brother did too."

I didn't respond.

"Anyway, bring your ass on in here and we'll see who's on the menu tonight."

I followed Buddy across the huge concrete floor in the direction of the crowd and the boxing ring. It wasn't my usual fighting space, seeing as how the NFA used a cage and it was an octagon shape, rather than a square. But fighting was fighting, and I'd trained in enough boxing rings to feel comfortable squaring up with anyone, anywhere, at any time.

"Back there's the changing room." Buddy pointed to a closed wooden door. "You can go change into your fighting clothes and by the time you come out, we'll have someone for you."

I headed in the direction he pointed, hiking the strap of the duffle bag I'd brought with me. Making quick work of getting out of the jeans and short sleeve shirt I wore, I changed into a pair of fighting shorts and nothing else. I took time to carefully wrap my hands. After doing a few rounds of warmups and some shadow boxing, I was ready to head out.

"Good, you're still here. We've got Tiny here, who's looking for a fight. Especially since you pissed him off at the door," Buddy told me as I moved closer to the ring.

I looked up and into the center of the square to see the same behemoth who had opened the door for me earlier, grilling me with his stare from the middle of the ring.

A slow, threatening smile spread across my face. I'd already sized him up. I could tell off the bat, he was the type of dipshit who thought his size made him unbeatable. For most people it might've worked too. But I wasn't most people.

I moved closer to the ring, jumping over the lines to enter.

"You liked talking shit at the door. Now let's see if you can back it up."

"Not a problem, you fucking Thanos wannabe," I responded.

His face morphed angrily as I laughed at my own joke.

"All right, you two. Forget that bull about having a clean fight." Buddy told us as he moved between the two of us.

I shook my head. "I'm not looking for a clean fight."

"Oh shit! That's Luke Skullcrusher McConnell," someone from the audience yelled, causing the rest of the onlookers to reply with a series of *oh shits* and *wows*.

I ignored the audience.

"You heard it, Skullcrusher. Your rep's on the line now," Buddy taunted.

"I've got no problems taking down a washed up NFA fighter tonight," Tiny charged.

Heat filled my belly at the sound of his laughter. I glared at Buddy, willing him to get whatever announcement he needed to make over with, so I could wipe the floor with this motherfucker.

"Listen up, you know the rules, Tiny. Skullcrusher, down here, we only have one rule. No hitting in the face, unless a son of a bitch absolutely deserves it. Then all bets are off. Everything else is basically a free for all." Buddy turned to Tiny. "You ready?"

He nodded while intently staring at me.

I returned the favor.

"McConnell?"

"Ready."

"Fight," Buddy yelled before leaping out of the way, allowing Tiny and I to move in closer.

He took a few bullshit swings at me, which I was easily able to dodge and move out of the way. As he moved, I took in his speed, which hand he let dominate his movements, mobility issues he had. All of this gave me insight into the ways in which I could easily and quickly overpower him.

The first blow I was able to land was a sidekick to his knees, forcing him down to a kneeling position. Then, I rained a series of hooks and jabs to both sides of his body, landing in his ribs. Unfortunately, I got sloppy and he recovered quicker than I thought, landing his own punch to my right side. I'd been working on my balance and coordination with Syd, and when I stumbled, instead of falling, I merely took a few steps back.

"That's all you got, you fucking pussy?" I challenged.

He made a deep noise at the back of his throat before charging me, obviously pissed.

That was when I side-stepped him and pushed him from behind, sending him into the ropes, but I didn't back off there. From behind, I grabbed him by the throat, forcing him down to his knees again. I struggled to get my arm firmly around his throat from behind, to effectively put him in a headlock. He wasn't in the mood to go down easily.

He was able to break free of that hold by twisting my arm around. He had me by the arm, an effective arm lock, but I was no stranger to this move. Nor was I a pussy about to give up this fight.

Instead of giving in like he'd expected apparently, I stepped one foot up on the corner poles that held the ropes together and used the momentum to propel my body into a backflip. Thereby twisting my arm around so it was right sided again. At the same time, Tiny lost the hold he had on my arm and let it go, allowing me to maneuver.

As soon as I landed on two feet, I sent a jab to the center of his chest and then a right hook to his left ribs. The howl of pain he let out, let me know this was his sensitive spot. So instead of letting up, I kept going—another sidekick landed at those same ribs.

Tiny grunted and barked in pain, but he didn't quit. Which, if nothing else, I could respect an opponent who'd fight until the end. We kept at it, blow for blow. When Tiny got pissed, he took a swing at my face. That made me laugh out loud, right in the middle of the ring. My cockiness earned me an actual blow to the face when he swung again, landing a hook to my jaw. As soon as it landed, I felt the blood start to fill the inside of my cheek.

"Motherfucker." I spit the blood out onto the floor of the ring, before charging Tiny. The taste of my own blood propelled me. I side-swiped Tiny's leg, plunging that behemoth to the ground before landing on top of him and wailing on his ass. He tried to counter but it was useless. All I saw was red until I felt hands pulling me off.

"Get the hell off of me," I snarled, still wanting to take my pound of flesh.

But as I was pulled off, Tiny stood, breathing hard and staring across the ring at me. A cut from over his eyebrow caused blood to trickle down the side of his face.

"You're done, McConnell. Good fight."

I turned to see the guy known as Buddy giving me a hard glare. His eyes were telling me it was finished. And though, tension still moved through my veins, I knew this fight was over.

I nodded. "Who's next?" I challenged, looking around.

Buddy's eyebrows raised briefly. "You want to go again?"

I nodded. "That's what the hell I came here for. To fight." That and to forget the woman at the hotel I stayed at. If I was down there fighting, I wouldn't be in close proximity to her. That was exactly what I needed.

Buddy shrugged. "It's your career on the line. Who wants a chance to take on NFA's own Luke Skullcrusher McConnell?" He looked out to the audience, questioning.

A series of hands raised, and Buddy looked back at me.

"Line 'em the fuck up."

Syd

"What the hell am I doing?" I asked myself for at least the fortieth time, that night. No, wait, it wasn't night. Looking at my watch, I realized it was nearing three o'clock in the morning.

My ass should be asleep. I should be in bed, resting to wake up the next day and go shopping with Luke's sister-in-law, Grace, like I said I would. We were going to find something for me to wear to their opening, after Grace insisted I attend. That's what I should've been doing. But what was I actually doing?

Pacing.

Like a dumbass, I stood in front of Luke's hotel room door, pacing back and forth, waiting for him to arrive. I hated to admit that I'd been there for over an hour, like a damn neglected wife waiting for her cheating ass husband to arrive home. Or worse, a parent whose rebellious teenager snuck out late thinking no one would notice.

I loathed the idea and yet, I couldn't move away from the door. I tried to force myself back to my own hotel room, to mind my business. Had even been successful on a few attempts, but then I just ended up walking in circles in my own room, and at every noise or person I heard in the hallway I peaked my head out to see if it was Luke. Around two a.m. was when I finally gave up and decided to pace outside his room, waiting.

Why was I waiting?

Good question.

I told myself it was because Luke was my trainee, it was my responsibility to ensure he kept on his strict diet and workout regimen to prepare for his next fight. However, that was nonsense and I didn't even bother to try to convince myself it wasn't. Luke had been fighting for most of his adult life. He knew what limits to push and not push to ensure he'd be able to train, I supposed.

No. The truthful reason I waited outside of Luke's hotel room was because I was curious. More than curious, actually. I was driven by a need to know he was all right. He'd been quiet throughout most of our dinner with his brother.

At first, I thought it was because I'd intruded on his time with his brother and sister-in-law. But the more I thought about it, the more I recognized he'd been behaving this way even before this trip to Williamsport. Maybe that's why I got on that plane to come here in the first place.

Honestly, the truth was that I didn't want to admit why I was so concerned about Luke and what would make him stay out nearly all night, when we had an early morning workout session scheduled. I bit my bottom lip, thinking of the possibility he could've been out with a woman, and simply enjoying himself. That thought alone almost sent me back to my room with my tail between my legs.

Of course, that was the likeliest of answers. Luke was a good-looking man, a professional athlete who was in great shape. And a grade A asshole. Women flocked to men like him. Why wouldn't he be out with a woman at this time of night?

That realization had my stomach sinking. There in that hallway, standing in front of his door, I had to admit to myself that somehow, I'd gone ahead and developed an attraction for the man I was supposed to be training.

Dumbass.

Yup. I couldn't even refute that snarky voice in my head who called me names. I was a real fool for this one.

Yet, I continued to linger in front of his door, working up the dignity to turn my ass around and get back to my hotel room before anyone else saw me.

Then, just like that, the hotel's elevator doors parted and Luke stepped off. Though his head was down, and I could only see his profile, I knew it was him. The way my heart rate picked up and the butterflies in my belly danced, my body knew who it was without seeing his actual face.

When he did lift his head and turned to look down the hallway toward his room, an involuntary gasp escaped my lips.

"What the hell happened?" I blurted out as he moved closer, the purple bruising around his eye and swelling becoming more evident.

"What the hell are you doing out here?" He barked, looking me up and down. "Dressed like that."

I looked down, having forgotten I was out in the hallway, dressed in my light blue shorts and button up cotton pajama set. With my matching bootie slippers.

"Waiting on you," I answered back almost as sharply.

"Why?"

He had the nerve to be angry. As if he hadn't just come back to the hotel at three in the morning with a bruised face.

"Don't answer that. Go back to your room, Syd," he growled as he inserted the plastic keycard into his own room's door, pushing himself inside.

I did the very opposite of what he'd wanted me to do, and charged inside after him, slamming the door shut behind us both. I didn't give him a chance to remove the leather jacket he wore, as I charged over to the center of the suite's living room, taking his right hand into the both of mine, lifting it to get a clear view.

I deepened my frown when I saw the swelling and bruising around his knuckles. I did the same with his left hand and it was the same there.

"You've been fighting. Where?"

"None of your business." Snatching his hand free, he removed his coat and tossed it onto the couch along with the duffle bag he held. He then removed the short sleeve shirt he wore. That too, was tossed onto the couch.

"I'm your trainer. It's my damn business what you do!"

His sharp gaze moved to me. The flash of anger in his eyes was almost alarming and... erotic.

My body responded in kind and I had to fight from raising my hands over my breasts to stop him from seeing the way my nipples pebbled beneath the cotton material of my top. I mentally kicked myself for forgetting to put on a damn bra before leaving my room.

"There are no legit fighting gyms open at this time of night, so that has to mean you weren't fighting at a gym. You were fighting in an underground ring?"

He stood tall, folding his arms over his massive chest and again, I fought to keep my eyes planted on his face, and not to move any lower. The last thing I needed was for my knees to go weak.

"What's it to you?"

"Luke, you know the NFA has strict rules against fighting in any underground fights. What if word gets out or someone snapped a picture of you fighting tonight? You could be suspended. Your career could be over. Hell, you could even be sued. Do you want that? Is that what you're trying to do?"

"What the hell is it to you?" he roared, sending me a couple of steps back.

But instead of being scared, I became pissed off.

"What the hell do you mean, what's it to me? I don't get up at five fucking o'clock in the morning to write up workouts for you, to study the latest research on recovery and workout techniques, to scout out the best grapplers in our area to work with you just so you can screw it up."

"What the hell for?" he yelled. "You get paid either way. Why the hell are you putting so much time and effort into all of this?"

"For you! You idiot!"

Four words.

That's all it took.

Most people will say the last two were an insult.

But Luke was good at reading between the lines. Because his response wasn't another smartass comment, or an angry retort hurled my way. No, his reaction was so much worse.

In two long strides, Luke was in my face, his massive hands curling around my arms, pulling me to him as his mouth slammed down against mine. The contact pulled an immediate groan from my lips. My entire body sighed in relief, as if this was very the thing it'd been begging me for, for weeks now. The kiss wasn't gentle. It wasn't kind and endearing. Two things I doubted Luke could ever be.

It was insistent.

And gritty.

And messy.

And perfect as hell.

I shouldn't have been so surprised at how skilled Luke was at kissing. I really shouldn't have been stunned at how my body completely opened up to him either. It was receptive to whatever it was he wanted to do. My lips opened, allowing his tongue to enter my mouth, moving along the length of the roof, causing my entire body to sizzle with a heat that was totally foreign to me.

"Shit," I cursed when Luke walked us backwards until my back pressed firmly against the door of his hotel room.

"That's why the fuck I went out to fight tonight," he said through clenched teeth, panting as he fought to catch his own breath. "Because it was either fight or bang on your door until you opened it and fuck you until you couldn't see straight."

A literal pool formed between my legs. If my pussy lips could talk, they would've screamed out *YES* to everything he'd just said.

"Luke—"

"I'm going to give you five seconds to get the hell out of my hotel room, Syd. After those five seconds, if you're still here, I'm going to carry you to my bedroom, strip your ass bare, turn you over and shove my cock so deep inside you, you won't know where I start and you end."

"Luke."

"One."

"We."

"Two."

"Shouldn't."

"Three."

"Um."

"Four."

"Five," I purred at the same time he did, wrapping my arms around his neck and pulling his face to meet mine, while he lifted me by the hips, wrapping my legs around his waist.

Again, he wasn't gentle as he damn near threw me onto the bed, his body coming down over mine. His hands were everywhere, seeking out buttons and undoing them all before moving lower to the waistband of my shorts. It took one hard tug with his left hand and before I knew it, my shorts were down and around my knees. He moved his hand quickly to my core, seeking out my swollen button while he continued to kiss the living shit out of me.

I arched my back and neck, my body seeking more of his rough attention. The calloused nature of his hands only served to increase the feeling of his body rubbing against the most sensitive part of mine. I moaned into his mouth and he swallowed it down, seeking out more. The hairs of his beard aided in increasing the mounting tension as it tickled my skin when he moved his head down the side of my neck.

He moved his right hand to my left breast squeezing it, causing me to jolt in an erotic pain-pleasure episode. It took no time at all for Luke to do just as he said he would, stripping me completely bare. Of course, he received no resistance at all from me, save for my arms and hands getting in the way as I tried to undo the belt buckle and button of his jeans.

His entire body stilled as he let out a hiss of air when I reached inside his pants, wrapping my hands around his massive shaft. I would love to say I never imagined what Luke would feel like, like this. That would be a lie.

My dreams had me imagining what length and girth he was, and even my vivid imagination was no match for reality. My mouth instantly watered at the thought of putting him in between my lips, but Luke had other plans.

He quickly removed my hand from his pants, lifting my wrists over my head with one hand while he used his other one to pull his wallet from his back pocket, and pulled out a condom. Tossing his wallet to the floor, I watched him tear the golden package open with his teeth, pulling out the latex that would sheath him as he entered me.

It was a necessity. I knew it was. I'd never foregone this very important step in protecting myself sexually. But there was something inside me that regretted, just a tiny bit, I wouldn't get to feel him in his entirety.

That thought wasn't given long to marinate in my mind before I found myself flipped onto my stomach. He moved his hands to my waist, holding me securely upright on my knees.

"Don't move your hands," he growled low in my ear.

Goosebumps rose along my arms and I was filled with a sense of anticipation, unlike any other I'd felt before.

"Luke," I screamed when he pushed inside me with one powerful thrust of his hips.

His response to my calling his name was a grunt and withdrawal of his hips before surging back in. My knees began shaking along with the quivering in my belly. I arched my back and let out a groan from the depths of my core. Luke leaned down over my body and again covered my lips with his, even as his body continued to pound into mine.

I was breathless, shaking and soaking wet in between my legs. He moved his hand to my belly, pressing firmly against it, pulling my back to his abdomen. I lifted my hands over my head, intertwining them around his neck and pulled at his hair. He growled against my lips, while moving one hand up to pinch my right nipple. And that was it.

That was the final stimulation I needed to send me spiraling into my first orgasm of the night. Luke swallowed down my screams, as if he was feeding off of them. His hips kept pumping, as the muscles of my core flexed around his rod, pulling his orgasm from his body.

"Shit," he groaned.

It was the sexiest sound I ever heard, and my body reacted to it yet again.

That was the first of many orgasms between the two of us that night.

CHAPTER FOURTEEN

The Morning After

Syd

So what happens now?

I wasn't even fully awake, and that question lingered on my mind. What the hell had I gotten myself into? This wasn't supposed to be a part of the plan. Not by a long shot.

Never was I supposed to have fallen into bed with Luke freaking McConnell. He was supposed to be my foot in the door of the training world. Along with a ticket to some information I was trying to get. That's it. Now, I was lying naked in his bed, after having my body thoroughly satisfied over the past few hours.

"You're thinking too fucking loudly," he groaned, his voice deep and full of sleep, disrupting my thoughts.

"How can I think too loudly?" I replied, laughing as he turned over and tossed a heavy arm over my waist, snuggling up closer to my body.

"Hell if I know, but you're doing it." He moved his hand underneath the sheet that covered my body, squeezing my thigh.

"That makes no sense, Luke." I'd meant my comment to be a snarky retort, but it came out as more of a purr.

"And it really doesn't make any damn sense that after I gave you three life changing orgasms last night you're up this damn early, interrupting my sleep." He snuggled his face into the crook of my neck, his warm breath moving over the skin of my shoulder, causing more goosebumps to rise.

"Two… it was only two life changing orgasms."

"You forgot the one I gave you that put you to sleep." He moved his hand up my thigh to cup my ass.

An involuntary sigh passed through my lips. "Oh yeah," I crooned, remembering that final orgasm. His face had been between my legs that time.

"Oh yeah," he mocked, lifting his head to nip at my earlobe with his teeth.

I shivered before turning fully onto my back to stare up at him. I winced at the sight of his swollen and purple and blue left eye. Lifting my hand, I cupped his cheek, running my thumb against the lower portion of the bruising.

"I should kick your ass for what you did last night."

A smirk appeared.

"For forever changing your life with this dick."

Rolling my eyes, I punched him in the shoulder. "No, dummy. For going out and jeopardizing everything you have by getting into an underground fight." *And for harming that beautiful face of yours.* Thankfully, I shut my damn mouth before that last part escaped it.

"It was more than just one fight," he countered.

I shook my head and sat up on my elbows. "You know that's not the smartest thing to do, right? Please tell me it's not something you do regularly."

Luke huffed before moving away from me to the side of the bed, climbing off of it.

"You sound like Pit," he grumbled.

"What?"

"Nothing. If I knew you were going to bitch about my fighting, I would've let you keep quietly drowning in your own thoughts this morning."

"I'm not bitching. I'm reminding you of what you have to lose."

He stood at the side of the bed completely naked. "Consider me reminded."

I swallowed as my eyes moved down his body, ogling the contours and indentations his layers of muscles made. The tattoos served to highlight how ripped he was. But even with the tats I could make out some of the bruising he'd sustained the night before.

"How many fights did you get into?"

He pushed out a breath, cracking his neck. "Syd."

"How many?"

"Four."

My eyes bulged. He'd taken on four contenders the previous night and then come back to the hotel and still fucked me like a stallion.

"Did you win?"

"Every single one."

"You better have."

"Why? You were going to take 'em on if I didn't?"

I rolled my eyes and tossed the sheets off of me before getting up to look for my discarded pajamas.

"What are you doing?"

I peeked up from the floor, searching for my clothing to watch Luke give me a confused expression. "I have to go back to my room to shower and get changed for the day. Grace and I are supposed to be doing some shopping while you and Jacob do whatever you guys were going to do to prepare for the opening tomorrow."

"After my workout session."

I shook my head. "Not happening."

"Grace can wait. Isn't that what you brought your ass here for? To make sure I got my workouts in?" He slowly moved around the bed, not apprehensive at all about being completely nude, standing before me with a semi-erection.

"This isn't about Grace." I forced myself to maintain eye contact with him. "After the bullshit you pulled last night, you need to rest and recover."

He let his eyes carve a pathway down the length of my body, darkening as they went.

"And stop looking at me like that," I snapped, pressing my hands into my hips.

"I'll look at you however the hell I want."

My body displayed its treachery when my nipples hardened at the baritone in his voice. However, I quickly side-stepped him as he reached for me. "No. We'll use the hotel's gym to do a short restorative yoga session and I'm going to find some ice for you to take an ice bath before you go out with your brother. Meet me there in ten minutes," I ordered, quickly putting on my own pajamas before heading for the door, without looking back.

If I had, there was a good chance I would've talked myself out of leaving and an even better chance I would've spotted Luke's heated gaze on my backside. That also would not have helped my possibility of exiting the room any sooner.

Ten minutes later, Luke and I met at the hotel gym's doorway.

"You're on time. Good."

"You said ten minutes."

I nodded, appreciating that ever since that one encounter with him being a few minutes late, he'd been a stickler for time. Even after what happened between us the night before.

"The hell is restorative yoga?" He asked as we entered.

"It's a slower paced yoga session where you hold the poses longer and use more props to support your body. It allows your body to do less work while still getting a good stretch. It's great for recovery, which you need." I leveled a hard glare at him, still angry about the fact that this was even necessary.

"Save your stares and speeches, I know I fucked up."

I blinked.

"What? I can admit when I'm in the wrong."

That pulled a laugh out of me. "Since when?"

He smirked. "Last night." He wiggled his eyebrows.

Rolling my eyes, I waved him off, as I showed him to the small space of the gym, I'd set up with a few yoga blocks and mat.

"Shit," he grunted when he moved to stretch out a particularly sore spot.

"That's what your ass gets. I couldn't get my hands on enough ice for an ice bath but there is a jacuzzi here in the hotel. I booked you some time in it, in about twenty minutes," I told him as I looked up at the mounted clock.

"No time. I'm meeting Jacob."

"Wrong again. I texted Grace and told her to let your brother know, you needed another hour. Problem solved."

Luke shrugged. "Whatever. Can I get off this damned floor, now?" He asked at the same time he pushed out of the pigeon position I had him holding.

"Maybe we should incorporate more yoga into your training," I wondered out loud.

"Fuck no."

Ignoring Luke, I grabbed my cell phone out of my pocket and made a note to look up a yoga instructor I knew, once we got back home.

When I looked up from my phone, I found his eyes locked on me. The same expression he gave me the night before right before we kissed came to mind. My heart hammered in my chest, remembering the ways in which he made me scream the night before.

I shook my head and said, "You need to head to the jacuzzi. Third floor."

"I know where it is." His voice was thick, and his penetrative gaze never left mine.

The air around us swelled with something new. It vibrated with a new tension that'd always been there but now it bubbled to the surface and spilled over.

There was no stuffing this genie back into its bottle. Not that I wanted to. Again, that was the damn problem. It seemed, neither one of us wanted to turn back, and that made this whole situation that much more complicated.

"Did you get the fighting out of your system last night?" I asked.

"I'm not going back out to fight tonight if that's what you're really asking."

I nodded. "It is."

Luke moved close, taking my chin in between his thumb. He held our faces mere inches apart.

"I told you why I went out last night."

"Because you were trying to avoid knocking on my door."

He shook his head. "Not knocking, Syd. Breaking that motherfucker down. This shit has been driving me crazy for weeks and you bringing your ass to Williamsport didn't help matters."

I tucked my head, grinning, before looking back up at him. "I should apologize."

"Save it. We both know you wouldn't mean it. And I wouldn't accept even if you did." He stared into my eyes for a long moment. There was so much life behind those brown pupils. So many questions that desired to be answered. Both his and mine.

"What does this mean, Luke?" I had to ask because the question was nearly choking me.

He shrugged. "Shit. Hell, if I know."

"Am I still your trainer?"

He looked at me like I had two heads.

"What? You thought I was gonna fire you because we fucked?"

I winced at the way he mentioned it, but I nodded.

He gazed upward a smirked playing at his lips. "I should, shouldn't I?"

I punched him in his shoulder. "Remember that sexual harassment suit you were oh so nervous about before hiring me? Try to fire me and see what happens."

He rose. "My girl likes to play dirty, huh? I like that shit."

The muscles in my stomach clenched and my body warmed all over at the underlying growl that appeared in his tone.

"Fuck with me and we'll see how dirty I can get," I retorted. Why did I say that? My knees immediately went weak at the look in his eyes. "You need to head to the jacuzzi," I told him just above a whisper.

"Are you coming?"

The deep richness in his voice felt as if it reached down into my belly and warmed me from the inside out.

"No." I cleared my throat and shook my head. "The recovery is for you. I don't need to be there. Make sure you do the full hour," I said before taking a step back and picking up the yoga blocks and mat to return them to their rightful place.

I kept my focus on the gym equipment even as I heard Luke's footsteps exiting the gym. Not until the click of the door closing, signaling his exit did I let out an exhale.

"What the heck am I going to do now?" I murmured while heading back to my own room.

***

"Do you enjoy working at the hospital?" I questioned Grace as we strolled down the sidewalk of the outside mall, close to the center of Williamsport's downtown area.

"I love it. I'm going to miss it once I start at our practice full-time."

"Yeah, I bet, but it's so exciting for both of you."

Grace looked over at me, a nervous smile on her lips. "It is but scary at the same time. I mean, I've barely started my nurse anesthetist program and that'll take at least eighteen months to complete, if I'm lucky. Add helping to get the practice up and running, and still being a newlywed…it's a lot on my plate but I can't wait."

I smiled. Grace and Jacob's official opening party was the following evening. Her family would be arriving in Williamsport in a few hours.

Wordlessly, I nodded my head in the direction of a little ice cream stand that was open. "I've got a taste for some cookies and cream," I commented.

"They've got the best ice cream. Chocolate chip cookie dough is my favorite," Grace added as we got in line.

"Have you turned in your resignation at the hospital yet?"

"For now, I'm going to be doing some per diem hours there. We hired a nurse anesthetist for the practice until I'm licensed. She'll be working with Jacob when he operates for the next year or so and I'll assist." She laughed. "Sounds crazy, right? Two jobs and going to school?"

I shrugged. "I've heard crazier."

A look of excitement crossed Grace's face.

"If you have any questions on running a business, feel free to ask," I offered.

"Remind me of what your business is again?"

"It's called ParaSquad." I quickly explained the business to Grace as we ordered and then received our cups of ice cream, before continuing our perusal of the outdoor mall.

"Then you work in healthcare yourself."

I nodded.

"And you're a trainer for mixed martial arts athletes?"

"Just Luke so far. He's my first client, actually."

Her eyebrows lifted as she gave me a surprised look. "What made you go into training athletes? Don't you need a degree for that?"

Shrugging, I said, "I've been doing some sort of martial art since I was a little girl. I've always enjoyed the art of fighting. The strategy behind it all. My mother hated it, but I watched any and every boxing match, wrestling or MMA bout if it was on the television.

"In college and grad school, while working as a paramedic, I also took classes in kinesiology, physical therapy, and nutrition."

"That's an interesting mix," Grace commented.

I nodded, agreeing. "I was never certain of exactly what I wanted to do with all the information I learned but still wanted to utilize it in some way. Through ParaSquad, I'm able to fulfill my passion to help others, and training allows me to utilize passion for fighting and the knowledge I've acquired."

Grace nodded. "It's interesting how you were able to weave together your different interests like that."

I agreed, inclining my head, while spooning another scoop of ice cream into my mouth. "Hopefully, it'll work out and I'm able to get Luke in the shape he needs to be in to win his next bout."

"It's for the championship title, isn't it? With a Dominguez or—"

"Rodriguez," I corrected, laughing.

Grace gave me a sheepish look. "I don't really follow the NFA that closely. Jacob does to keep an eye on his brother, but I do so in passing."

"No worries at all. It can be a brutal sport to watch if you're not used to it."

"Aw man, you're so right about that. So much blood and broken noses and everything. I mean, I'm a nurse so I'm used to seeing that sort of aftermath, but knowing people voluntarily get into the ring and do that stuff for fun or to make money." She visibly shivered. "I tell Jacob that maybe he should advertise at some of the local fights, right? Have a big ol' placard on the wall of the arena that reads, come and see plastic surgeon, Dr. Jacob Reynolds to fix that broken nose of yours or correct your cauliflower ear."

Grace and I laughed.

"I can picture it," I said before remembering something she said that stuck out. "Did you say Dr. Reynolds?"

She turned to me with a furrow in her brow. "Yeah."

"As in Jacob Reynolds."

She nodded slowly.

"That means you're Grace Reynolds."

"Yup. As non-traditional as I might be in some ways, I dropped my maiden name to take on Jacob's last name."

"Right... so that's Jacob's last name but Luke goes by McConnell," Grace and I said at the same time.

A number of questions filled my head at that point. There could be a simple explanation for why two brothers had two different sur names. Until my mother officially changed my last name when I was twelve, I had a different last name than my younger brother.

Maybe Luke and Jacob had different fathers. Neither one of them had mentioned anything about their parents the night before over dinner. Admittedly, I'd found it a bit odd, but suspected it was yet another topic that was off limits with Luke. Of course, that was before he and I had taken our relationship to the next level.

"They have different last names," I finally said out loud to Grace.

The look on her face said with that one simple question, I'd moved into uncomfortable territory.

"They do," she responded slowly. "If you want to know any more about that, I suggest you speak to Luke about it."

I sagged my shoulders feeling frustrated. "I was afraid you'd say that. Getting information out of him is like getting blood from a stone."

She let out a wry laugh. "Trust me, that is definitely a family trait."

"Hm-hm." I started walking again but was stopped by Grace's hand on my forearm.

"Tread lightly with Luke."

My gaze moved from her hand on my forearm to meet her eyes. "I'm only his trainer." The words were even difficult to get out, as if my own body were physically rejecting the lie.

She gave me a once over, her eyes revealing she didn't believe a word I'd just said. I should've remembered as a nurse, she had developed a keen sense for reading people. Most of the 'medics and nurses I'd come across, who were great at their professions were that way.

"You and I know that's not the whole truth." She shrugged and held up her free hand. "And I'm not looking to get into your business. You two are adults. I'm just offering a little bit of wisdom from my own experience. Being loved by my husband is the greatest thing that's ever happened to me in my life. But it does come with its challenges. Many of which are a result of how he was raised."

I started to ask Grace for more information. What did she mean, how he was raised? Did it have to do with why I'd had such a difficult time finding any information about Luke's past? But Grace shook her head, silently conveying she was done talking about this subject, for now.

Sighing, I let the questions die on my tongue. If I wanted to know more, I'd have to go directly to the source. Silently, I questioned if it was even fair of me to do so when I was harboring a secret of my own.

"Thanks for the heads up, Grace."

"I'll add one more piece of advice. If Luke loves anything like his brother. I mean, if he's even one-tenth as giving, caring, protective, and kindhearted as Jacob, then he's worth the challenges."

My brows lifted in surprise at the seriousness I saw in her eyes. She meant what she'd said. At first, it was hard for me to imagine the man I'd met the night before, the way she described.

Jacob didn't speak much to myself or Luke. He came across as serious and closed off. But then I remembered how his demeanor shifted as we pulled up to the house and he saw Grace standing outside waiting. His body language changed and a smile—one wouldn't think him capable of at first appearance—crossed his face.

A smile that met his eyes. I totally could see where Grace was coming from. Jacob was a man who saved his love for a select few. In my experience, people like that had learned somewhere along the line the outside world wasn't safe. I wondered who or what had taught him that. More importantly, I wondered if Luke had learned the same harsh lesson.

I thought about Luke since the first time I'd introduced myself to him. All of his smartass comments that were obviously designed to keep people at arm's length. Then there was the night before.

When he'd admitted the reason he went out fighting at an underground group was so that he could keep away from me.

Yes, Luke had learned the same mistrust of others.

I wondered if the lessons he learned would extend to me, and if so, how much would it hurt when he shut me out?

CHAPTER FIFTEEN

You Date?

Luke

"Slow it down, Luke."

I ignored Syd's yelling from ringside and circled my sparring partner, ready to take his ass down.

"You're moving in too quickly," she called again as soon as I moved in for a headlock with Antonio.

"Fuck," he grunted.

A smile pursed my lips when I realized I had the fucker right where I wanted him. Spinning and dropping down on my back, I locked my legs around his neck. In less than fifteen seconds, once my legs began tightening, he tapped out, and I released my hold.

"What the hell was that?" Syd's angry rant came, dampening my high.

I frowned, glaring at her. "The hell do you mean? I just kicked his ass. Did you see that leg lock?"

Rolling her eyes, she shook her head. "I told you to slow it down. Take it easy."

"For what? I won."

"Yeah, with Antonio. But had you been up against a better grappler, they would've taken you down with the amount of your left side you exposed. No offense, Antonio," she finished, holding up her hand and looking over my shoulder to the guy I beat.

That, for some reason pissed me off, and I found myself, taking her by the arm and leading her across the gym floor to my office, slamming my door behind me.

"Luke, what the hell? Don't man handle me," she insisted snatching away from me.

"That wasn't what you said three nights ago."

Her eyes bulged and her jaw tightened. My cock twitched. Angry sex was the best sex, in my opinion.

"Don't you dare look at me like that. We're at work," she insisted through gritted teeth.

"Not my fault my mind keeps picturing you on your knees, back arching, in front of me as you take all of me."

"Luke!"

I gritted my own teeth, running my hand through my hair. What the fuck was happening to me? Nothing, and I mean, *nothing*, had ever gotten in the way of me fighting. I could always drown out all the crap that was going on in my world, and focus on the fight, whether in the cage, or here at the gym. Now, in a matter of weeks, the only thing I wanted more than to fight was Syd.

"I think you need to take up yoga."

I blinked and gave her an incredulous look. "You're still on that bullshit? First, dancing, now yoga. Are you training me to win a fight or to be the perfect date?" I twisted my head, cracking my neck. I still didn't see the purpose of those damn lessons, but I continued to show up them.

She narrowed her eyes and slammed her hands against her hips. "The lessons are working. And you're taking yoga."

"Why? If this is necessary for my training explain it to me." I crossed my arms over my chest and stared.

She pursed her lips, lifting her head to the ceiling. "Must you fight me on everything?"

"Yes."

"Fine," she said, dropping her hands. "Yoga. Not only will it help with your flexibility and mobility. More importantly, one of your weaknesses in the ring is that you move too quickly. You've got superb reflexes, and anyone can see they're honed. But you're too reactionary. Looking to get it done too quickly. Patience is, more times than not, the name of the game. You're quite impatient, Luke. Yoga might help slow you down a bit. And the flexibility will aid in your grappling."

"I don't need slowing down," I countered.

"You do. I wasn't kidding when I said if you had been paired with a better fighter that shit you pulled against Antonio wouldn't have sufficed. That reminds me, we're going to need to get you some better sparring partners. I've been calling around and I have a few who are interested in training here at Peak Fitness."

Nodding, I said, "Bring 'em down. We'll see what they got."

"And the yoga?"

"No fucking way." I shook my head adamantly, crossing my arms over my chest.

"Great. I've already spoken with an instructor from a local studio. I used to attend his classes. He's A1."

"Did you hear what I just said?"

"I did, but I'm ignoring you because I'm your trainer not the other way around. And don't you dare say something smart about you being my trainer in the bedroom or whatever you were about to say," she commented sternly, pointing a finger at me with narrowed eyes.

A deep chuckle moved up my chest and pushed past my lips. Shrugging, I said, "I'll save it for another time."

"I bet you will."

I grabbed the T-shirt I'd worn to the gym from the back of my chair and pulled it over my head.

"Hey, your masseuse will be here in thirty minutes."

"I'm aware."

"Good. I have to head to work. Oh, and we need to discuss this exhibition fight I want you to do. It's next month."

I blinked. "First you say I'm fighting too much now you're setting me up fights before the title match? Make up your damn mind, Syd."

"My mind's made up. You'll be taking on Luca Morelli," she said as I plopped down in my chair.

"Why?"

"He's a better grappler than you and we need to see how you do in the cage after what we've implemented so far."

"That's not taking on too much?"

"Trust me."

I snorted, but didn't say anything. Syd's training had been unconventional up until that point. I couldn't say for sure whether or not it worked, or if it would give me what I needed to win against Rodriguez, but I didn't feel compelled to argue about it right then.

"Luke. What—" she yelped when I pulled her by the wrist, bringing her body to me. Sitting in my chair, I sat her on my lap. Syd, turned her head to stare out the window. I guessed looking to see if any of the other gym goers or instructors had noticed the semi-intimate move.

Fuck them. I thought. They'd inevitably find out sooner or later that our relationship had gone beyond trainer-trainee. Why not now?

"We haven't been on a real date yet."

Her eyes bulged at my whispered words.

"You date?"

"Hell no."

She laughed.

"But I will for you."

Truthfully, I didn't even know if I knew how to date. I'd gotten by for years with so little effort. Dating seemed more like a hassle than anything else. The women I went out with always knew what the deal was.

Syd stopped laughing. She stared down at me, a question lingering in her eyes. The very same eyes I'd avoided looking directly into for so long. Now, it was as if my body made up for lost time because I couldn't stop staring at them.

"Where?"

"The NFA fight Friday night."

"Are you feeding me too?"

"In more ways than one, Syd."

Those full ass lips broadened into a smile and it took all my strength not to completely clear my desk and bend her ass over it. I had to remind myself that my office was completely visible to everyone else in the gym. I was a man who was open and up for many things but sharing Syd's body with others wasn't one of them. Even if she'd been down for it.

I hadn't touched Syd since that first night. The following days had been spent with Jacob and Grace, celebrating the opening of their practice.

"I have to go."

"You should before I kick everyone else the hell out and lock you inside."

"That sounded strangely like a threat."

"More like a promise, babe."

Her eyes widened for a second and it was then I realized I'd actually gone ahead and given her a pet name. Not out of being condescending or naming some random body part of hers that stuck out to me in lieu of remembering her actual name.

Shit!

Something was happening and I wasn't all too sure whether I wanted it to or not.

"I'll see you later. Five thirty, sharp. The yoga instructor will be coming by later this week."

The words barely registered as I watched her turn and my gaze fell to her round ass that was particularly prevalent in the high-waist maroon pants she wore. The four-inch heels she had on helped to highlight the roundness of her backside, not that it needed much assistance. Syd was stacked. The image of her in those pants lingered in my mind long after she exited the gym.

Syd

"Hey, Syd. Can I speak with you?" A familiar male voice asked as I headed for my car in the gym's parking lot.

Pausing, I lifted my keys from my purse and stared back at Greyson, giving him a smile. He and I hadn't talked much since our initial encounter. However, there were times while I was working with Luke that I caught him staring at the both of us. A hopeful look was in his eye.

"Sure, but you'll have to make it quick. I'm on my way to work."

He nodded. "Um, I was wondering about your plans for Luke and the Rodriguez fight."

"My plans?" I questioned, confused. "What do you mean?"

"Well, what type of training are you doing with Luke? I've gone to him over my concerns regarding your training, but he brushes me off."

"Your concerns," I drew out the two words, thinking them over. "You don't think I'm doing a good enough job by Luke?"

He stood up a bit taller, reaching his full six-foot even height, as he peered down at me. I took a step backwards and lifted my chin, staring him in the eye.

"I didn't say that, you did. He's taking a big risk by letting a woman train him in the first place. Not to mention you have so little experience. I've been doing my research and aside from some Judo and other fighting classes you're pretty light in experience in the fighting world."

"How inexperienced was I when I put you on your backside when we sparred?" I asked and raised my eyebrow.

Luke had mentioned Greyson vied for the spot as his head trainer before I showed up.

"Greyson, you're a good karate instructor but Luke needs someone who's better adept at groundwork." I kept my voice neutral, trying my best to keep my annoyance to a minimum.

Greyson, also lacked a certain confidence that a trainer needed. There was no way he could cut it as Luke's head trainer. Luke would run right over him.

"A few years of judo doesn't make you a grappler," he said, moving closer.

"Over fifteen years," I corrected. "More than a decade of judo, also studying some Brazilian Jiu Jitsu and working with three of the top trainers in my sport, and MMA, during much of that time." I recanted my history in the fighting world. "Not to mention." I paused, when I realized I almost said too much.

"Not to mention, what? You're sleeping with him," he said through clenched teeth.

Heat rose up the back of my neck. "Watch your damned mouth. I'll ignore this tantrum since it can't be easy watching me do the job you obviously wanted, but don't ever speak to me like this again."

Clenching my keys tightly in my hand, I backed away from Greyson and strode in the direction of my car. Even as I got in, I watched him eyeing me for a few heartbeats with clenched fists before he turned and headed back toward the front of the gym.

Sighing, I reminded myself I had enough problems with getting Luke to fully trust me as his trainer. The last thing I needed was to worry about some low-grade karate instructor who let his jealousy get the best of him.

CHAPTER SIXTEEN

First Date

Syd

I'd been on edge ever since the night before. I was looking forward to going out with Luke on a real date. Something that didn't center around his training.

It was the conversation I planned on having with him later in the evening I wasn't looking forward to. I didn't know how to soften the blow of my truth. More so, it was the fact that I withheld it from him for the past two months I suspected would piss him off the most. He wasn't a man who trusted easily.

I wondered how long it took him to trust his last trainer. He rarely ever spoke to me about Banks. I'd wanted to ask him a thousand questions about his former mentor, but I held back.

At the moment my mind really began spinning with the different possible outcomes of the night, there was a knock on my door. I let out a huge exhale of air and walked across the hardwood floors of my condo. I smoothed my hands down the black, fitted skirt I'd chosen to wear for the night. Quickly fluffing my curls, I realized how ridiculous this all was since I'd seen Luke two hours earlier at his second workout of the day.

"Hey," I greeted, pulling my door open with a smile on my face. My stomach immediately began quivering with butterflies. Damn, he looked good. Yes, I'd seen him earlier, but I swear every time I looked at him my belly did gymnastics. Especially when he slowly and carefully glided his eyes down the length of my body. They darkened with each second that past.

"Have I told you how fuckable heels make you look?" Those were the first words he spoke since I opened my door.

"Seriously? That's what you say to someone on a first date?"

He dropped his lips, frowning. "Why start with the pretenses now? Especially since I've already heard what my name sounds like spilling out of your mouth while I'm balls deep inside you."

"Okay, that's enough of that. I assume those are for me?" I pointed at the bouquet of flowers in his hand. Naturally, I found it utterly shocking he'd put in so much effort as to pick up flowers for me. Sunflowers, no less, which happened to be my favorite.

"They sure as shit ain't for me." He pushed the bouquet into my hands as if they were burning a hole in his palms.

"Thank you. Come in," I said, stepping back and widening the door. "I'm going to put these in water, and we can head out."

He nodded, looking around my open floor plan condo.

"Nice place."

I smiled, looking around at my pickled wood entertainment center and earth toned furniture and pieces, as if trying to see it anew through his eyes.

"Thanks."

"You ready?"

I nodded and a tiny gasp escaped my lips when he reached his hand out, taking mine into his. It was the most unnatural, natural thing I'd ever experienced. Luke paused, stopping to stare down at our joined hands as if trying to solve a riddle. After a moment, he continued walking, but he didn't release my hand either. I was forced to lock my door with one hand while he held my handbag with his free one.

"I booked a reservation at the restaurant in the Radisson Inn by the arena. I figured from there we could park once and then walk over to the fight after dinner."

"Good planning. They have a lot of vegan options for you too. I've eaten there a couple of times for business meetings."

"Yeah?" he questioned as he held the door of his SUV open for me to get into the passenger side.

"Yup."

He closed the door and then passed around the back of the car to get into the driver's seat.

"What business meeting did you have over that way?"

"With the NFA, actually."

He peered over at me, after pulling out of the parking space in front of my building. "What business was that?"

"For ParaSquad. Last year, Tanisha and I spent a good amount of time negotiating with the executives of the NFA to work out a contract."

"What type of contract?" His eyes were on the road, but his question was filled with interest.

A smile of pride touched my lips. I sat up a little higher in my seat. "ParaSquad is now the exclusive on site first responders for the NFA's local fights."

Luke shifted his gaze to me briefly before looking back to the road ahead. "So, you'll be working the fights?"

I shook my head. "Not *me* per se. Obviously, if I'm training you and you're fighting, I can't work for ParaSquad at the same time. However, my company, yes. Our employees are trained to handle the relatively minor issues that may come up with spectators who get too rowdy and injure themselves."

Luke nodded. "Do you like owning your own business?"

The question caught me by surprise. I wasn't expecting it for some reason. It was almost as if Luke went out of his way *not* to ask too many questions, so this sudden interest left me a little confused.

"Yeah, I love it actually."

"What about it do you love?"

I shrugged. "Working for myself and making my own hours is great. Not always, of course. Being the boss often means working late hours or getting up early when I want to sleep in. There are also the times when I have to cover a shift when an employee unexpectedly has to take off. But I get to serve people, help them when they need and I'm not so much confined by policies and red tape like if I were working in hospital administration or healthcare policy making somewhere."

Luke nodded. "It's why I own my own gym. Even after fighting I'll be damned if I work for someone else."

"After fighting? Are you thinking about retirement?"

He glanced over at me before turning back to the road. "I'm not dumb enough to think my time isn't limited. Every athlete has a window. Especially those of us who get the shit kicked out of us for a living."

"So you've got your retirement plan all set up?"

"Not quite, but I'll be sitting pretty enough that I can take my time figuring my shit out."

"When do you think—"

"We're here," he stated abruptly, cutting my question off.

Looking around, I recognized immediately that we were in front of the Radisson, where the restaurant was located.

Luke placed the car in park, lowering the window to speak with the valet before turning to me. He shifted his head, looking through the passenger window and nodded. The door on my side opened as one of the Radisson employees opened it to assist me out.

"Hands off," Luke said abruptly, taking my hand from the employee. How the heck he got from out of the car to my side so damn fast was a mystery.

"Thank you."

He snorted and I stifled my laughter.

"I hope you're hungry. This place was tough as hell to get a reservation for tonight."

"Is that right?"

"You bet your sweet ass. I pulled a few strings." He glanced down at me and grinned.

A chill ran through my entire body and it took all of my good sense to bite down on my tongue and refrain from telling him we could skip dinner and the fight to go back to my place or his. Didn't matter which as long as it was private. But I couldn't do that. I held back, trailing Luke, my hand in his as we followed the hostess to our seats near the back of the restaurant.

"It's quieter back here," he said as he looked across the table at me, as if seeking my permission or something.

"It's great. This place can get loud, especially on nights like this where it'll probably get pretty busy."

He pushed out a breath, appearing relieved.

Another smile touched my lips.

"Is it awkward that we're doing this?" I asked, suddenly lowering the menu from in front of me.

His forehead creased. "Doing what?"

I waved by hand between our two bodies. "You and me. Dating." Realization donned on his handsome face. "You're not used to any of this are you?"

I was expecting one of his usual smartass comments. The type that always emerged from his mouth when anything got too close to the truth, but instead he answered with.

"Not even a little bit." He ran his left hand through his hair, making himself look a little less put together, again, another turn on. "I don't know what the fuck you're doing to me."

My entire body stiffened at his abrupt honesty, and the unwavering stare that accompanied it. His jaw was rigid, dark eyes meeting mine and his words hit me like a ton of bricks. His eyes searched mine for something. A sign that I was out on this ledge with him, maybe?

"For whatever consolation this might offer, you're kind of doing the same thing to me." My own words came out above a whisper.

But when Luke was about to respond our waiter interrupted.

"Red wine for me," I ordered.

"Seltzer water with lime," Luke requested.

I raised an eyebrow his way.

"No alcohol while training."

I nodded respecting his decision. Even though the fight was still over three months away, Luke really was taking his training seriously. Not that I hadn't thought he would, but there's something incredible about seeing it up close. He even complained less about the dancing lessons I continued to put him through.

"We're ready to order now," Luke informed the waiter.

He ordered the mushroom risotto with pan seared broccolini as his side, while I chose the swordfish and steamed vegetables in a buttercream sauce.

"You know the butter essentially defeats the purpose of steaming the vegetables," he told me as the waiter disappeared.

I tossed him a one-sided shoulder shrug. "Someone's jealous they can't have a little bit of butter?"

He gave me a half smile. "Maybe."

My heart rate increased inexplicably.

"Nice to know I'm not alone," he finally said after staring at me for a while.

I blinked trying to recall what he was referring to. My chest warmed, remembering our conversation before our waiter interrupted. At least a thousand questions came to mind to ask him. I wanted to know so much more about him, but had no idea where to even start, or how to start without scaring him off. I felt guilty even wanting to ask when I still hadn't told him my truth as of yet. I chose to go with a safe question instead.

"How're Jacob and Grace doing?"

"Fine as far as I can tell."

"Are you two close?"

"Define close."

"Talk often, visit frequently, share vacations, I guess. Don't you know what it means to be close to someone?"

His gaze hardened as he placed his arms on the table, leaning in closer to me. "Yeah, I know what it means, I guess." He shrugged and shook his head. "But that ain't the case with me and Jacob… not yet anyway."

"Yet?"

Luke wasn't given time to answer when the waiter brought out our food. That particular conversation was dropped as we ate, mostly in silence. However, I peeked across the table every other minute or so, searching for something from Luke. More often than not, his dark irises were on me as well. He wasn't even shy about it either.

"When's the last time you took a woman out?" I questioned, picking up on our previous conversation.

He chuckled. "Define *taking a woman out.*"

"That long, huh?"

He shrugged. "Too many think a date actually means I'm interested."

I didn't know how to feel about that comment.

"Don't get all up in that pretty head of yours, overthinking shit. It's different with you." He stared directly into my eyes.

A smile that rose from the tips of my toes, met my lips.

"I'm liking it."

My smile faltered as we once again paused staring at one another. No words were spoken, but a whole volume was communicated through that one look. It wasn't until the waiter delivered our check that we were forced to break eye contact.

Luke handed over his card and a handful of minutes later, we were exiting the restaurant. Luke, not so casually, moved so that he placed his body in between me and the street. Unlike the first time we shared a meal, he moved in closely.

I found myself melting into his embrace when he lifted his long arm, placing it around my shoulders as we continued walking in the direction of the arena. It was then I started to think maybe it wouldn't turn out so badly once he found out my secret.

"Oh shit, you're Skullcrusher McConnell," The young twenty-something guy, taking tickets at the door exclaimed.

"No shit," Luke grunted in response. But his demeanor didn't put off the young guy who laughed and took it in stride.

"You're my favorite NFA fighter. Can I get your autograph?"

"Sure kid. You got a pen?"

The guy quickly pulled a marker from his back pocket and presented Luke with his own ticket stub to sign.

Luke did so and handed the stub and marker back to the guy.

"Thanks, man. I always heard you weren't that friendly in person, but thanks for this."

Luke shook his head. "Don't make a big deal out of it, all right?"

The guy nodded, a huge grin still covering his face. "Yo, I wanna fight like you one day. I'm working here to save money to hire the best trainers and shit."

"What's your name?"

"Carl."

Luke snorted. "Shit name. You're gonna' have to come up with a better one. Good luck, kid."

Luke wrapped his arm around me again and escorted us through security, who upon recognizing him, didn't bother checking us or making us go through the metal detector.

"Do you always get this type of preferential treatment?"

He nodded. "When I bother to show up to an actual fight. I haven't been to an NFA fight in which I wasn't one of the headliners in years."

"Why not?"

He shrugged. "You want popcorn or anything?" I shook my head. "Let's find our seats. We're in the front row."

"Best tickets in the house. Nice." I rubbed my hands together, feeling excited to get to see an actual fight up close. It'd been months since I was only a spectator. The last couple of NFA fights I'd been to were either to meet with NFA execs or as a hired contractor on behalf of ParaSquad to help ensure the safety of the fighters and the audience. I was looking forward to being able to sit and watch the fight, as well as the company I was with.

"You sure you don't want anything?" Luke asked again once we reached our seats.

"You're starting to act like a real date or something."

"This is the real thing, babe." That word again. I wonder if he recognized he was using it so much.

Not long after we settled, the lights lowered, informing us the fight was about to start. When the spotlight hit the center of the cage, the audience around us erupted into cheers and applause. They were ready to get this thing started.

"Does this get you excited? Make you wish you were in the cage yourself?" I asked, feeling the excitement from the crowd around us.

Luke shook his head. "Used to. Now, I drown it all out. They're background noise, I can turn up or turn down depending on my mood."

Pausing, I took a look at his profile as he stared ahead at the cage. His face was set, determined, and while I couldn't see his eyes directly, I could feel the tension that came off of his body, as if he was imagining himself stepping inside the cage. It was as if there was a change taking hold inside of him, even without his permission.

Luke was innately a fighter. Not one simply due to his years of training and the bouts he'd won, but a fighter, born and bred. Through and through.

"Are you watching me or the fight?" he asked before slowly turning to me.

I was struck speechless for a few breaths at the intensity in his eyes. Slowly, however, my lips parted and I retorted, "I can do both."

He dropped his eyes to my lips, biting his own lower one. He moved his hand, the one that'd been resting against the back of my chair, to my shoulder, massaging it with his fingers.

"Be careful, Syd."

Damn.

Every thought in my brain scrambled and I couldn't discern a wish from a plea, from a request. Luke's eyes slowly rose to meet mine again.

"Watch the fight. What comes later will come."

I swallowed and my stomach muscles tensed with fear. Just that quickly, I remember what I had to tell him later that night. I nodded and turned back to the cage where the two fighters were circling one another. I still felt heated from the inside out. As if someone had flicked the switch to my internal thermostat, turning it all the way up. Luke's hand never moved from my body, his fingers continued brushing up and down my arm throughout the entirety of the fight.

I loved the sport of mixed martial arts. Loved watching athletes at the top of their game go at it and fight for dominance, but that night I couldn't give a shit about who was inside that cage. All I could focus on was how things between us would change.

By the time the fight ended, I sighed in relief, needing to get out of the arena.

"My place or yours?" He asked, staring at me with a gleam in his eye.

"Yours."

***

Luke's place was closer to the arena than mine. That was the main reason I said his. The way my skin burned with the need to be touched, I didn't know how long I could wait.

"I say something funny?" He asked, glancing over at me from the driver's seat.

"You're driving fast as hell."

He nodded.

"And your panties are wet as hell. It's in both of our interests I make this drive as short as possible."

I smiled, agreeing there. Peering down at his large hand on the gear I squeezed my thighs together. Pushing out a breath, I leaned over and turned on the radio, needing a distraction.

Luke gave me a look before turning his attention on the radio. He reached over and turned the volume up.

"Is that the band Rejected One?"

He turned to me briefly with a wrinkled brow. "You listen to alternative rock?"

"A little. The lead singer's pretty cool. Tak—"

"Tak," he said at the same time I did. "The little shit actually made it."

I was surprised at the pride in his voice. I narrowed my eyebrows. "Do you know him?"

He threw me a glance before finally nodding. "He's part of the crew. Kid's like a little brother. Crazy as fuck but hell of a musician."

"What crew?"

Another one of those looks from him came my way, as if debating on how much to tell me.

"The assholes," he said and chuckled. "My crew."

Suddenly, I thought back to my first day as his trainer. "Is that guy Pit part of your crew?"

He snorted. "Sure is."

"And you call yourselves the assholes? On purpose?"

He laughed. "It has a ring to it, no?"

I rolled my eyes at his prideful grin. "Where'd you all meet?"

"Bridge Lake."

I nodded, recalling the university he attended before dropping out. Spurred on by this revelation, I pushed for more.

"It's you, Pit, and Tak?"

"Can't forget Deacon, Skittles, and Kelex. Although, Kelex's ass is MIA half the time." His jaw tightened.

"Skittles. That's a funny name."

"Don't let her hear you saying that. She's the biggest ass out of all of us."

"Her?" Hearing him refer to this Skittles chick with affection in his voice sent a jolt of jealousy through my belly. Before I could fully express to myself what that envy even meant, Luke's deep chuckle pulled me from my thoughts.

"What?"

"Your face. Don't think too much into it. Skittles is batshit. She'd be too much of a fucking headache for me. Besides that, there's also the fact she's about to marry Pit."

I pushed out the breath I'd been holding.

"But she is protective over all of us, and lethal." He gave me a side-eye before turning onto his street.

"Is that a warning?"

He shrugged. "Take it how you like because I'm done talking about their asses. Why don't you bring that ass here," he growled at the same time he pulled into his driveway, parking.

It took me a moment to realize we'd gotten there so quickly. Thinking about how fast we'd arrived was lost when Luke reached over, wrapped his hand around the back of my head and pulled my lips to his.

The kiss reignited the burning in my low belly that desperately wanted him in between my thighs. I groaned almost painfully when he pulled away to get out of the car. Following suit, I climbed out of the car and met him in front, his lips falling to mine again.

We somehow managed to make it inside of his place, in a tangle of arms and legs. After flicking on the light, Luke pulled my blouse out of the waistband of my skirt, connecting the tips of his fingers with the skin of my belly. My breathing grew erratic, from the way his mouth stole every ounce of oxygen I somehow managed to breath in.

Suddenly, I was lifted and on instinct I wrapped my legs around something hard. His waist.

We were moving. Or rather, Luke was moving and I, like the tide that has no say in whether it flows with the movement of the moon, was carried away with him.

I shoved my fingers into his hair, digging in to massage his scalp. He moved his hands from my waist down to my backside, gripping it and me closer to his body. He carried me up the stairs.

If common sense had been on my side, I would've stopped to consider this man was carrying us both. I should've offered to walk, but that would require breaking the connection we had. I wasn't too keen on that, and by the way Luke held firmly to me, he wasn't either.

I didn't know how much later, could've been five seconds or ten minutes, but there was a loud thumping sound and then Luke's feet padded against a carpeted floor.

Bedroom. We were now in his bedroom.

Slowly, his grip loosened from my body and my legs slid down the length of his waist, thighs, and finally to the floor. He never broke the kiss.

His hands went to my waist and I raised my arms, allowing him to easily remove the blouse I wore. After tossing it to the ground, he went for the clasp at the back of my skirt, while I reached my hands underneath the shirt he wore. Feeling the hard planes of muscle and flesh there, I moaned.

Pushing his shirt overhead I examined his tattoos again. The one on his chest of a car wreck that read 'Asshole 4 Lyfe' stood out.

"Is this for your crew?" I asked with my lips against this, covering the tattoo with my palm.

"Enough questions," he growled against my lips before stripping me of my skirt.

Though dismayed by his response, when he made decisive work of disposing of my bra, exposing my hardened nipples to the cool air, I forgot about anything aside the pulse of need passing through my body.

Luke pulled back and strutted over to the nightstand by his bed, pulling a condom out of the top drawer. I snatched the contraceptive from his hand before going to my knees in front of him.

Looking up, I caught the surprised expression on his face. Grinning to myself, I unbuttoned his jeans and pushed them along with the briefs he wore all the way down. A rush of air flew from my mouth when I was almost smacked in the face by his member. We hadn't been together since the first time and I'd convinced myself that I'd over exaggerated how big Luke was in my mind.

But no. The man was packing.

My mouth watered as I leaned forward, licking the tip of his cock. He sucked in air and his body tensed, emboldening me. Instead of taking him fully into my mouth, however, I bent even lower, and ran my tongue down the underside of his member.

"Fuck, Syd," he whispered.

My nipples pebbled to the point of pain.

While not one to brag, I knew giving head was one of my specialties. I was good at it primarily because I enjoyed pleasing my partner. Studying Luke's body, I listened for every groan and tensing of his body, to learn what he enjoyed. I worked, getting his dick nice and soaked in my saliva before sliding my lips firmly around him. I bobbed head up and down his length, being careful not to let him get too deep, since this was only a warmup.

Luke's hand moved the back of my head, pulling my hair.

"Easy, Syd, unless you want me to detonate in your mouth."

Looking up at him with his cock still in my mouth, I slowly began to pull back. Luke's gaze locked with mine. His jaw clenched tightly, and he looked as if he was barely holding onto the shred of control he had.

He took a step backward allowing his cock to spill from my lips on a popping sound. Swallowing, I tore open the condom wrapper with my teeth and rolled it over his girth before standing.

As soon as I rose to my feet, Luke tugged my body flush against his, kissing me, before he pushed me down onto the bed. My gasp of surprise barely got out before he climbed over me, pressing me back against the bed.

"Luke," I yelped when I heard a tearing sound. "You ripped my panties."

"So," he said before stealing another kiss.

I wanted to tell him these were one of my favorite pair, but I became too consumed with excitement, when he used his leg to push my knee apart. He moved fully against my core, spreading my legs wide and positioning his dick against my opening.

Our eyes met as he leaned over me, his lips only a few inches from mine. He didn't move in for the kiss this time, though. He paused, staring me down. I could see the lust-filled gaze in his eyes, but there was another emotion in those brown pools of his. I couldn't identify it.

"Oh," I gasped when he finally pushed inside of me. My belly caved from the fullness I felt. It took a few deep breaths to allow my pussy to expand and accommodate his girth. As soon as I did, Luke pulled back, almost completely pulling himself free before surging forward with his hips.

My low back came off the bed at the intrusion. He did it again. I panted and struggled to restore my breathing to normal as he invaded every single one of my senses with his monstrous cock.

"What the fuck are you doing to me?" He asked, peering down at me while intertwining our fingers.

I would've responded if I could, but I didn't know what the hell he was doing to me. I curled my legs around his waist and lifted my hips against his thrusts. Luke grunted and finally lowered his face to meet mine. He kissed me deeply before moving lower, trailing his tongue down my neck.

Every piece of my body tingled with electricity. When I couldn't take it anymore, I pushed up, surprising Luke, as I used my leverage to flip us over so that I was on top.

"What the fuck?"

I laughed. "Judo black belt remember?" Not waiting for his response, I lifted my hips and lowered them, beginning to ride him. I moved my hands to my hair, massaging my own scalp the same way his cock stroked my insides with every rise and fall of my hips.

Luke moved his hands up my waist, squeezing as he went, until he reached my boobs. He plucked and pinched my nipples, bringing my body to the brink of my climax. My breasts were especially sensitive. Always had been.

I moved my hips faster and when Luke took another opportunity to pinch my nipples, my body couldn't hold back anymore. The tremors that began in the soles of my feet, moved up my legs and exploded in my low belly. The rhythm I'd set with my hips faltered as ripples of pleasure rushed through my veins.

I yelped when I found myself on my back, once again.

A deep chuckle emitted from Luke's lips. "Judo or not, you'll come on your back for me."

His new positioning allowed him to move his hips in a way that caused the end of his cock to rub against my clit, on each thrust.

A second orgasm quickly built and crashed through my body and I found my back bowing off the bed. In my passion-induced mental fog, I heard Luke grunt as his body stiffened. His orgasm nearly ignited a third climax of my own. But my body was spent.

CHAPTER SEVENTEEN

Exhibition Fight

Syd

"You sure this is the right thing for him to do?" Lenny questioned as he pulled me into the hallway from Luke's changing room.

"Luke always says you have bad timing."

Lenny grinned and shrugged. "Better late than never, right?"

"I suppose. To answer your question, yes. I'm sure he should be doing this. We've trained for weeks for this exhibition. He's ready. This fight will give us a good gauge on what he might be weak on. What we'll need to tune up on over the next few months to prepare for the title."

Lenny nodded. "That makes sense. You're his trainer so I trust your judgement. I wanted to check."

I smiled, placing my hand on his shoulder. "You're a good friend, Lenny."

He nodded. "I've been told."

I laughed lightly before pausing. I sometimes wondered what kept Lenny so loyal to Luke. On the outside, their friendship was built on Luke's condescension and snark often aimed at what was supposed to be his good friend. Lately, however, after being privileged enough to get to know Luke better, I could see how someone could be loyal to him. I still wondered about the inner workings of their friendship at times.

"Can I ask you something?" I finally blurted out, my wondering getting the better of me.

"Sure."

"You and Luke... how did you two be become friends?"

Lenny smiled.

"It's that you two seem so different."

"We are." Lenny pushed a hand through his dark, almost jet-black hair, and not for the first time I noticed how handsome he was. Lenny kind of had a nerdy yet sophisticated look going on.

"High school."

I lifted an eyebrow, not realizing they'd been friends for so long.

"One day, junior year, I was getting my ass beat by one of the school bullies named Shark. Not an uncommon occurrence in those days. When Luke walked into the bathroom, I expected him to join in. He already had a knack for being an ass."

I snorted. "Never would've guessed that."

He chuckled. "Yeah well, he surprised me that day. Told the guy to leave me the hell alone. When Shark got pissed off about it and went after him, Luke took him down. After that, he challenged anyone who thought it was a good idea to pick on me. They decided to leave me alone." He shrugged. "When I went to thank him, he said, *I didn't do it for you, jack face, and don't get all sappy over it either.*"

"Now that sounds like Luke," I said.

Lenny nodded. "It is, but you know, I kept hanging around him after that. We became friends. He kept me from getting my ass beat and I did his homework." Lenny chuckled at the memory. "We ended up going to the same college. He dropped out, but once he started earning money in the NFA he paid for me to go to law school. Afterwards, I started my own firm primarily representing him and his interests. I've since taken on other athletes and entertainers, but Luke is more than just my client, obviously."

I stared at the small grin on Lenny's face. I could see in his eyes he had a tremendous amount of love and respect for his friend.

"He can definitely still be an ass… they all can."

"They?"

He nodded. "He's told you about his Asshole Club, I'm sure."

I nodded.

"Yeah. I don't know the others that well, but that's one thing that brought them together. Their love of being the biggest shit stirrers in the room. That and the accident."

"Accident?" I was reminded of Luke's tattoo. The one with the scene of a crashed automobile around the 'Asshole' tattoo.

A look of concern crossed Lenny's face. "You'll have to ask Luke about that. I'm gonna' head inside." He jutted his head to the door.

I nodded, appreciative he took the time to tell me more about the man who waited inside.

I too, started to head back into the changing room to make sure Luke was warming up. I smirked at him telling the PT I'd hired recently, to fuck off when the guy was doing his job. And, when he did the same to David Novak, the yoga and karate instructor I'd added to his corner. Grumpy ass.

I smiled to myself.

"Focus, Syd," I said to myself, shaking my head.

As I entered the back room, I saw Luke stretched out on the PT table, grumbling about something.

"Quit your bitching. You have a fight you need to win," I harped, moving over to the side of the room where the physical trainer was warming up his muscles.

Luke snorted and turned to me. "Are you sure all these people know what they're doing?" He asked, eyeing his PT with suspicion.

"I wouldn't have hired them if they didn't." Placing my hand on Jeremy, the PT's, shoulder, I said, "Trust me, Luke. They're good at what they do."

He frowned. "Turn around."

"What? Why?" I asked, looking over my shoulder to see if anyone new entered the room.

"I wanna see your ass," he said, causing the PT to laugh.

"You're here to be my PT not my damn audience," Luke said to Jeremy.

I pushed out a harsh breath.

"Turn around, Syd. I need to see something." He lifted his eyebrows.

"Luke, get serious."

"I'm serious as a heart attack, doll."

"What'd I tell you about those pet names?"

"Can't remember," he said, shrugging as he sat up from the table.

Jeremy moved away, leaving Luke and me alone.

"Get serious. It's time to focus."

"I've been focused."

I was stopped from responding when the door pushed open and one of the arenas hired showgirls or whatever her job was entered with one of those edible arrangement things.

"A gift from the hosts of the fight," she crooned, not bothering to hide the fact that she was deeply ogling Luke.

Suddenly, I became very aware of the fact that he was only dressed in his spandex fighting shorts. All his glorious muscles and tattoos were on display for this wench to see. I scowled deeply at her.

Behind me, I heard Luke snort. "Quit staring, sweetheart, before my trainer here forgets I'm the one who's supposed to be fighting and drags your ass into the cage. Trust me, you don't want to be on the other end of that fight," he warned her.

The chick then turned scornful eyes on me. Lucky for her, she didn't say anything as she placed the arrangement down on the center of the table and exited without another word.

Tramp.

I turned back to Luke. "Did you ever sleep with her?"

He shrugged, nonchalantly. "I'd have to see her from the backside to remember."

I shook my head and rolled my eyes.

No sooner than that thought crossed my mind, he pulled me into him again, dipping his face to my ear.

"No worries, Syd. As soon as this fight is over it's you I'm taking home. I might even let you give me a rub down."

I pushed out a harsh breath. "Rub downs are your PT's job. But if you're lucky, I might let you touch my butt later."

He lifted his eyebrows. "Might?"

"I said what I said."

A cocky grin covered his face.

"Enough of this, let's go," I said at the same time there was a knock on the door.

One of the arena's staff, pushed the door open and nodded. "They're ready for you."

"It's go time," Luke said, hopping off the table.

"Okay, it's time you both get out," I said, clapping my hands and looked at both the PT and Lenny. "David, you ready?"

David nodded, carrying the towel and the robe over to Luke. I stood back as David assisted Luke in putting on the robe. Lenny and the PT exited and it was just the three of us. Luke's cutman for the fight was already waiting out by the cage. David exited ahead of us.

When it was Luke and I left in the room, I palmed his face with both of my hands.

"Remember, this is an exhibition. Only three rounds. Your job is to size Luca up, assess his weaknesses, learn what you can and end this shit as quickly as possible. Follow our training plan, okay? No fuck ups and don't try to get cute."

A slow, lazy smile spread across his face. "I love it when you talk dirty, Syd."

Pushing the tremors that coursed through me at the deepness of his voice, I shook him by the face. "I'm serious, Luke. If you get seriously injured during an exhibition fight because you came out too strong or weren't paying attention, it's not that tramp from earlier I'm going to be pulling into the cage. You hear me?"

He surprised me by pressing a kiss to my lips. "Got it. Can I go kick his ass now?"

Stepping back, I dropped my hands. "You may."

Luke moved to the door, pulling it open for me to pass through first.

Luke, David, and I started for the aisle to make our way to the cage where Luke was to fight, with me leading the way. The cheers of the crowd grew louder with each step we took.

This wasn't the main arena where most of the NFA's fights took place in the city, but it was still a decent size, allowing for close to a thousand spectators to come and watch the fight. Pretty much every seat in the house was filled. Not particularly large by the standard of Luke's usual fights, but large enough.

The crowd really erupted once the spotlight shone on our group and they realized Luke Skullcrusher McConnell was in the room. A shot of electricity flowed through me and suddenly I grew nervous.

I had only been training Luke for three months and this would be a test of whether or not the skills we'd begun implementing worked. It was risky to try to change a fighter's style so late in the game. Luke was more a boxer than a grappler, but he needed better groundwork to win another title belt. This match against Morelli would test him in ways he may not even realize.

I had to push against the doubt building in my mind. I started to fear that our growing personal relationship might be a distraction from the training he needed. That fear had grown for some time. Ever since we came back from Williamsport. To be honest, it was part of the reason I wanted Luke to take on this exhibition fight. It would be a test not only of his grappling, but of whether or not he took my training seriously.

The roar of the crowd, quickly pulled me from my thoughts as we entered the arena. I had to put personal matters aside right then.

Luke

The chants from the crowd echoed around me, but internally all was silent. Now was the time to put my training to use.

"Ready?"

I grinned. "Another day at the office."

She nodded.

I glanced over to find Grant, my cutman for the fight, nodding in my direction.

David stepped behind me and removed the robe that had been draped over my shoulders. I bounced around on the balls of my feet for a few moments, shaking out my arms, to keep myself limber and ready.

The ref nodded as he entered the cage.

I peered across the cage and caught sight of Luca Morrelli. He was six-six, three inches taller than my six-foot-three frame. He was more on the slimmer side, which also aided in his speed, something he and Rodriguez had in common. I'd watched plenty of footage of him, in fights, in training, and in interviews. I knew his style in and out. He loved a takedown. His grappling was good, but as I thought about all the work Syd had been pouring into me, I knew mine was better.

I moved my gaze upward to see the scowl he threw my way. He was a mean son of a bitch too. I guessed he'd perfected that expression as a method to intimidate opponents. Didn't work on me, however. I'd been going up against fuckers bigger than me my whole damn life. The bigger they were the harder they fell was the one thing I learned to be true of them all.

The commentator stood at the center of the cage and began making his introductions. I barely heard him announce Luca's full name or the cheer of Luca's fans that were in attendance. I did, however, watch as the dumb fuck lifted his hand, waving to the crowd.

The announcer went on to introduce me, and while I drowned most of it out, I did hear the chants and cheers grow louder. The most important sounds were the ones that came directly behind me. I could hear Syd as she urged me to keep focused and rely on our training.

A slow, meticulous smile started at the corner of my lips, spreading across as I glared at Luca. He still wore the scowl, but the look in his hazel eyes was as if an alarm went off in his head. My smile made him nervous.

Good.

"All right, gentlemen, bring it in," Mike our ref, insisted.

Luca and I closed in on Mike from either side of the cage. Behind me, I heard the door of the cage seal shut.

"We're gonna' have a nice clean fight, gentlemen, all right? Three rounds. Touch fists," Mike insisted.

Luca held out his right hand and I quickly rapped at his knuckles before pulling back.

"Okay, step back," the ref announced.

"Let's see what the fuck you got," I growled.

He scowled.

Everything went silent as I stared into Luca's eyes.

In the blink of an eye, the bell rang, Mike jumped out of the way and Luca, dumbass that he was, went in too quickly with a left hook. I easily ducked the punch and jumped back, stepping out of arms' length, making him have to come to me. Luca attempted to feel me out, implementing a couple of punches and forward kicks.

Every shot he took missed. Luca wasn't a boxer, but it'd been the first fighting technique I'd learned. From the looks of it, he wanted to establish his dominance early on. Yet, he had no real defense for my strikes. His aim was to try and get me to the ground. The first time he attempted, I elbowed his back causing him to loosen his grip. Once he released me and stepped back, narrowly missing my right hook to his face, I saw the caution in his eyes. That was the sign to me that underneath all that bravado and scowl, he wasn't as confident as he put on. I suspected he knew he didn't have the stuff to be in this cage with me.

"You need to give it up, McConnell. You're old as shit," he taunted as we moved in.

Baring my mouthguard I went in for an uppercut to his chin but missed.

He chuckled. "See?"

It was right then I popped him in the nose with an uppercut. It started bleeding and the crunching sound I heard led me to believe it was broken. That didn't mean Morelli was out for the count. Plenty of guys, including myself, could continue to fight and do some serious damage even with a broken nose. Letting up could've led to a catastrophe on my end.

"How's that for old, motherfucker?"

He made a move, going for my legs for the takedown. As soon as my back hit the ground, I rolled out of the way, standing. Mike stepped in between us, briefly stopping the fight to assess Luca's bleeding nose. I watched as the ref carefully looked over Luca, asking him if he was okay to continue the fight. I rose my fists again as soon as Luca nodded in the affirmative.

The rest of the first round went on like that. Luca attempted a few more takedowns but I was able to scramble out of them and get to my feet to keep the fight where I wanted it.

"One down, one more to go," I stated, smirking to Syd and the rest of my corner.

Syd frowned as David wiped my face with a towel and looked over my face, assessing any bruising that may need tending to.

She shook her head. "Don't get too cocky. This guy's still a hell of a grappler. He's trying to get you to the ground. If he does again, perform the arm bar we've been working on. He doubts your grappling skills and he won't be expecting it. All right? You've got two more rounds in there. Be smart."

I pushed David and the cutman away from me and grunted. "Not if I win this one." Which I was certain I would. I felt too good and I'd barely broken a sweat in that first round with Luca.

"Any other advice?"

"Listen to me, Luke. Morelli might not be able to go toe to toe with you but don't doubt his game, okay?" she insisted.

"Sure thing." I tossed her a wink, which only caused her frown to deepen. I didn't know what bug crawled up her butt, but I didn't have time to think about it. The bell for the second round went off and I moved back to the center of the cage. Luca and I glared at one another.

His team had stopped his nose from bleeding and covered the cut above his right eye with a small amount of petroleum jelly.

Good.

The last thing I wanted was that fucker's blood on me.

"All right gentlemen, let's fight," Mike yelled, jumping out from between Luca and me, allowing us to advance on one another.

This time around, I was the first one to take a swing. Unfortunately, I missed Luca's jaw by less than a centimeter, barely grazing his skin. He was able to turn that missed punch into a shove at my back shoulder, allowing him the advantage of getting behind me for a take down.

We both landed on our backs with Luca's arms wrapped around my waist. He tried to maneuver to put me in a headlock, but I countered with an elbow his rib to loosen his hold enough to escape the headlock.

"Arm bar," Syd yelled from outside the cage.

I ignored her, knowing that I could bring this fight back on our feet. Pushing away from Morelli, I hopped up on my feet and swung a right hook, missing his jaw by centimeters.

Morelli chuckled. "Washed up. You're too slow, Skullcrusher," he said my stage name with scorn in his voice. "Everybody knows you don't have what it takes anymore."

For a second his words got the better of me, and I was caught off-guard when he landed an uppercut against my ribs. As I stumbled, he went in for a leg sweep of my right leg, taking me down to one knee.

"Shit," I cursed before narrowly missing the left cross he directed my way. He was able to get off a shot at my ribs right when the bell ending the second round went off.

Pissed, I sauntered to my corner, ripping my mouth guard out while peering across the cage at Luca and his team.

"Don't touch me," I growled at David when he went to put an ice pack against my upper back.

"Luke, why didn't you do the arm bar?" Syd asked, moving in front of me.

I didn't answer. I kept staring.

"Look at me," she said, getting closer. "This entire round he's going to try to get you to the ground. He knows you are tired. When he does, do what we've practiced. He often leaves his right arm open, giving you the perfect opportunity for an arm bar."

Still, I didn't respond.

"Luke, do you hear me?"

Grinding my teeth, I curtly nodded and put my mouth guard back in. The bell for the third round rang.

"Fight," Will yelled for the third time of this match, jumping out of the way.

I zeroed in on Luca, going in for a right jab right off the bat. He ducked it and swung, kicked at my lead leg. The kick stung but it only pissed me off more, especially when he grinned when I grunted. I took that opportunity to fake him with a slip to the left and then a right uppercut to the jaw. It landed perfectly.

Luca stumbled back and I seized the opportunity to advance. While I landed another shot at his ribs, he was successful in getting his arms around my waist. We toppled to the ground. When he went to move over top of me, I wrapped up his left arm, making it useless as he tried for a chokehold. He was tough, though because he scrambled and was able to get to his side, giving him more leverage to either stand or move over me to climb on my back for another choke out attempt.

"Arm bar," Syd yelled from my corner.

I growled as we both tried to regain leverage, trading elbows and knees from the awkward position on the ground. I grew angrier with each second that passed, recalling Luca's words from earlier. He continued to talk shit as we wrestled.

With less than a minute left in the round, I was able to land an elbow to the side of his head that stunned him. It enabled me to move out from underneath his body. I climbed on top and sat on his torso and began wailing on him with the old ground and pound. Morelli could do nothing but cover his face with his arms.

"That's it!" Mike yelled as the third and final bell sounded.

As soon as I stood Mike lifted my arm, declaring me the winner. I grinned, looking to my corner. I caught David and even my cutman clapping and smiling at me. However, when I moved my gaze to Syd's the frown on her face caught my attention.

I tossed a wave to the crowd before stepping out of the cage.

Washed up my ass.

While we made our way to the back room, Lenny, clapped me on the back of my shoulder, congratulating me. I stared at Syd's backside as she walked ahead. She hadn't said a word since I stepped outside of the cage.

"Can you all give us a minute?" She asked of everyone once we entered the room.

Lenny nodded and held the door open as David and the PT exited, leaving Syd and me.

"What the hell was that?" She asked, folding her arms over her breasts?

I cocked my head to the side. "That was me winning."

She gave me a scornful look. "That was you not listening to a word I said."

I made a sound at the back of my throat before turning to the table at the far side of the room. Taking a seat, I stared at her.

"Luke, you didn't take a word of advice I said."

"I didn't see his arm open."

"Bullshit," she cursed. "He was wide open. You had ample opportunity to go for the arm bar and yet you chose not to listen."

"What the hell does it matter? I won," I said, holding my arms up. I ran my hand through my hair.

"It matters because Morelli isn't half the grappler that Rodriguez is. Tonight was about you testing your grappling skills.

Yet, you chose to rely on what you know, your old game. We've discussed this."

"I swear to… Syd this is bullshit. So what? I didn't try your little arm bar, trick. I got the W, didn't I?"

"Little trick?" Her arms fell to her sides.

My stomach dropped at the look she gave me. It was a mix of disappointment and anger. I braced myself for a tirade that I just knew was coming.

Instead of yelling and ranting, she pushed out a huff of air and yanked the door open, leaving the room without another word.

I fought every instinct that reared up in me to go after her.

CHAPTER EIGHTEEN

What's Going On?

Syd

"That's awesome, Aeryn. Thank you so much," I said into the phone, feeling relieved. "We'll be there next week. Thanks again," I told my old friend and mentor before hanging up the phone.

Sighing, as I looked up and ran my hand through my hair while staring out of my office's window.

"What's that look all about?" Tanisha asked, walking through my office door, and taking a seat in the chair in front of me.

"I just got off the phone with Aeryn Reese."

Her forehead wrinkled. "That name sounds familiar."

"It should. The man taught me most of what I know when it comes to Judo. He was my instructor for many years."

"Down in San Diego? At that studio you used to go to?"

"Dojo."

She waved me off.

"Yes. To answer your question. He's agreed to my bringing Luke down there to train for six weeks."

"Aren't you his trainer? Are you giving him over to your old teacher?" She asked.

"No, I'm still training him, but he needs something more. He has a few quality sparring partners here in Los Angeles, but in San Diego, at Aeryn's dojo we'll have access to higher quality challengers, which is what Luke needs."

"*We?* You're going with him?"

I nodded.

Tanisha tilted her head to the side. "When were you going to tell me, you were going to be gone for a month and a half?"

"Today. I just needed to clear it with Aeryn. He can get real territorial over his dojo. I've thought about it for some time. That exhibition fight last week helped me decide. Aeryn finally said yes today."

"And you have to go to San Diego with him for this training?"

I shrugged. "Of course. I'm his trainer. Why're you looking at me like that?"

Tanisha's side-eye spoke volumes. "I don't know about martial arts and all of that. What I do know is that you're planning on going away for six weeks with a man you started off training and are now sleeping with."

I sighed and pinched the bridge of my nose. "It's not like that, Tanisha. I wouldn't take this time off to train with Luke unless it was absolutely necessary. Besides, I won't be gone the entire time. San Diego is only a two hour drive from here. I can come back and forth when needed. Also, I'll have my laptop with me. You'll be able to get ahold of me for anything emergent."

"I figured you planned all of this out already. I'm not worried about work. We've got plenty of staff to take care of any assignments that might come up. My real issue is what's going on with you and Luke," Tanisha said, staring at me with her head tilted to the side.

Lifting my hands, I shrugged and shook my head. "I'm his trainer."

"Don't give me that bullshit, Syd. You're training that man outside of the gym, too. Don't play with me."

I sagged my shoulders and shook my head. "I didn't mean for this to happen. It kind of came out of nowhere. And now, I think this thing between us has gotten in the way of his training."

Tanisha lifted an eyebrow. "How so?"

"He doesn't listen. That exhibition fight last week proved it. I still don't think he trusts me when it comes to his training. He refused to follow my direction in that cage when he had the perfect opportunity to perform a move we've practiced repeatedly."

My chest tightened at the disappointment and guilt that twisted in my gut. Maybe Luke's lack of trust in me as his trainer was due to the fact that I'd let our relationship turn personal so early on.

I sighed again and frowned at the thought.

"And I'm assuming Luke doesn't know about your connection to Banks? Or that his old trainer is partially responsible for why you decided to go into MMA training?"

The tension in my gut tightened at Tanisha's words. There was also that issue. I clutched the silver pendant around my neck.

"No, he doesn't know. Not yet."

"Because your scary ass hasn't told him."

"I will," I retorted, releasing the pendant and pointing the pen in my other hand at her.

"When?"

I huffed. "Soon. We're at a pivotal time in his training and I don't want him any more distracted than he already is."

She eyed me, suspiciously.

"I've never met Luke, but from what you've told me about him, he isn't someone who likes secrets. He won't appreciate being lied to."

"I haven't lied to anyone. You make it sound so duplicitous."

"It kind of is, Syd. A lie of omission is still a lie."

I rubbed my forehead, feeling like shit. It wasn't supposed to turn out like this. I'd had no intention of ever getting personally involved with Luke SkullCrusher McConnell. I'd wanted to tell him the truth from the beginning, but he was so skittish around new people. Luke didn't trust very many and I didn't want to take any chance he'd turn me down as his trainer.

"I'm going to tell him at the right time. The training he'll have in San Diego will take his grappling to another level. He'll be more ready for the Rodriguez fight and by then, I'll feel more comfortable disclosing the truth. We need to put aside personal matters for now."

"Oh, this secret is too personal and will distract him, but the distraction of your pussy is okay?"

"'Nisha," I yelled, throwing a pen from my desk at her.

She laughed as she caught the pen just before it hit her in the forehead. "Just sayin'. My advice would be to tell him as soon as possible. But I'm going to drop it for now because your hardheaded ass loves learning the hard way."

"Since when?"

She frowned, giving me a *bitch please* look. "Since I've known you. Do I need to list off the number of jerks you've dated in your time? You do remember Stephen, right?"

I groaned and waved her off. "Anyone you dated before the age of twenty-one doesn't count."

"Girl, you were twenty-three when y'all started dating. That man had an ego the size the state of Texas and loved telling anyone who would listen the size of his bank account."

"Stephen was proud of his career, that's all."

"Don't play with me, Syd. He was obnoxious as fuck. Then there was Gerard. That French actor you dated last year."

"Okay, Nisha. You don't have to list off all my past romances. Besides how did we even get on this conversation?"

"Easy. I'm pointing out your long, storied history of dating assholes. You pick men who take pride in not giving a shit about anyone else."

"Luke isn't like that."

"He's not? By your own admission he's closed off and carries his fuck you attitude with pride. And you sought him out to train. Now you're sleeping with him."

"What are you getting at?"

"Maybe you're seeking somehow to get closer to the father you never knew by sleeping with him."

Shaking my head, I pulled a face. "No, Nisha. That's not it. Let's drop it, please?"

"Fine but be careful is all I'm going to tell you, Syd."

"I heard you the first time, Tanisha."

CHAPTER NINETEEN

San Diego

Syd

"If you wanted to take me on vacation, all you had to do was say so," Luke said, grinning down at me, as he got out of his car, in the parking lot of the bed and breakfast.

"Ha, ha," I replied with a deadpan expression.

"Why the hell did we take separate cars down here anyway?"

Glancing over at my car, in space next to his, I shrugged. "We needed space. Plus, you'll be here for six weeks, but there'll be times when I have to go back to LA for work."

He frowned. "Whatever," he grumbled as we started for the front entrance of the McReynold's Bed & Breakfast. "You sure you're not still trying to stick it to me for the Morelli fight?"

Glaring at him over my shoulder as I stepped through the door that he held open for me, I replied, "Oh no, I'm still pissed about that. But trust me, if I wanted to get payback, I'd be a lot more creative than having us take separate cars for a two hour drive." I patted his cheek.

He grunted and caught my hand in his. When I thought he would release it, he held on as we walked to the counter. My stomach tied in knots and my skin warmed. Guilt warred with desire. I still wondered if our personal relationship was a hindrance to Luke's training. Yet, I couldn't put my feelings for him on the back burner.

I had to pull my hand free as we approached the counter. It took less than five minutes for us to check-in, and the B&B's staff offered to take out bags up to our rooms.

I started for the staircase that led up to the second floor. "Great. We can head over to the dojo so I can introduce you to Aeryn and everyone, and then have dinner here so you can get to sleep early."

"What the fuck is this?"

I stopped short and turned, looking up at Luke. He held up the card I'd given him, giving me a curious look.

"It's a key card."

He frowned. "Don't play dumb. Why do you have a different room than I do?"

Glancing over my shoulder as someone passed, I stepped closer to Luke. "Because we need separate rooms." I turned and continued up the stairs to the second floor.

"Why?" He asked right on my heels.

"Why what?" I asked, staring down as I looked in my purse for my cell phone, once I reached the top of the stairs.

"Syd," he called, stopping me by grabbing my arm, spinning me to face him. "If you're still pissed about Morelli, you need to get over it."

Rolling my eyes, I place my hands on my hips. "I told you I am still pissed about that fight but nothing I'm doing here is out of anger."

"So, you're not making us sleep in separate rooms because you're upset?"

I shook my head and grinned. "Funny, I didn't think you'd mind having your own space for the next six weeks."

He ran a hand through his hair, moving his gaze over my head. He had a far off look on his face for a moment. "I'm surprised as hell too," he mumbled.

"What?"

He shook his head and stepped closer, bringing our fronts to touch. He ran a finger down the length of my jaw.

I shivered.

"This," I said, stepping back, out of his reach. "Is why we need separate rooms. You need to focus on the training you will receive here. Aeryn and his team are some of the best in the state. They taught me most of what I know and here you'll have access to better grappling partners than in LA."

He deepened his frown. "None of that explains why we need separate rooms."

I parted my lips to answer but I was still surprised that he pressed this hard for us to share a room. Luke liked his space.

"No distractions," I said, finally. "These six weeks will transform your fighting. If you let it. I don't want our personal relationship getting in the way of that," I said, honestly.

I watched as the muscles in his jaw tightened. I moved closer, taking his hand in mine. "Trust me, Luke."

He took a long, hard look at me, remaining silent for longer than I cared for. He searched my gaze with his own. Finally, he nodded. "Fine. If I'm here for six weeks and not getting any ass, it better be worth it," he said.

I tossed my head back and laughed.

"It will be. I promise."

CHAPTER TWENTY

Waltz With Him

Syd

"Aeryn," I called, running to catch up with my former mentor, in the parking lot outside of his dojo. "How's he doing?"

I'd had to return to Los Angeles for a couple of days to do some work for ParaSquad. I returned to San Diego after two days away, and my first stop was to the dojo.

Aeryn gave me a scathing look before gesturing with his arm toward the parking space that was supposed to be reserved for dojo employees.

Glancing over, I spotted Luke's black Maserati parked directly in front of the dojo.

"He refuses to park anywhere else."

I tried to stifle the smirk from my lips. "He's like that. What about his training?"

Aeryn shook his head. "He's still not getting it. He wants to muscle his way through every move, and he doesn't listen. I almost had to stop him from getting into a sparring match with Jay yesterday."

I slumped my shoulders as I began following Aeryn toward the front door. It'd been like this for the entire two weeks we'd been training down here. Luke kept relying too heavily on his boxing skills. He wanted to stand toe-to-toe with his opponent. Most of the time he could outmatch them in this way, but in my gut, I knew he needed more tools in his arsenal. He refused to listen.

Stepping inside the dojo, I heard the grunts and growls of the two men rolling on the ground in the cage at the far corner of the gym. I instantly made out Luke and one of the other dojo students, grappling.

"At least he's here on time every morning," Aeryn said as he followed me over to the thirty foot octagon, set up exactly like that of an NFA cage.

In my peripheral, I could see a few of the other students standing around, outside of the cage, championing either Luke or the other guy. A speaker set up on one of the tables at the back of the dojo, blasted hip hop music. A standard style choice in the dojo to help get the fighters amped up even during training sessions and workouts.

I stood for a moment and watched the grappling inside of the cage.

"No, Luke. You have to counter," I yelled.

He quickly peered back at me over his shoulder before continuing with the move he'd been trying to make.

However, Tomas, his opponent, was slippery and managed to get out of Luke's hold.

I slapped the cage with my hand in frustration. "Counter, dammit."

Luke didn't listen as he and Tomas continued to take one another on. Glancing over, I saw the clock overhead counting down in big red numbers. There were thirty seconds left in this match up. At the very least, I hoped Luke could hang on until time ran out. No such luck.

Tomas pulled out from a triangle hold Luke tried to maneuver, and got ahold of Luke's right arm.

"Shit," I cursed, seeing the arm bar from a mile away. I wanted to yell at Tomas to get the hell off him, but I held back. I had to use restraint to keep my mouth shut.

"Fuck!" Luke growled when he was forced to tap out or have his arm broken by the arm bar.

When Tomas let him up, Luke threw his gloves across the cage in frustration.

"Can you give us the room, please?" I asked Aeryn, who stood a few feet away from me. He'd watched the fight as well.

He gave me an uncertain look but then nodded. "Yeah, we needed to do some conditioning outside anyway."

"Thanks." I watched as Aeryn, Tomas, and the three other students who'd been present trickled out the back door of the dojo, to the back parking lot where they typically conditioned and did drills.

I headed for the sound system and connected it to my phone's Bluetooth. I pulled up the Waltz playlist, I'd made some time ago and pressed play.

Before entering the cage, I kicked off my shoes and headed inside the octagon. At that point, Luke sat in the center of the cage, his elbows perched on his knees, staring straight ahead, at nothing.

"Dance with me," I said, holding a hand out.

He slowly raised his gaze up to meet mine and I had to fight not to shrink back from the scathing look in his eyes.

"This is bullshit."

"Get up and dance with me, Luke."

"What are you doing?"

I sighed and gestured with my hand again. "Get up."

"Don't fuck with me, Syd."

"I'm not. Take my hand, Luke."

He eyed the hand I still held out to him for a heartbeat longer, before finally standing on his own. I moved closer, wrapping one arm over his shoulder, and holding out my right arm long ways. Slowly, he took my hand in his and we assumed the dance position we'd learned months earlier. Luke took the lead, as usual.

"Let's dance."

I waited in silence, the music still playing in the background, loud enough for us to hear it. He sighed, but eventually took the initiative of the first step and then the second, until we were moving around the cage, circling it in a waltz.

"If any one of those twat waffles comes back in here and says a motherfucking thing about this, I'm busting their heads."

I laughed. "No, you won't because you don't want to get suspended or kicked out of the NFA before your shot at Rodriguez." I paused and narrowed my eyes up at him. "That is, if I don't strangle you first."

He lifted an eyebrow, challenging me with a smirk playing at his lips.

I curled my toes and reminded myself of the need to focus on the agenda at hand, not his lips.

"You want to know my favorite fight ever?"

"Sonnen versus Silva," he said quickly, avoiding looking me in the eye.

I reared my head back and blinked. "So, you do listen when I speak."

He captured me with his gaze. "In spite of my better judgment."

Sucking my teeth, I punched him in the shoulder, garnering a small smirk from his lips.

"Anyway, yes, Sonnen versus Silva. You know why?"

"No, but I bet my left nut you're going to tell me."

"Because, for one, it's a thing of beauty. Sonnen was stellar in that match. He had Silva on the ropes, so to speak. In their case, on the fence. The whole fight he looked as if he were going to pull it out. The great Anderson Silva was on the verge of losing his title belt. And we know how that ended."

Luke, cavalierly said, "Silva pulled it out in the end, keeping his champion status."

"Right. But it was how he did it. He hung in there, round for round with Sonnen. And in the end, it was his grappling that won him that match. Sonnen tired himself out throughout the fight.

Silva held on, got the lock, and submitted Sonnen. The last ninety seconds of that fight are what won it."

"Is there a point to this trip down memory lane?"

"Yes. Spin me to your left."

He frowned, dipping his eyebrows.

"Spin me to the left, please."

He pushed out a breath and moved his arm to spin me in the direction I asked. I braced my right foot, stopping the spin before it started.

"Go ahead, spin me," I instructed, staring him in the eye. He did so, only this time when I tried to brace my right leg again, he moved his arm in such a manner that I had no alternative but to spin in the direction he guided me.

"That's it," I said, smiling.

"What?"

"What did you just do?"

"I spun you. Like you asked."

"And when you came up against resistance?"

"I forced you."

"Right." I clapped my hand against his shoulder. "You didn't give me the option of moving in any other direction than what you wanted. When dealing with a dance partner who refuses to take your lead, you force their hand. In the cage, your opponent is your dance partner. They are not going to take instruction well. So, you have to force them to go and do what you want. That's how Tomas was able to arm bar you just now."

He stopped moving, keeping his attention on me. However, his look had gone from scathing to indifferent to interested.

"Those dance lessons weren't a waste of time. You learned how to counter your opponent's bodyweight, to the music." I jutted my head in the direction of the speaker. "Take what you learned and put it in the cage. Because when you go up against Rodriguez, the fight will go to the ground, and you will need every bit of what you learned to beat him."

Luke's nostrils flared as he inhaled and for the first time, I got the impression that what I said was sinking in.

"Waltz with him, Luke."

CHAPTER TWENTY-ONE

Talk Shit Get Hit

Syd

"Yes. Now, that's how you clear a bitch," I shouted and banged my hand against the cage as Luke locked up Gabriel, another one of the student fighters at Aeryn's dojo.

It'd been four weeks since my return and our dance refresher course in the middle of the cage. Since then, it was as if a switch flipped in Luke and with his grappling. He still had a ways to go but he'd become more attuned with his positioning on the mat and locking his opponent out of place.

"Hell yeah," I encouraged when he was able to use his leverage to force Gabriel onto his right side, allowing Luke to gain the upper hand and perform a chokehold on him. Within seconds, Gabriel tapped Luke's arm, signaling his defeat.

"Shit, you smell like a damn dumpster," Luke said as he stood up with a cocky smirk on his face.

Gabriel gave Luke a scorching look, to which he shrugged. "Not my fault you smell like the asses that've been wiped along the bottom of this cage. Next time, keep on your feet."

"Thanks, Gabriel," I said stepping in the cage in between him and Luke before Gabriel got tired of Luke's taunting and said something back.

Gabriel nodded at me and snorted before walking off.

Turning to Luke, I said, "Cocky, much?"

He shrugged. "I have reason to be. That's my third take down in two days."

"It's almost as if you've got a good trainer or something."

I let out a laugh when he pulled me into his body. "She's a pain in the ass but she might be on to something."

There were only a few students left in the dojo and Aeryn had gone home for the day an hour earlier. As I stared up into Luke's eyes, my body warmed from my belly up through my chest. I dropped my gaze to his lips, hating that'd it'd been weeks since I felt them on mine. Though I was proud of myself for sticking to my rule of no sex during this training. I wanted Luke to focus and to take this time and me seriously.

"What're you doing tonight?" He asked.

Lifting a brow and cocked my head to the side. "Not you."

He chuckled. "Bullshit you aren't. Tonight, is our last night in San Diego. Final day of training. Six weeks are up, Syd."

Grinning, I replied. "So, it is. You had something in mind."

"There's one of those axe throwing places a few miles from here." He jolted his head toward the corner of the dojo where a few of the remaining students sat around. "A few of them went the other night."

I nodded. "Romeo's Axe Throwing. I know it."

"You been?"

I shook my head.

"Good. We're going tonight."

"Is this you asking me?"

"Yeah, asking, whatever. Have your pretty ass dressed and ready in an hour."

I gasped when he smacked my backside and gave me a wink before exiting the cage. I started to remind him of my no sex rule, but I stopped when I remembered he was right. That was our final night in San Diego, and truth be told, I wanted to go out with him, in a capacity other than being his trainer.

Which was how I found myself, an hour later standing in front of my hotel's mirror, studying my profile, ensuring the jeans, boots, and low-cut top I'd chosen fit perfectly.

***

"You're becoming quite the gentleman," I said as Luke held the passenger door open for me get out. I laughed at the look he gave me.

"Get out of the damn car," Luke said.

The drive to the axe throwing spot had taken only about fifteen minutes.

"Thank you," I said stepping inside of Romeo's Axe Throwing while Luke held the door open.

We were greeted by loud yells as patrons at the far end of the building cheered for someone or something. Seconds later, the loud thump of what I presumed to be an axe hitting one of the wooden targets, sounded.

"You wanna throw or eat first?"

"Throw." I was ready to get my hands on an axe. I'd seen a few of these axe throwing houses in Los Angeles but hadn't been to one yet. Romeo's had spaces for the axe throwing at the far end, while the main entrance entered the business' restaurant and bar section.

It had a rowdy sports bar feel to it. Many of the patrons who were eating, either sat at the bar and watched one of the mounted televisions or danced to the EDM playing in the background, at the far end of the bar.

"Good. We'll work up an appetite," he said as we moved to the counter.

When my body warmed, it took me a moment to realize it was because Luke had wrapped his arm around my waist, pulling me closer to him. I swayed a little, moving in closer to his hold while he reserved our axe throwing space and our table for later.

"We've got a forty-five minute slot at booth six, but we have a ten minute wait," he said, his fingers firmly digging into my waist as he looked down at me.

"Hm. Let's use those ten minutes wisely."

He turned his head sideways, giving me a curious glance at the same time I took his free hand into mine and lead him over to the dance floor.

He rolled his eyes and smiled. "Always trying to get me to fucking dance."

I laughed. "Don't worry. This time it's not a training session."

He chuckled and pulled my body into his. He cupped my hips with both hands, grinding his hips against mine. My breathing hitched and I suddenly felt my skin vibrating with need. How I was able to keep my hands off him for six weeks is a testament to my will power. Luke had a magnetic draw to him. For me, at least.

"You want to fuck the hell out of me right now, don't you?" He asked against my lips.

"Sort of." No sense in lying about it.

"Good. 'Cause there's a lot of nasty shit I want to do to you, Syd. Six weeks is too long."

"I agree," I said, moaning and lifting my arms around his shoulders. Luke ran the tip of his nose down the side of my face and the length of my neck, sending tingles coursing through my body. He pressed a kiss below my ear before biting my earlobe.

I shivered and my pussy muscles tightened.

"We're not going to make it to dinner if you keep that up," I whispered in his ear.

"You can be my dinner," he quickly replied.

Right as I'd been about to take him up on that offer, the buzzer he'd been given at the counter went off.

"Let's go throw some hatchets."

"Axes," he corrected and smacked me on the ass as he moved to the side allowing me to lead the way in the direction of our booth.

After a quick tutorial and explanation of the safety measures, Luke and I were able to begin our throwing.

"If we're throwing axes, we have to up the ante."

I wiggled my eyebrows and turned to him. "What'd you have in mind?"

He smiled and my belly quaked at that look. "Every time I hit the bullseye, you shed a piece of clothing."

I bulged my eyes and glanced around the space. The booth we were in sat directly in the middle of the axe throwing space, which meant there were three booths on either side of ours.

"No chance in hell."

He frowned. "Chicken?"

"Don't taunt me. We're in public. I'm not taking my clothes off."

He glanced around and shrugged. "You're right. I don't want any losers in here seeing your goods. For every bullseye I make, you owe me an on-demand blow job."

My stomach rumbled in excitement. Before I could answer, however, laughter sounded from my right side.

"I'd love to see what that mouth do," a guy, the next booth over said, smirking at me. One of the guys he was with laughed.

"What the hell did you say?" Luke asked, moving out of our booth to stare the guy down.

"I'm just sayin' that's a sweet piece of ass right there. I'd make a wager for her to get on her knees for me too if I were you," he said and busted out laughing as if he told the funniest joke ever.

He was clearly drunk and didn't comprehend the heat coming off of Luke's glare.

"What? Don't get mad, buddy. Hell, I'd take her home and—"

"That's enough," I interjected when Luke's fists balled at his sides. He'd moved closer to the jerk and I became fearful that he'd forget himself and swing on this guy or something.

I got in between the guy and Luke and pushed him away and back over to our booth. The idiot behind me whistled.

"Damn, those jeans."

I rolled my eyes and glanced over my shoulders. "You don't know when to quit do you?" I asked, doing my best to hold Luke back.

"Let it go. He's not worth the trouble. You have a hell of a lot more to lose than he does," I reminded him.

Luke continued to glare at the guy over my shoulder.

"Calm down. Let's do what we came here to do, okay? It's our time to have fun."

Slowly, his gaze cleared, and he peered down at me.

"It's your turn. The sooner you hit the bullseye, the sooner you get to put your dick in my mouth," I whispered in his ear.

I smirked at the gleam my comment sparked in his eyes. Luke surprised me when he bent low and brushed his lips against mine.

"You've got a way with words."

"Words aren't my specialty," I teased. "Hit the bullseye and I'll get a chance to remind you what is."

Somehow that managed to get Luke to forget about the jerk next to us and focus on the axe throwing. The forty-five minutes went by quick, and in that span of time, Luke hit the target four different times.

"Hope you know how to do face yoga. I don't want you getting lockjaw before you make good on your promise."

I laughed as we walked in the direction of the table he had reserved earlier for our dinner. "You never said it had to be all in one night."

"No, we're definitely spacing them out. Shit, I might even request one in the cage after I take that title from Rodriguez."

"Ha. You win the title, and you might get lucky."

He chuckled as we sat down to eat. The food was fairly good and surprisingly, they had vegan options available to suit Luke's meal plan. He was still on board with the change to a plant-based diet and so far, it worked for him.

We talked about his training, some of the guys at the gym and even the time I'd spent training there, before and during college.

"That was delicious," I said and tossed my napkin onto the table next to my empty plate.

Luke started to reply but one of the passing patrons' booming voice cut him off. I rolled my eyes recognizing the same jerk from earlier. He was even louder then he'd been down at the axe throwing booths.

"Some people need to learn how to handle their alcohol," I said before turning to Luke. When I did, I saw the look of fire in his eyes as he stared the man down while he passed us. Slowly, Luke took another sip of his iced tea, but his eyes never wandered from the man at the bar.

"Forget him." I reached under our table and grasped Luke's thigh.

He turned to me. "What?"

"I said never mind the jerk at the bar. Tell me more about your crew," I encouraged. He'd started telling me about some of the stuff they'd done over the years of their friendship. A part of me became envious at the adventures they'd taken and the trouble they got into together. Maybe I was more jealous of the way Luke's voice filled with affection when he talked about them. I don't think even he realized it.

"Yeah," he said before turning away, looking over toward the bar again. "They're cool," he said, sounding distracted. "I need to take a leak before we go," he said abruptly, standing from his seat. "Stay here."

"But the bathroom's that way," I called as he walked left while the bathroom sat at the far right side of the restaurant.

I watched as he moved closer to the bar. The douchebag from earlier sat at the bar, talking as loudly as he had been when he passed our table. My heartbeat sped up and I hoped that Luke wasn't about to do anything stupid.

Luke

I ignored Syd's attempt at redirecting me to the bathroom. Instead, I kept my attention on the cocksucker who'd talked shit earlier. With the amount of red I'd seen when he looked at Syd with that fucking glint in his eyes and laughed, it amazed me that I hadn't lashed out right then. I had too much on the line, though and I knew it.

But that fucker was still going to pay for disrespecting the woman I was with.

"Hey, buddy," I said, slipping my arm around one of the other dudes at the bar. He was big and burly as hell. He'd be perfect for what I had in mind.

He turned and frowned at me. "Do I know… oh shit, are you Luke McConnell?" His eyes grew wide.

I smirked. "Oh shit. I thought you were someone I knew," I said while slipping my arm down and to the wallet that hung out of his back pocket. Deftly, I moved his wallet behind me, putting it in my left hand. "But yeah, that's me. McConnell."

"Hell, I knew it," he said, his expression turning friendly. "Fuck what are you doing out here? Aren't you in training for that Rodriguez fight?"

Briefly, I glanced over my left shoulder and was satisfied to see the shit talker from earlier sitting directly next to me. His back was turned toward me, and he loudly talked in the face of some broad. I placed the wallet in my hand into his back pocket, making sure to be as discreet as possible. He didn't seem to notice what I'd done.

"I am. Been down here training for a few weeks," I said in my friendliest tone to the burly dude on my right.

"Pssh, man. That's going to be one hell of a fight," burly dude said. "I think you can take 'em."

"You think so?" I asked, almost convincing myself that I gave a shit about this conversation.

"Yeah. Here, what are you drinking?"

"Nah, I couldn't," I said.

"No, please. You're a legend."

I gave him a mock frown. "I'm not certain about that, Tiny, but if you say so." I chuckled. "How about whatever's on tap."

"Sure thing, I'm about to close out my tab anyway." He waved the bartender over and ordered a beer for me before he reached back to grab his wallet. He frowned.

"Something the matter?" I asked as the bartender slid the beer in front of me.

"My wallet." He patted both of his back pockets and then his chest although his T-shirt didn't have any pockets.

I stepped back and peered down at the floor, around the stools as if trying to look for the wallet.

"Oh shit, excuse me," I said, bumping into the cocksucker behind me, none too gently. "We're looking for my friend's wallet."

Cocksucker turned and started to stand as if going to help look too, and as soon as he did, Tiny's wallet fell out of his back pocket and onto the floor.

"Is that my wallet?" Tiny asked, his voice booming as he moved to pick it up. As soon as he flipped it open, his face turned beet red. "You tried to steal my wallet."

I was barely able to jump out of the way fast enough before Tiny swung and punched the stuffing out of cocksucker. I stifled my laughter as I stood back and watched as cocksucker's friends from earlier tried to intervene. Tiny began swinging on them too. He was pretty decent at fighting. But when another side fight broke out, I discreetly made my exit.

"It's time to go," I said and pulled Syd up from the booth by her arm, before taking out my own wallet and tossing enough cash to cover the bill and tip on the table.

CHAPTER TWENTY-TWO

Tommicus

Syd

"What happened in there?" I asked when Luke practically pushed me outside the door, and we started for his car.

"Shit's about to get real in there."

"I see that. Oop," I gasped when a loud thud sounded as someone busted out of the door we'd exited. Glancing over my shoulder, I saw it was two men whose fight seemed to spill out into the parking lot.

"Did you start that?" I asked when he held the car door open for me.

"Get in."

I sighed and did so. Luke slammed the door and crossed the front, getting in the driver's seat.

"Now, do you want to tell me what happened?" I asked as he made a right turn out of the parking lot.

"That cocksucker from earlier needed to learn a lesson." He shrugged. "And since I can't put my hands on him, I had to find someone else who could. Anyway, he'll wake up tomorrow with a sore jaw and a fucked up eye socket."

I laughed and shook my head. "I can't believe you did that. He was nothing more than a drunk jerk."

He glanced over at me. "First rule of shit talking, make sure you can back it up."

"Is that your rule?" I asked, leaning over to get closer to him.

"Damn straight. That's especially true for a motherfucker talking shit about my lady."

I sat up straight and stared at his profile.

"What?"

"You called me your lady."

He quickly looked over at me again before turning back to the road and shrugged. "Yeah."

I stared, waiting for him to say more. He didn't say anything else but the air in the car had shifted. The same arousal that'd burned its way through my body on the dance floor, earlier, made a reappearance. Not that it'd ever gone away, but it was reignited by his comment.

"Turn down this street," I said.

He looked at me with pinched eyebrows but did as I asked.

"At the next light, you're going to make a right turn and take that road all the way down."

Luke continued to take my direction until we came to a hilltop that ended on a dead end.

"Park over there," I said, pointing toward the dirt lot.

"What's this place?" He asked, glancing around.

"Here is where I make good on your first of four blow jobs," I said, reaching over to undo the buttons of his jeans.

"Syd…" he called, not finishing whatever he'd been about to say once I reached my hand into pants and pulled him free.

"Hmm?" I asked before spitting on the tip of his dick and then using my tongue to swirl it around.

Luke inhaled sharply. His cock began to harden in my hand as I continued to massage the tip with my tongue. Luke leaned over and pulled the lever to move his seat back, giving me enough room to work.

I moved closer and took all of him into my mouth, bobbing my head up and down on his member. I moaned around his cock when he palmed the back of my head, guiding the movement of my head and neck. I got off on the smell of his and my own arousal intermingling in the air around us.

Using my hand that rested on his knee, I reached down and undid the clasp of my own jeans. But before I could stick my hand inside my panties, Luke stopped me.

"Uh, uh, Syd. That pussy is all mine to please."

With the quickness of the practiced athlete he was, Luke pulled himself from my mouth and pulled me up by my shoulders, kissing me until I grew dizzy.

I pulled back panting. "Please tell me you have a condom?"

He grinned in that way that I loved so much. Yet, instead of reaching for his wallet, he opened the car door, and got out, his hand tugging mine. He damn near drug me over the center console, to get out on the driver's side with him. As soon as I exited, he pressed my back against the side of the car. He pulled his wallet out of his back pocket and retrieved a condom, displaying it between our two bodies.

"I'm like the fucking boy scouts. Always prepared."

"I don't think they're referring to condoms when they use that slogan."

His response was to pull my lips against his. As we kissed, he pushed my jeans down and over my hips, as I did the same for him.

Kicking my shoes off, I stripped the jeans off completely and wrapped my legs around Luke's waist. He plunged into me.

Tossing my head backward and arching my back, I let out a wild scream. I didn't think about the fact that we were outside or that while we were in a secluded spot, anyone could turn down this road and find us in this position. All I cared about was the way Luke worked his hips.

"Shit, you feel so fucking good," he said against my neck.

"Don't stop. Don't ever stop," I begged while he thrusted his hips again. I tightened my thighs around his waist and dug my fingers into his shoulders, holding on for dear life.

"Six damned weeks, I dreamt about this pussy."

I called out his name while he ravaged my body. My orgasm hit me quicker than I expected, as if my body had waited for this release and couldn't hold back.

When my pussy muscles clamped down and around Luke's rod, his body tensed, and his hands tightened around my thighs. He squeezed me firmly when his orgasm tore through him, pulling a loud yell from him. It was the sexiest sound I'd ever heard.

"Shit," he panted, pressing his forehead against mine. I could still feel him pulsing inside of me, even through the barrier of the condom. "How's that for waltzing?"

Laughing, I said, "You'd be champion in my book," before taking his face into my hands and kissing him.

***

"I can't believe I had sex with you out here." I laughed and turned to Luke, as we both laid on the hood of his car. Luke's phone sat in between our bodies, playing *Disfunction*, an album from the band Rejected One.

"This was the popular hookup spot when I was a teenager."

Luke turned from looking up at the sky to stare over at me. "You snuck your freaky ass up here with a guy?"

"More than once. I actually lost my virginity here." I laughed when he stared. "Jealous?"

"Possibly."

I waved my hand. "Don't be. I was young and dumb as all hell. Tommicus Wilkens. He was a complete let down. After that, I swore sex was overrated."

He snorted. "Your first mistake was fucking a dude named Tommicus."

He laughed when I elbowed him in the side. "I was seventeen. You can't hold it against me."

"I might," he said, catching my hand in his and intertwining our fingers.

"Please. Like you don't have a few duds in your past you'd like to forget. Oh wait, never mind, you probably don't remember half of the women you've slept with."

"Not their names." He shrugged.

I shook my head.

"They don't matter anyway." He turned fully on his side, keeping my hand in his hold.

Turning on my side to get a better view of him, I stared into his eyes and he looked back. There was so much depth in his eyes I swore I could stare forever.

"Why'd you start fighting?" I asked.

He looked away briefly, his nostrils flaring and lips tightening. I could feel tension fill his body when his fingers tightened around mine. He took so long to respond that I started to think he wasn't going to. I held my breath and silently wished that he wouldn't clam up on me again. Not this time.

"My mother made us."

"She put you in martial arts classes?" That would make sense. Lots of parents start their kids off in karate or something to get them to partake in a physical activity when they are young. But it was the tone of voice Luke used when he said those words that led me to believe it was something a more sinister than a loving mother putting their child in a sport.

"No." He pushed out a deep breath, before connecting his gaze with mine again. "The sick bitch made Jacob and I fight."

I curled my brows and reared my head backwards. "Why?"

He shrugged. "Over anything. If the dishes weren't cleaned right, because I got a shitty report card, fuck, if it was raining and she wanted sunshine, she forced us to fight one another."

"What the hell?" I asked the question more to myself than of Luke.

"She was twisted with a desire for control. To the world she made us out to be the perfect family, but when she didn't get her way she'd yell, curse, make us fight, and when one of us refused, she'd resort to hitting us herself. Always body shots, though. Never in the face or head where it might be visible to someone else."

"What about your father?" My throat tightened at the idea of Luke growing up with such a witch.

Luke shook his head. "He was off building his career and upholding the Reynolds's name to give a shit about what his wife did at home." He clenched his jaw.

"Reynolds. Like your brother."

He nodded. "I changed my name after I dropped out of college. The Reynolds's are involved in politics and shit back in Washington. I didn't want to be associated with the bastards."

I pushed out a breath, finally getting my answer as to why Luke and Jacob had different last names. And why their relationship seemed so strained. I still couldn't fathom that life.

"Someone had to know what was going on. A teacher, other parents, somebody?"

He snorted and shook his head. "A teacher once asked me about the bruising on my ribs, he saw when I changed for gym class, but I told him I'd gotten it rough-housing with some friends.

"Jacob left when I was twelve. The physical abuse stopped then, but she still told me in one way or another I wasn't shit. Every single day."

I tightened my hand around his.

"I'm sorry, Luke."

He shook his head. "Don't sweat it. She's dead," he said it so cavalierly that I knew it impacted him more than he wanted to let on.

"When did she die?"

"Last year. I went back to Washington to make sure. Not the funeral. I couldn't stomach that bullshit. People standing around crying for her when she was a witch in sheep's clothing. I showed up at the gravesite after the funeral. My bastard father was there. Jacob, too."

He shook his head and turned to lay on his back again, staring up at the darkness above. He placed our intertwined hands on his chest. I moved closer and laid my head on his shoulder.

"I'm sorry." Those were the only two words I could think of to say.

"Don't get all in your feelings. It happened a long time ago."

Lifting, I moved up and pressed a kiss to his lips. "It shouldn't have happened at all," I said before laying my head back down.

"My mom left my real dad when I was still young. I don't remember him that much." My chest tightened. And I reached for the silver pendant around my neck.

Luke didn't say anything, but he raised our hands and pressed a kiss to my fingertips.

"She remarried when I was seven and never spoke of my biological father."

"Is that why you haven't been to see her since you've been in San Diego? Don't they live out here?"

I nodded against his shoulder. "Yeah. But my stepdad travels a lot for work and mom often travels with him. They've been out of town. My little brother, Mitch lives on the East Coast. He stayed there after college."

"You're not close with your family?" He asked.

"I am. To an extent. I have my life and they have theirs. What about you?"

"I haven't spoken to my father since my mother's funeral and don't plan on seeing him until I'm standing over his grave."

I lifted my head and looked down at him, surprised at the venom in his voice. He claimed it all happened a long time ago but the anger in his voice revealed that it was still fresh.

"I have a different family."

"Your crew?" My question hung in the air as the crooning from Rejected One's "Dissension", played in the background.

"Yeah."

"How did you become so tight with them? Didn't you say you all hated one another at first?"

He chuckled. "Yeah, we did. Then the accident happened."

I remember his tattoo and Lenny mentioning an accident. "Tell me what happened."

I felt Luke shift his body as if looking down at me, but I continued to stare out into the night. After waiting a few heartbeats, he began talking. He told me about the race that almost killed two of his crew members, Kelex and Tak, and bonded the rest of them.

"That night changed all of us, in one way or another."

"How did it change you?" I asked.

"It showed me that life can end in the blink of an eye. And it gave me what I needed to rip off the final hold my mother had over me. I broke off contact completely with my family and began living life on my own terms."

"Is that why you live out here while the rest of your crew lives in Vander City?"

He pushed out a deep breath. "I moved out here to train with Banks."

"Banks died two years ago," I said before I could think better of it. Inwardly, I cringed as soon as the words passed my lips. I was certain Luke would clam up and refuse to talk about his former trainer.

Instead, he sighed and said, "I've considered moving back. I had Lenny hire a realtor and he sent me a couple of places he found."

My stomach tightened at the idea of Luke moving so far away. Clearing my throat, I asked, "What about Jacob?"

"What about him?"

"Would you move closer to Williamsport?"

He snorted. "Nah. We're still working through our shit."

We remained silent for a moment before I said, "Parents can do a number on us all, can't they?"

He made a sound at the back of his throat.

"Speaking of parents, there's something…" I trailed off when suddenly, a pair of headlights nearly blinded me.

I held my hand over my eyes, squinting to see who the headlights belonged to.

"The fuck?" Luke sprang up, looking as if he was ready to fight.

"Evening folks," a male voice called as he got out of the car.

I pushed out the breath I'd been holding when I noticed the lights attached to the top of the car, once the officer turned down the headlights.

He began approaching us with his flashlight.

"What's going on here?" He asked.

"Taking in the view, officer," Luke said, arms folded across his chest as he leaned against his car, legs crossed at the ankles.

"Well, this is private property." The officer turned to the far right and shined his flashlight in the distance. When I followed the direction of his action, I noticed the sign that read 'No Trespassers.'

"Didn't see it."

"We were just leaving, officer," I quickly said before Luke could get too defensive. "Come on, Luke," I said.

He glanced back at me before he started for the driver's seat. I was already buckling up my seatbelt by the time he closed the door.

The officer waited for us to pull out of the spot we were in and start down the road before following us out.

After a few minutes of silence, Luke began laughing.

"What?"

"If he'd been thirty minutes earlier, he would've caught you with your pants down."

I slapped his shoulder. "I wasn't the only one with my pants around my ankles, jackass."

He laughed louder before snagging a hold of my hand and pressing a kiss to the back of my palm.

"Thanks for these six weeks, Syd."

I grinned. "Hang on." I pulled my hand free and retrieved my phone from my pocket to open the notes app.

"What're you doing?"

"Writing down today's date and time. You just thanked me. Who knows when the hell that'll happen again?"

He cut me a side-eye. "Yeah, you definitely need to write that shit down. Don't bank on it happening again."

I smirked.

"Don't forget you still owe me three more on-demand blow jobs. Don't think I forgot. Maybe I'll drop in at your office and have you give me at least one of 'em while I sit at your desk."

"Shut up." I laughed.

He tugged my hand again, pulling it into his lap as we drove. The past six weeks were desperately needed for Luke's training, but they'd also shifted something deeper between us.

CHAPTER TWENTY-THREE

Press Conference

Syd

I shut down my computer for the day, grabbing my handbag and tablet and locked up my office for the night. Walking to the garage where my car was parked, I pulled out my phone and texted Luke to let him know I was on my way.

Trivial as it might've been, I was excited to stand in Luke's corner as he did his first press conference with me as his trainer. Luke wasn't particularly thrilled at the idea of welcoming all the cameras and reporters into his gym, but he recognized the necessity of it. Correction, once Lenny had made it clear that doing at least one press conference was required for him to receive any sort of payout for this fight, he reluctantly agreed to do it.

On my way over, I made the decision to tell Luke the truth. Not before the press conference but the following night after the date I planned for us. I'd lay my cards out on the table and let the chips fall where they may. I expected his initial reaction to be anger but given the trust we had built, I hoped he'd understand why I didn't share with him my connection to Banks from the beginning.

"What took you so damn long?" Luke grumbled as soon as I stepped inside the gym.

"Calm down. It's only a few cameras and some harmless reporters."

"I am fucking calm. When the hell are they leaving?" He asked, turning to face the front of the gym.

The reporters were setting up their cameras and recorders in front of the tables and chairs where Luke and his opponent Manuel Rodriguez would sit.

"It'll be okay, Luke. Don't look anyone directly in the eye," I quipped.

A small smile appeared, and he pushed out a heavy breath. "Whatever. I don't like this many people in my space." He scanned the crowd of reporters and people from Rodriguez' team with his eyes.

"They'll be gone soon. You should be used to this by now. This isn't your first rodeo."

He frowned as he pinned me with his gaze. "And I still don't like 'em. Reporters all ask the same questions. You'd swear they all shared one brain."

"Please promise me you're not going to lunge at any reporters today," I said, wrapping my hand around his forearm.

He dropped his eyes to my hand. "I don't make promises I don't plan on keeping."

"Luke."

He grinned at me. "Don't sweat it. These fuckers may share one brain cell but I'm not about to risk this fight on their simple asses."

I let out the breath I'd been holding and released his arm. I watched as he turned and started for the front of the room. I moved to follow but movement out of the corner of my eye caught my attention.

Turning my head, I caught Greyson staring at me through a slanted gaze. I noticed his stares more and more lately. The closer we got to the fight it seemed the more he realized he didn't have a shot at being Luke's trainer.

Dummy. If he had any sense at all, he would've tried to get on my good side, and asked to be a part of Luke's training team. But he resorted to lame stares or scowling at me whenever I passed him.

I rolled my eyes at his pettiness and moved to the front of the room and taking a seat in one of the empty chairs. This press conference would drum up some anticipation for the fight. Butterflies stirred in my belly. Luke wasn't the only one on edge due to this press conference.

Luke

"Luke, that was a tough loss you suffered at the hands of Ronaldo Caldwell more than five months ago. Can you tell us how you've trained differently to prepare for this next fight with Manuel?"

My gut tightened with slight tension. I hated being reminded of my losses, even those that happened months or even years earlier. But as I pushed out a breath, I turned my head and caught sight of Syd, staring at me. I relaxed my shoulders and let out a smile that I couldn't hold back.

"I've learned to dance," I said, confidently, still staring at Syd.

Her lips twitched and her gaze shone a little brighter at my comment.

"Uh, do you want to run that past us one more time? Dancing?" The same reporter questioned.

It was on the tip of my tongue to tell this guy to get lost, but I bit my tongue when Syd gave me a slight shake of her head.

Sighing, I ran my hand through my hair and answered, "I've changed up my training a lot. But I'm putting in some quality time in the gym and paying close attention to form and technique." There that was a politically correct answer—one that sounded good but didn't reveal too much.

When I turned to look back at Syd, the smile on her face warmed my insides. I let my gaze linger on those plump lips for a second longer than necessary.

"Anything else you care to tell us about your training?" Another reporter asked, drawing my attention.

"I've added a few changes to my regimen since the Caldwell fight, working on my weaknesses, and some dietary adjustments to aid recovery time." I wasn't about to go into detail for these buzzards. Give them too much information and they'd circle in on any one detail and pick it to death, analyze it and before you knew it, your opponent had your entire strategy pegged.

"Dietary changes? Such as?" Another reporter questioned.

I took a quick glance in Syd's direction before answering, "Taking meat out."

The commentator who stood at a podium in between the two tables nodded in my direction.

"Not eating meat. The hell type of training strategy is that?" Came from the table on the other side of the commentator. There were a few chuckles heard around the room.

"Manuel, did you have something to say?" The commentator questioned.

"I wanna know what type of bullshit training this guy's doing?"

"Why don't you bring your bitch-ass over here and find out?" I growled rising from my chair. That caused a number of other people from my side and Rodriguez's side to get up and move in between the two of us.

He didn't get too close though, which I knew he wouldn't.

"Calm down, Luke," Lenny implored in my ear.

I shook him off. "I am calm." This was all for show. Yeah, I hated these damn things, but the forced aggression was good for the buildup. The hype built audiences.

I clenched my fists as camera lights clicked around us.

"Let's all calm down. There'll be plenty of time for fighting in the coming months," the commentor said.

Everyone took their seats again, but I continued to glare at Rodriguez.

"Next question." Someone from Rodriguez's side yelled.

"Yes, this one is for McConnell. It's long been known that your long-time trainer and friend, Daniel Banks died going on two years ago, and you haven't announced the name of a new head trainer. Do the changes you've made to your training regimen indicate that you've hired someone new to fill the position?"

My entire body stiffened at the mention of Banks. I should've been expecting it, but it caught me off guard. I hated talking about Banks with people who didn't know him. Glancing over at Syd again, I noticed her cupping that silver pendant she always wore.

"Yeah, I hired someone new," I answered while still staring at Syd. She seemed to look nervous as her eyebrows rose in surprise. I wondered if she was anxious about being on camera.

"Are they here? We'd love to get to ask him some questions," the reporter continued.

"Her," I corrected.

"Excuse me?"

"My trainer's not *a him*. It's a her." *Douchebag.*

"Syd?" I called.

Still looking slightly bewildered, Syd rose from her chair and moved around the table to my right side. I started to wrap my arm around her, but the flashing of a camera reminded me we were in fucking public. I couldn't believe I'd nearly forgotten that.

"Syd? Was it?" Another reporter stood and asked.

She nodded. "Yes. Syd Quinn."

"How long have you been working with Luke?"

Syd peered down at me. "A little over five months now."

"And how is the training going?"

"Very well. Luke has made stellar progress and we're confident that—" Syd's full response was cut off when laughter from the other side of the room sounded.

"What the fuck is this?" Someone from Rodriguez's team questioned. Rodriguez snickered.

"A fucking broad is your trainer now? Banks would be rolling over in his grave."

That was the last thing I heard before I stood up, knocking chairs and almost the podium out of my way to get to Rodriguez and any other cum stain on his team who thought it was funny to talk shit.

This time it wasn't for show.

"Luke. Calm down!"

"Come on, motherfucker. Let's get this party started right now," Rodriguez yelled as he stood behind three dudes who looked bigger than he did.

I was half ready to barrel through all three of them to get to him. But then her hand on my arm stopped me.

"Luke, you'll get your shot at him. Take a breath. Relax," Syd said low enough so only I could hear. "He's not worth messing up your payout. You know that."

I did, but I had plenty of money. I didn't give a shit about a payout as long as that smirk still lingered on his cocky ass face.

"This is bigger than a payout anyway. This is for your title," she reminded me.

I blinked and turned to stare down at her. The heat that had risen through my chest began to cool enough for me to use reason. Swallowing the remaining anger, I took a step back, uncoiling my fists.

The commentator quickly made his closing remarks, ending the press conference. I still stood there, eyeing Rodriguez.

"That's going to be a great clip for the nightly broadcast," the old fart commentator said. "Thanks, Luke." He grinned, sticking out his hand for me to shake.

I dropped my eyes to his hand and then turned to glare at Rodriguez again. The commentator walked off after a few seconds. Around me the reporters began packing up their shit.

"Hey man, no hard feelings, right?" Someone from Rodriguez's camp came over to me grinning.

I started to tell him to fuck off, but then I thought better of it. Grinning, I took his offered hand in mine, squeezing it tightly.

His face turned red as I pulled him in closer to me. "Tell your fucking lackey that if he or anyone on his team ever disrespects my lady again, I'm going to fucking choke the living shit out of them. I don't give a fuck if we're being filmed or not." With that, I released the dickhead's hand and watched as he gathered himself, before heading back over to the door where Rodriguez stood.

I glared at both of them as they exited the gym, along with the rest of his crew.

"They were trying to get under your skin. You let them," Syd scolded, giving me a searing look.

"You know how delectable you look when you're all pissed off like this?"

"Luke, be serious," she hissed.

"I am being serious. I wanna fuck the shit outta you, right now."

"I swear to God." She stomped her foot and my cock jumped. Damn, I needed to hear her moan again and soon.

"Luke, we need to talk. I—"

"Luke," Lenny called from behind Syd, approaching us both. "That was great, man. I mean, you were a little more on edge than I would've liked or recommended, but Gregg's right. Your response will be a good five second clip for the sports reports tonight and going into the weekend. I'm already fielding calls from three different companies who want to offer you sponsorship deals for the fight. We need to talk this through."

"Dammit, Lenny you really have piss poor timing," I growled.

He frowned, looking between Syd and I. "Was I interrupting something?"

"No."

"Yes."

Syd and I answered at the same time, causing my face to morph into a scowl.

"You weren't interrupting at all, Lenny. Go ahead and talk with Luke. I have to head out anyway to finish some work at home. Don't keep our guy out too late. He's got an early morning workout scheduled." Syd tossed me a wink, before grabbing her handbag from the chair where she'd been sitting earlier, and headed in the direction of the front door.

To say everything inside me wanted to call her back. I wanted to pull her to me and let her know that she'd come home with me and sleep in my bed that night. Yet, she was right.

I needed to talk with Lenny about business. It was also probably a good idea to keep my distance from her for the night. Especially since I knew the following night, we wouldn't have the distractions of Lenny and this fucking press conference.

CHAPTER TWENTY-FOUR
Rope A Dope

Luke

"You made me shower and change to bring me up to the damn roof?" I asked, standing behind Syd right before she pushed open the door that led to the rooftop of my gym

"No," she said, glancing back at me before opening the door.

When she did, I cocked my head to the side and surveyed how she'd transformed the top of my building. The barebones space that was usually occupied by nothing but a couple of lawn chairs, was covered in artificial grass, new low-sitting deck chairs with huge pillows and at the center of the space sat a square, wooden table with candles on it. The most interesting feature, however, was the huge screen set up in front of the chairs.

"This is what I made you shower and change for. Besides, you smell horrible after two hours of rolling on the mats. Ouch!" She yelled when I smacked her ass.

My stomach growled. "You better have brought food to this little shindig. As delicious as your pussy is, I need actual calories if we're going to be up here fucking. Shit," I cursed when she smacked my stomach. "Careful, you don't break a finger doing that. My pain in the ass trainer has me on this plant-based diet that has me ripped as fuck."

She grinned. "She's noticed," she said, her eyes trailing down to my torso and back up. "But we're not here to fuck."

I frowned. "Pity."

"Shut up." She took me by the hand, and I followed as we walked over to the chairs.

It was then I noticed the projector that sat at the far side of one of the chairs.

"I've got you covered with food," she said, releasing my hand and uncovering the plates on the table. "I got you one of those vegan burgers you said you liked so much."

"The Better Meat ones?"

She nodded.

"Hell yeah," I said, moving closer, noticing that she also got waffle sweet potato fries, knowing I preferred them over regular fries. "Thanks."

"Where's my phone?" she asked, looking around.

"Fuck off," I replied, knowing she was messing with me for thanking her again. "What'd you get?"

She nodded to her plate. "Fish sandwich and fries. Oh, and…" She paused as she moved around the side of the chair, to pick something up.

"Beer?" I asked when she held up an ice bucket filled with bottles of my favorite craft beer.

"I know you don't drink while training but I figured we could make an exception for tonight."

"What's tonight?"

"We're watching one of the greatest fights in history."

I lifted my gaze to the sky and groaned. "If I have to hear you talk about that damn Sonnen versus Silva fight one more time, I might put a bullet through my brain."

"Morbid much?"

I chuckled and folded my arms across my chest.

She shook her head and placed the bucket down next to the table. "I didn't say my favorite fight. We're watching yours." She smiled and jutted her head at the chair closest to me. "Sit. The projector's all set up. We're watching a documentary on it first."

My stomach growled again, and I snatched the Styrofoam platter holding my food off the table before sitting. Seconds later, the blank white screen filled with the words, 'Manila: The Philippines.'

Turning to look over at Syd, I caught her smile.

"Thrilla in Manila?"

"What? You think you're the only one who listens when someone speaks? I remember what you said when I asked what your favorite fight was that day."

"C'mere," I said, pulling her to me with my free hand when she went to sit down.

"Luke, you're going to spill your food."

"I got it," I said, moving my platter out of my lap to make room for her to sit. "We're watching this with you right here."

"You better not spill anything on me."

"I'll make sure to lick it off if I do."

She squirmed a little in my lap, adjusting. I sat back in my chair. The chairs were large enough that there was enough room for her to fit on my lap and I could eat comfortably.

"I never knew the full history of the rivalry between them," Syd said about thirty minutes into the documentary.

"Banks told me a little bit about it."

She stiffened and turned to me.

"Pass me one of the beers."

"Please?" She looked at me expectantly.

"Please."

She rolled her eyes and passed me a beer before setting her platter back on the table. She leaned back against me and I wrapped my free arm around her, palming her belly.

"Frazier would've died in that ring," I said, staring ahead at the screen.

"You think so?"

I nodded and took a swig from my bottle. "It was about more than pride. That man had his whole life turned upside down and interrupted over Ali's accusations."

"He was a major shit talker. Reminds me of some else I know." She reached around and poked me in the stomach.

Laughing, I caught her hand and laid it across her stomach, covering it with my hand again.

"Ali was king of talking shit. A poet and a boxer."

"But he backed it up."

I nodded. "Exactly. He's the greatest heavyweight of all time. Put anyone past, present, or future in the ring with him in his prime and they're going down."

Syd was quiet for a few moments. "Yeah, I'd agree. I think Tyson would give him a run for his money though."

I shook my head and grunted. "Not likely. Tyson's footwork couldn't match Ali's."

We talked throughout the remainder of the documentary, comparing Ali and Frazier's styles. Syd knew her shit. I already came to recognize that months ago. When she'd shown up at my gym months earlier, I wrote her off as another gym groupie looking to get banged for the bragging rights of screwing an NFA fighter.

I'd hired her as my trainer mainly to prove she was full of shit. That plan backfired like a mother, since over five months later here she was seated on my lap, my arm tightly wrapped around her hip, and analyzing fight styles better than any of my gym instructors. Not to mention how much more my ground game improved in the time we'd worked together.

"What?" she asked when I unintentionally made a sound at the back of my throat. She peered back at me with concern.

I shook my head as I stared her in the eyes—the same eyes I'd avoided for the first month she trained me.

"Everything's changed."

Her eyebrows dipped and she parted her lips, but her phone rang. "Hold that thought."

I watched as she snatched her phone from the table, answering it.

"Brandi, hey?" She paused, listening to whoever this Brandi chick was. At least, it better be a chick. I'll be damned if any son of a bitch called her this late in the day and she answered in my face.

Jealousy.

Syd glanced over at me when I snorted at my own inner thoughts. Yeah, I was jealous. An emotion I never thought I'd ever become familiar with.

"Okay, I'll come pick 'em up in an hour. That should be enough time, right?"

She paused.

"Okay."

"Who was that?" I asked as soon as she hung up.

"Brandi. One of my employees. She's working at the NFA Minor fights tonight and needs me to come pick up some of our work supplies. She has to go out of town for a family emergency."

"We need to go?"

She shook her head and waved her hand. "Not yet. The fights aren't over yet. We've got some time. Besides, we haven't gotten to the actual fight yet. Let's cut the documentary short."

She moved over to the projector turning off the HBO documentary and replaced it with the actual 'Thrilla in Manila' fight. When she retook her seat in my lap, I didn't think twice about it.

We watched the fight, silently at first. But quickly, the both of us got into it, cheering for one opponent or the other, despite knowing the outcome already.

"Rope a dope," I yelled at the screen when Frazier got Ali against the ropes. "Banks loved this part." I smiled at the memory of my former trainer, retelling the match, almost moment by moment. "Ali used it to tire Frazier out, leaving him vulnerable for the counter."

We both continued commenting back and forth as the fight went on.

"Get up," Syd cheered when Frazier went to the ground for the final time.

"He's out," I replied with my eyes locked on the screen.

Syd sighed as the screen went black. "That was a thing of beauty."

"Which is why I don't understand how this isn't your favorite fight ever. It has everything. History, drama, all that bullshit women like and two opponents who could actually fight."

She rolled her eyes upward and stood. "You act like I said it was a crap fight or something. It's not my favorite ever, but it's in the top five."

"It should be number one. No exceptions," I said as I stood and helped her clean up our dinner.

We bickered back and forth all the way down to my car and on the way over to the arena where Syd had to pick up her work supplies.

I only realized that I wore a legitimate smile on my face when I spotted my reflection in my rearview mirror. I almost didn't recognize myself. There was something different in my eyes.

It's love, shithead.

"What happened?" Syd yelled when I hit the brakes.

"What?"

"Why'd you slam on the brakes like that?"

Because I think I'm in love with you.

"You didn't see that damn dog run across the street?"

"What? Where?" She glanced around at the street searching.

"He must've passed. People need to keep their animals locked up," I mumbled as I continued driving down the pedestrian street, toward the arena. I shook off my earlier thought, putting it out of my head.

CHAPTER TWENTY-FIVE

Have To Tell You Something

Luke

I watched the sway of Syd's ass as she stepped onto the elevator. The only thing keeping me from reaching out and touching her was the two heavy bags of medical supplies in both of my hands. I followed her and crowded closed. We'd picked up the supplies from the arena and we now dropping them off at Syd's office.

"Now would be the perfect time to collect on my debt."

She frowned and wrinkled her forehead. "What debt?"

After hiking one of the duffle bag straps onto my shoulder, I trailed a finger down her cheek. "My next on-demand blow job."

She widened her eyes before pushing me away. "Not here. No way." She shook her head.

"You're right. The elevator's not where I imagined you taking me into your mouth, anyway. Your office is where I want to see you on your knees."

"Luke, get outta here," she said, laughing, pushing me away when I pressed against her.

The elevator dinged and I exited behind her to follow. The view from behind her was a sight for sore fucking eyes as she strutted down the hall in the direction of the glass door that read "ParaSquad" in black letters.

She held the door open for me.

"Where's your office?" I glanced around the darkened lobby.

"Not happening," she said side-stepping me and starting for the hallway to the left.

We came to a door, which she used a key to open. I recognized it as a closet space for the medical supplies the company kept on hand. Placing both bags down on the floor, I moved to one of the shelves.

"Show me what you know, Mr. I *was once a paramedic*," Syd challenged.

"You think I don't know my shit?"

"It's been a long time since you were in college."

I grinned and shook my head, pointing at the tubes that were placed in a yellow bin. "Tubes for oxygen masks." I pointed to the next bin. "Bandage scissors. Don't look like much, but they're the best thing when you need to quickly cut through gauze and shit." I pointed to the next bin. "Endotracheal tubes. Your employees better be the real deal if they're using endotracheal tubes. At the very least you could be sued if they don't know what they're doing and worst-case scenario, you could end up in jail if shit goes left.

"Resuscitator BVM. I've still got an old one of them lying around my place somewhere," I said as I pointed at one of the bins behind her. "It's the same mask I used on a teenage girl who'd lost consciousness after drinking too much one night. She lived. Kept the mask as a reminder since I quit a few weeks later."

I dropped my hand to my side as I stared at Syd.

She turned from looking over her shoulder. "So, you're legit."

"Guess so." I stepped closer, crowding her in the little space she had between the metal shelves that held all the medical supplies. Raising my hands, I wrap my fingers around her hands and trap them between my body and the shelves.

"Now about that blow job."

"Luke, this is my job."

"And?" Letting go of one of her hands, I bring my hand to her throat, clutching it, not tightly, but enough that Syd's eyes sparked with arousal. My dick jumped against the zipper of my jeans. I pulled her to me by the throat and kissed her harshly.

The kiss pulled a moan from her lips and she lifted on her tiptoes, her body begging for more. My cock twitched again.

A surge of need pulsed through me. I swear every time we kissed or fucked, I wanted more of her. After those six weeks in San Diego, her ass was lucky I didn't chain her to my damn bed. Somehow, I managed to get through training day after day without bending her over in the middle of my gym, but shit, I only had so much restraint in me. Her office would be the perfect place to get relief from the ache in my pants.

"Wait, wait," she panted, pulling back, moving her hands to cup my face.

"The hell?" I growled.

She smirked.

Again, my cock responded to her.

"We can't have sex in my office, and we need to talk."

"How about we fuck first?" I dipped my head for another kiss, and she pulled back laughing.

"Luke, I'm serious. Not here."

Grumbling, I lowered my hands from her body and took a step back.

"I need to pick up something from my main office and then we can leave."

"Make it fast."

Reluctantly, I watched as Syd exited the storage closet, leaving me to trail behind her. Again, watching that ass in the skirt that would be on my bedroom floor not soon enough.

Entering Syd's office behind her, I watched as she turned on the light over her glass desk, moving behind it, looking through some files that were stacked on top. I entered further, giving the entire office a look around. It was a decent size.

Not too small, but not a corner office. There were a few photos that faced away from me. One by one, I picked them up. The first photo was of Syd at her college graduation with a woman who she resembled enough for me to discern it was her mother. The smiling man on the left, I assumed to be her stepfather.

The second photo was of her and another woman who I didn't recognize, both wore graduation caps and gowns.

"This is Tanisha?" I angled the photo so she could see it.

She smiled. "That's her. You'll get to meet her at the Rodriguez fight. She bought a front row ticket. She's not one for fighting but she said she needed to come out and support me training my first champion."

"You? I'm the star of the show."

Syd rolled her eyes as I sat the frame back down. But when I went to lift the next frame, Syd slapped her hand over mine, stopping me.

"You don't need to see that one," she said.

"If it doesn't need to be seen, why's it on your desk?"

I flipped the photo over and froze, staring at the image in front of me. The photo looked to be at least twenty years old, probably closer to twenty-five. There was a man in his late twenties or early thirties, smiling as he pushed a young girl on the swing. The girl had tawny brown skin, and huge curly pigtails laughed open-mouthed, baby teeth on display.

I wrinkled my forehead as I shifted my gaze back to the man in the photo.

"Banks?" It was him. The image was at least two decades old, but I'd recognize my mentor and the man who was more like a father to me than my own fucking father, anywhere.

"Why do you have a picture of my dead trainer on your desk?" I asked out loud but didn't look up at Syd for the answer.

Instead, I shifted my gaze to the little girl in the picture. She had to be around three or four, fuck if I knew.

I shook my head in disbelief. Slowly, I trailed my eyes up and over to Syd, who stood silently, watching me. Those pupils that revealed a hundred different things at once spoke volumes.

"What the hell are you doing with a picture of you and Banks on your desk?" I asked again, staring her in the eyes this time.

A part of me hoped there was some sort of logical explanation. Maybe, her parents had taken her to a fight as a kid and they happened to capture this picture of Banks showing off. But as soon as the thought formed in my head, I knew it was bullshit. Banks didn't even like kids. In the years we'd worked together, he never once took a photo or even smiled at a kid.

"It's an old picture." She attempted to reach for the picture, but I snatched my hand back causing her to catch air instead.

"Why are you in this picture with Banks?"

Yeah, the image was old, and the girl was young. But the eyes and the mole on the right side of her mouth. They were all the same. The same eyes that stared back at me from across Syd's desk.

"He's my father," she finally admitted after a long stare off.

That admission took the breath from my lungs. I glared at the photo again, trying to put two and two together.

"Your father."

Syd didn't respond immediately. Not until I peered up from the photo, glaring at her, silently demanding an explanation.

"I told you, my mom left my real father when I was too young to even remember him. I never saw him after she left. She refused to tell me much about him and she's always been sketchy on the details. Something about not wanting to live being the wife of a fighter or trainer."

"Sketchy? As in lying to your face for months, sketchy?"

She sagged her shoulders and pushed out a deep breath. "It's not like that."

"Not like you looking me in the eyes and not saying anything about Banks being your father? Even after I told you all the shit about my dysfunctional ass family?"

Disgusted, I tossed the photo back onto her desk carelessly, causing a few of the files to spill onto the floor.

"Luke, I was going to tell you. I tried to tell you."

"You should've tried harder." I paused before saying, "He told me he had a daughter."

Her mouth clamped shut.

"He told me he hadn't seen her in years but that was it." I stepped back from the desk, shaking my head, and started for the door.

"Luke, where're you going?" Syd demanded, running in front of me, placing herself between me and the door.

"The fuck outta here."

"Please, don't. Look, I know—"

"Know what? That you're a lying, scheming, conniving…" It was on the tip of my tongue to call her out of her name, but I held back. God only knew why.

"I didn't lie."

"Lie of omission is still a lie." I started to move around her to get to the door again, but Syd stepped to the side, blocking my path.

"I just wanted to find out more about him. To somehow get to know him."

"So, you thought fucking Banks's championship fighter would, what? Bring you closer to him? Kind of a fucked up way to mend your daddy issues, sweetheart," I snarled.

Pop.

The stinging on my left cheek was immediate. I curled my hands into fists as my entire body filled with tension. The sting of betrayal and radiated throughout my chest. It had more of an impact on me than the slap she'd given me. I narrowed my gaze.

"Stay the entire fuck away from me."

"Luke, don't walk away."

I damn near dislocated my arm, pulling out of her hold when she reached for me. "Keep your hands the fuck off me. And don't bother showing up to my gym on Monday," I informed in a lethal tone, looking back over my shoulder. "You're fired."

CHAPTER TWENTY-SIX
Brought This On Yourself

Syd

Frowning, I stared at my phone, my thumb hovering over the call button, daring myself to call him again. Yet, as my thumb began to lower, the sound of my office door opening pulled my attention away from the screen.

"You're still in here staring at that damn phone?" Tanisha asked in an annoyed tone as she pushed her way into my office, moving to the chair across from me and plopping down in it.

"Don't you know how to knock?" I tossed my phone onto my desk before planting my elbows on it.

Tanisha looked over her shoulder toward the now opened doorway and shrugged. "No one's here. You didn't have any meetings on your schedule and your phone line wasn't lit up, so I knew you weren't on a call. Figured you'd be in here pouting. And look at you," she said, disgusted, looking me up and down. "Just as I suspected. Bags all under your eyes." She shook her head.

Frowning, I tossed her a middle finger. "Aren't you supposed to be my support system at a times like this?"

She blinked and placed both hands on the arms of the chair, pushing herself to sit up straight. "I've always got your back. You know this. Which is why I told your ass to tell that man the truth from the beginning."

"I was going to tell him," I defended myself.

"Right, but not before you slept with him."

Rolling my eyes, I sighed heavily because she had me there. "My goal never was to sleep with him in the first place."

"Uh huh, that's right. You just tripped and accidentally fell on his dick."

"Shut the hell up."

Tanisha laughed as she caught the pen, I threw her way, instead of letting it knock her in the forehead like I intended.

"Don't get mad at me because that man's denying you the D."

"Tanisha," I said in warning.

"Okay, okay." She held up her hands as if surrendering. "I needed to mess with you a little because you did bring this on yourself."

Pushing out a breath, I admitted. "I know, I know. This wasn't my intention at all. I wanted... I don't know, to feel closer to the man who helped create me. All I have is this pendant and photo."

"And your love of fighting and MMA."

"That too," I agreed. "I don't know, a part of me thought getting close to Luke would bring me closer to my father. I thought I could pick up where Banks left off. Like, it would be in my DNA somehow. I didn't expect all of the rest to happen." I bit my lip.

"You went and fell for his ass."

I shook my head and raised my shoulder because Tanisha had nailed it. I wasn't ready to admit the words out loud, however. It hurt too much.

"Now, he won't even speak to me. He hasn't shown up to the gym since last Friday." That was five days ago.

"He's hiding from you."

I frowned because it was more like Luke was avoiding me than hiding. I couldn't help but wonder how his training was going, was he still keeping on top of his workout regimen, was he eating right, getting enough rest? Was he taking care of himself? And yeah, it was definitely more than a trainer concerned about the fighter she was training.

"He won't answer my calls."

"Duh."

"Who still says *duh*?"

"I do." Tanisha shrugged. "More importantly, you should've known he would react this way. Wasn't it you who told me the man already seemed skittish?"

"I regret telling you anything." If I hadn't, she wouldn't be here in my face with the *I told you sos*.

"No, you don't. Not really. Besides, you tell me stuff because you know I'm going to tell you the truth."

Pushing back in my chair, I sighed heavily, and stared up at the ceiling. Tanisha was right again. One of the things I respected the most about her was her honesty in telling it like it was. Yeah, I knew Luke was the skittish type when it came to relationships or getting close to anyone. At first, I hadn't told him Banks was my biological father because I didn't want him to think I'd shown up looking for a handout or something. I wanted an honest shot at training Luke based on my own merit. And in the process get to learn about the man who raised me until I was four years old.

"What am I going to do, Tanisha?" I asked, not really wanting an answer. However, Tanisha being Tanisha provided one anyway.

"First, you're going to stop sitting around here feeling sorry for yourself. Second, you're going to go apologize to that man for lying to his face, and then beg him for the opportunity to train him again. And whatever else you want." She twirled her hand in the air, frowning as she stood.

"I don't beg."

"Yeah, well, it might be time to put away your pride. How many times have you called him in the last five days?"

"Only three."

"Right, and how many times did you pick up your phone to call only to force yourself not to?"

I curled my top lip as I snarled at her. Tanisha laughed, clapping. "See? That man, has you sprung." She paused, laughing still. "Anyway, you obviously have feelings for him. And I know when you love you love hard."

I sat up, my back going ramrod straight. "Who said anything about love?"

She side-eyed me. "That tone in your voice did."

"I—"

She held up her hand. "No sense in denying it. Whatever, maybe you're not ready to admit it yet. Maybe it's not love yet." She shrugged. "Still, you've been moping around this office, snapping at our employees all week. Stop taking this mess out on us and go and find that man and apologize."

My pride wanted me to tell Tanisha she had it all wrong. That I didn't owe Luke an apology for a damn thing. I could easily twist the facts around and hold firm in the words I'd spoken to Luke as soon as he found out. That I *hadn't* lied.

A lie of omission is still a lie.

He was right. No, I hadn't verbally expressed a non-truth, but I wasn't totally forthcoming about my motives either. Yes, I knew Luke wasn't the trusting type, making it all the more necessary that I should've been honest from the beginning.

"Where're you going?" Tanisha questioned when I stood and began gathering my phone and my purse from the drawer of the desk where I kept it during working hours.

"To find Luke." He'd been avoiding his gym all week. Had turned off his phone, and even had told Lenny to tell me to screw off when I called him trying to get through to Luke.

"Good. Hopefully, you'll show up here in a better mood tomorrow."

I ignored Tanisha's comment because I was already figuring out which location I'd check first. Stopping at the gym wouldn't make the most sense since he hadn't been there in days. If I couldn't find him around town, my last alternative was to try to get ahold of his brother, Jacob, and see if he knew where Luke had gone. Maybe he was in Williamsport.

The fact that within the span of the five minutes it took for me to get from my office to my car parked in the building's garage, I'd begun moving my schedule around in my head to make room for a trip to Williamsport should've baffled me. However, I was determined. Tanisha was right.

I did love hard. And, while I wasn't ready to confess to actually being *in love* with Luke, I could admit to caring for him. At the very least, I did owe him an explanation. I hoped when I found him, he'd be open to hearing me.

I'm Sorry

Luke

"What?" I barked into the phone as I answered.

"Mr. McConnell?"

"Yeah."

"This is your driver, Sean…" the man said into the phone.

I released a breath and cracked my neck as he told me that he'd be in front of my door in twenty minutes for my pickup.

"Yeah, thanks," I murmured right before hanging up. I tossed the phone back onto the bed next to my suitcase and continued packing.

The previous five days were spent either laying low at my house or at the apartment I kept downtown. I'd never brought Syd to that place and when my own home started to remind me of the times she spent there, I went to the apartment.

I'd done everything to forget thinking about Syd. I'd blocked her number, stayed away from the gym, ran miles and miles on the beach to exhaust myself and nothing, not a damn thing worked. Hell, I even found my sorry ass at the Peach Pit, thinking that would do it. Yet, my mind kept comparing every chick I came across to her. It wasn't enough to get my shit together.

Finally, I made the decision to hightail my ass out of California for a little while. I had just under three weeks until the Rodriguez fight and I couldn't focus on training. Time away would do me some good.

"Ouch. The fuck," I growled when a sudden loud banging on my front door caused me to drop my suitcase on my damn foot. Luckily, I already had my shoes on. Snatching my cell phone from the bed, I tucked it into my pocket before heading for the door. As I raced down the steps, the knocking turned to the sound of my doorbell ringing throughout my house.

"For fuck's sake," I growled, ready to curse this driver out for being so damned demanding on my door. "What the fuck is your issue?" I said as soon as I snatched the door open.

Before me, Syd's eyes bulged in fear and surprise. My heart lurched against my chest and I tightened the hold I had around the doorknob.

Syd quickly rebounded from her surprise and she shoved me aside to make room to enter. I stood there for about two seconds, staring at the now empty doorway.

"You're letting all the cold air in."

Slamming the door and spinning around to face her, I glared. "We live in California. No cold air to let in."

She shrugged. "Something my grandmother used to say when I visited her in New York as a kid."

I gritted my teeth feeling angry and strangely excited to see her.

"Get the hell out of my house," I demanded.

"No." She folded her arms over her chest.

As if on their own volition, my eyes began trailing down her body, noticing the leopard print button up top she'd tucked into the black skinny jeans she wore with a pair of red high heels. A simple outfit, nothing special about it, but fuck all if I could get that message through to my body, which began to heat up.

"The hell do you mean, no?" I advanced forward.

She lifted her chin, defiantly. "I mean." She hesitated, but eventually blew out a breath, lowering her arms, holding them out at her sides. "You're being a stubborn ass by firing me and not even giving me the opportunity to explain myself. Grow the hell up."

This time it was my eyes that bulged. "Grow up? I'm not the one who lied. You are. I might be an ass, but I've always been upfront and honest about it."

She narrowed her eyebrows angrily. "Oh please. Come off it. You hide behind being an asshole because you don't want anyone to know the real you. You don't want anyone to get too close. Where's the honesty in that?"

I tensed for a heartbeat, before smirking and folding my arms over my chest. "Is this you thinking you've got me all figured out?"

She pushed out a breath and stepped closer, to which I responded by moving backward. She stopped. "I know you, Luke."

I glared at her. "If you knew me, you would've never fucking lied to me." Pointing at her, I added, "You would've known the one thing I never could stand is being lied to, manipulated, just like," I stopped before the words could come out.

"Like what?" She asked.

"Like, Anna. My mother," I seethed, gritting my teeth as the words passed my lips. The thought made my stomach rumble with nausea. I hated the woman that birthed me and to think of Syd as being anything like her stirred something ugly and deep in me.

She sighed. "I tried to tell you that final night in San Diego."

"Why the hell didn't you? You had ample opportunity," I yelled, feeling myself getting more rattled than I cared to admit. That night in San Diego, I'd opened up to her about my past, all the while she kept this secret.

"I was going to tell you once we got back."

"When?"

"That night. After our date."

I deepened my frown. "How convenient."

"It's the truth, dammit," she insisted, stomping her foot. "Did I or did I not tell you during that night I needed to talk to you about something? That we needed to talk?"

I thought back to that night and recalled Syd mentioning something about talking. However, my cock was too busy trying to bust its way through my jeans to put much stock into her comment. I had figured it was about training.

I ran my hand through my hair, looking away from her because my damn heart—the very thing I promised not to give to any woman, was softening.

"You could've told me from the beginning."

"Yeah right, Luke. What would've happened if I walked into your gym that first day and said I'm Daniel Banks' daughter? The one he hadn't seen for over twenty years before he died. Can you tell me about him? Oh, and by the way, hire me as your new head trainer."

"I would've told you to get lost."

"Exactly," She responded, exasperated.

"But at least I would've known the truth."

"What if I wasn't ready to tell you the truth? You know what it's like to keep family secrets. Is it easy to open up to a practical stranger?"

I didn't say anything because the answer was obvious.

"Thought so."

"Still doesn't make the shit right, Syd."

She turned her head away from me, placing her hands on her hips. There was a long pause before she turned back to meet my gaze. "It doesn't. I'm sorry, all right?"

"Fine. Now get out."

"Damnit, Luke." She huffed, folding her arms. "I knew you wouldn't make this easy."

"Then why the hell are you here?"

"Because despite all my common sense, I think you're worth it. I think *we're* worth it."

My body went rigid at that. There was an inward push and pull my internal senses began to engage in, a tug-of-war struggle between telling her to get lost, and demanding she stay and explain herself until I was satisfied.

Outwardly, I snorted. "Worth it."

"Yeah. You have an obvious contempt for getting too close with anyone, I think you're worth me coming here and telling you the truth."

"I don't have contempt for shit, except lying."

Syd cocked her head to the side. "Really? You treat your best friend like shit, you call your group of friends your *crew*, but in the over five months I've trained you, I've only seen one of them, and you've never mentioned visiting them. You have a contentious, at best, relationship with your brother. You barely remember a woman's name after you sleep with her."

"Never did that to *you*." I said.

She peered down at the floor. "No… you haven't," she finally admitted.

I didn't say anything as I watched her.

After a couple beats of silence, she looked down at my side and then back up at me. "Where're you going?"

Glancing down, I spotted the suitcase I'd nearly forgotten about. Before I could respond, my doorbell rang again.

I gave Syd one final look before turning and opening the door for my driver.

"Mr. McConnell," he said with a smile that instantly pissed me off even more.

I handed him my suitcase and watched as he headed for the car parked in front of my house.

"Luke, where are you going?"

"None of your damn business," I growled.

"You can't leave."

"You don't get to tell me what I can and can't do."

"You're at a pivotal time in your training. The Rodriguez fight is—"

"No longer any of your concern. You need to get out of my house," I said, my voice sounding cold to my own ears.

"I'm sorry, okay? I lied because I didn't want you to dismiss me right off the bat. I wanted you to give me a chance as a trainer. I really wanted the job, and to learn about my father through you. I had every intention of telling you once we worked together for a while but then it got complicated."

I grunted. "Complicated. The truth is never complicated, Syd." I stood there with the door open, leaning against it. "All you had to do was tell me the fucking truth from the beginning and allow me to make my own decision. You couldn't do that. Therefore, I can't trust you as my trainer, and I damn sure can't trust you as," I paused, swallowing the lump that tried to arise in my throat. "Anything else. It's time for you to leave. I have a flight to catch." I didn't look at her as I kicked her out.

Slowly she moved closer, pausing as she moved in front of me, but I refused to acknowledge her. In my peripheral, I saw as she slumped her shoulders before exiting. My stomach twisted in knots, but I didn't bother stopping to discern what emotions were running through my body. Instead, I secured the lock on my front door and moved with purpose toward the car that would take me to the airport.

It was definitely time for my ass to get out of the West Coast for a little while.

CHAPTER TWENTY-EIGHT

The Crew

Luke

The music from the bar blared even before I pulled the door open. When I did, the volume increased and a small amount of relief enveloped me.

Fuck Off. Though it'd been a while since I was last at Pit's bar, a sense of familiarity surrounded me as I entered. Slowly, I peered around the bar. Not seeing Pit, I knew there was only one place he could be. I started toward the back room that only certain people were allowed to enter.

"Rom," I nodded to the bulky dude standing out front.

"Luke," he nodded and opened the door, granting me access to the private room. Scanning the room, I found Pit seated at the round table in the center, his arm wrapped around Skittles.

Striding closer, I slipped my hand into my pocket. Pulling out the wad of cash in my pocket, I toss it onto the middle of the table as I approached.

"The hell?" Pit grunted, looking up at me angrily.

"That's for the invoice you sent me, fucker," I said, glaring down at him. I let my gaze travel over to the woman seated next to him, and nod. "Scarface. You're looking lovely this evening."

"Ah, sunshine. Good to see you, butt munch, but I have your fucking Scarface, bitch."

I chuckled and looked to Pit. "You sure you want to marry a woman with that kind of mouth?"

He curled his lips into smile. "You have no idea what that mouth can do. Fuck," Pit growled annoyed, as he turned his head to Skittles who'd just punched the shit out of him in the stomach.

"Don't try me with that bullshit, Will. He'll have you in the desert. Try me."

"Excuse me, but we were in the middle of something."

For the first time since approaching the booth, I allowed my gaze to travel over to the man seated across from Pit and Skittles. I frowned, recognizing the guy as a state senator or some shit. Pit always had one of these fuckers in here doing deals and whatnot.

"Get the fuck out, Jean. I'll get you want you need. This fucker has decided to grace us with his presence, which means we're done."

"Ro will see you out if you need," Skittles said when the dumb fuck didn't seem to get the message.

"I can always assist you out of your seat," I added just for good measure, cracking my knuckles. I was already in a pissy mood from the previous night's events. I didn't mind taking a little aggression out on this jackhole's face.

Wisely, he didn't say anything else as he slid to the end of the booth, rising, giving us one final look.

"The hell are you doing here?" Pit asked.

"I can't pop in to visit an old friend?"

"Cut the shit, Luke. What's that puppy dog look in your eyes about?"

I blinked, hating Skittles was able to read me so damn well. "No puppy dog look here, Taste the Rainbow. Just here to pay a debt." I gestured my head in the direction of the cash still lying on the table.

"What's that for?" she asked.

"Your fucking fiancé sent me an invoice for his impromptu visit to California."

Pit chuckled. "Sure as fuck did. You owed me for those flights. Nice of you to run my cash in person."

"Whatever. The hell are you two up to?"

"You mean to tell me you drug your ass back to town and didn't call me?"

I grinned looking up from the table to see Deacon standing, arms folded, glaring at me.

"Just got in. I was gonna' call. I need a place to crash. Especially since I can't stay with these two. I'll be damned if I listen to them screwing all night." I snorted at the image.

"You might learn a thing or two," Pit said.

Skittles sucked her teeth. "Move. I'm going to go grab a round of beers for the table. And a seltzer water for this guy since he's training."

I watched as Skittles rose from her seat to get our drinks, and Deacon took a seat next to me.

"Are you training for that Rodriguez fight?" Deacon asked.

I nodded. "Hmhm."

"How's the new trainer holding up?" Pit asked.

"I saw the last press conference you did. That chick is fucking hot. I guess that rule of never working with a woman went straight out your ass when you saw her?"

My hands tightened into fists and my stomach muscles clenched. I hated the comments about Syd. I came back to Vander City to get away from her and anything that reminded me of her. Now, my closest friends were all up in my shit about her.

"She's fine. Training's fine. It's all fucking fine," I mumbled.

Skittles arrived back at the table with three beers and the water, but I quickly snatched one of the beers, taking it to the head. When I lowered the now half-filled bottle to the table, three pairs of eyes stared back at me.

"What?"

"Since when do you drink while training?" Deacon asked.

I whistled and shook my head. That's what I get for coming back to the crew who knows me so well. They can read me like a damn book sometimes.

"I'm trying something new." Hell, beer is plant-based so it's not like I'm breaking my commitment. Again, my stomach clenched. Thinking of training or anything regarding training brought back thoughts of Syd.

"Aw shit."

I groaned and looked up at Pit.

"Fucking knew it. Saw it that day in the gym. Pay up," he said with his hands out to both Skittles and Deacon.

I narrowed my eyes when both Deacon and Skittles pulled out cash, placing it in Pit's hand.

"What the fuck is that?"

Pit gave me a cocky look. "After my trip to Cali, I told them about your new trainer. I bet them five big faces at some point you'd drag your ass back here looking all sorry and twisted over that one. Should've made it two stacks." He shook his head, looking remorseful.

"Glad to see you have no problem profiting off of my pain."

"Ha, then you admit it. Your panties are all twisted over some chick," Skittles said, narrowing her eyes at me, looking just as pleased as Pit to rub my damn face in the shit.

"I'm not admitting shit to you jackholes. Where's Tak?" I glanced over at Deacon, asking about our fifth wheel.

"Probably at the skating rink or wherever the kids hang out nowadays," Deacon joked.

"He now owes me five hundred from that bet too," Pit said.

"Assholes," I grumbled.

"You say that like it's an insult," Deacon responded, patting his chest over the tattoo we all had.

"Some would say it is," I said.

"They ain't us," Pit said before taking his beer to the head.

"Damn sure ain't. So, what's up with you?" Deacon asked, a serious look covering his face. "Impromptu trips are often for a reason. Last time you were out here it was just after Banks died."

"Damn, a man can't visit his crew once in a while? What is this? The Spanish Inquisition?"

"Or you could just move your dumbass back here already so you wouldn't have to hop on a plane to get to us when shit hits the fan," Pit answered.

I snorted as the muscles in my stomach tightened. I recalled Syd's words from the day before, as she mentioned how I kept everyone at arms' length, even my crew.

Is she right?

Moving back to Bridge Lake had been something I'd thought long and hard about. Yet, the realtor I had Lenny look up was on hold. He'd sent me images of at least four different homes and I'd put him off. Yeah, training was partially responsible for my procrastination, but if I'm honest, the truth was deeper than the title fight.

"Whatever." I shook my head. "Fuck that," I gritted out under my breath, remembering I'd come to Vander City to forget about all the shit on my mind, not dwell on feelings and shit.

"This must be serious. She must've done a number on you," Skittles chimed in.

I shook my head and finished the beer without confirming or denying. Yeah, I was fucked up over Syd's lies, but the last thing I wanted to do was talk about it.

"That conversation is off limits," I said, finally.

"Don't think your ass is getting out of here without coughing that shit up." Pit pointed at me, beer in his hand.

"What're you all doing tomorrow?" I asked, ignoring Pit's comment.

"Fucking," Deacon said.

"Breathing," Skittles said.

"Probably taking a shit at some point," Pit said.

"Good. I need to get my mind off of shit. Let's get high."

They all gave me inquisitive looks. Slow smiles spread over Pit and Deacon's faces.

"We're putting our skydiving licenses to use," I told them.

CHAPTER TWENTY-NINE

Sky Diving

Luke

"Damn, I love this shit," Deacon yelled over the engine of the plane and the rushing wind from the open door.

"You had to know I wouldn't let you down." I winked.

"The hell do you mean, *you*? It was half pint's connection who got us this fucking plane," Pit added.

"Aww, I'm finally getting credit for something around here," Skittles said.

"Was my idea, so both of you can fuck off very much," I yelled. Turning from Pit and Skittles, I looked to my left, on the other side of the open door stood Tak. "Kid, you doing all right?"

"I got your kid right here," he yelled back as he grabbed his junk.

I chuckled. "Be careful with that thing before you break it off."

"Are we doing this shit or not?" Tak asked, looking eager to take the plunge.

"Obviously. All because Luke's bitch ass is running from his feelings," Deacon yelled.

I tossed him a middle finger. Pit, Deacon, Tak, and Skittles all laughed at my expense.

"Someone needs to remind me why I'm even friends with you fuckers," I mumbled.

"We've reached altitude," The pilot announced through the speakers.

I nodded and did my best to ignore the fact that Deacon was right. I needed something like this to get my mind off Syd. Every time I thought about her my stomach clenched and my heart felt like someone had put it in a vice. The idea of even stepping foot in a gym to train had my throat closing up with tension.

I needed this jump more than words could express. All I wanted was to jump out of a plane with my crew and experience the rush of adrenaline that came with it.

"Let's fucking go," I yelled before checking one final time that my pack was secured to my back.

"Be our guest," Pit yelled.

"Say less." I took the plunge, jumping from the plane with my arms spread wide.

The rush of wind smacked me in the face. The rush was electrifying. All thoughts about Syd, fighting, title belts and any other bullshit left my mind. I heard a few more yells, telling me the others made the jump also.

I felt like I was moving through space and time. My body pulsed with electricity and adrenaline. Any thoughts I had when I jumped from the plane, were pushed aside as my body plunged toward the earth below. It was exhilarating and mind-numbing. Exactly what I needed.

When the time came, I pulled the string to open my 'chute. Once I did, I was yanked up, no longer being hurled to the ground beneath us, but more like carried gently. I preferred the hurling. As soon as the sensation of being thrown to the ground with the threat of death hovering around me let up even slightly, my thoughts went to who wasn't there with me to experience it. Even the shouts of Deacon, Pit, Skittles, and Tak as we landed one by one, didn't push them away.

"Who's up for going again?" I questioned as soon as everyone was back on the ground. I grinned when every single one of them raised their hands, laughing their asses off. This was my crew for a reason.

CHAPTER THIRTY

Skittles

Syd

"That's not how you do it, Vince," I scolded, as I took the papers, he stapled from him. "These need to go in the cabinet files, therefore they don't get stapled." Annoyed, I yanked open the top drawer of my desk to search for my staple remover.

"My mistake," he said.

Pausing, I looked across my desk at my office assistant. My stomach dropped at the frown on his face.

Shaking my head, I said, "I'm sorry," before pushing out a harsh breath. "It's almost six. I appreciate your staying late. How about you call it a day?"

Vince peered at me. I hated to see the concern in his eyes. While I didn't disclose the personal details of my life to my employees, everyone in the office probably could tell there was something going on with me. I'd been snapping at people for days, ever since Luke left to God knows where.

I hadn't tried contacting him after that night at his house. He made it abundantly clear that he wanted nothing to do with me.

And it felt like with every beat of my heart, the pain only grew, not lessened. Work was the only distraction I had. Which was why I sat there for the third day in a row, working well past the time of closing.

"We still have to create next month's schedule and prepare for that meeting you have next week," Vince said, interrupting my pity party.

I shook my head. "It's all right. I'm sure you have something better to do tonight than create a schedule. I'll do it."

"I have a better idea," he said, standing from his chair. "How about I order from the Italian place down the street? They have the best calzones. That'll give us some energy to keep working." He was halfway out of my office before I could respond.

"Get me sausage," I called as he started for the office lobby.

He waved, acknowledging that he heard me.

Maybe a cheesy, greasy, tomato sauce filled meal is what I needed to get me out of my funk.

"Yeah, right," I mumbled to myself. I'd eaten enough carbs to last me the year, in the form of my favorite danish, at least one full carton of ice cream, and greasy fries the other night for dinner to help stuff my feelings. It didn't work.

"And who are you?" I heard Vince say from up the hall.

I shot my gaze to the clock mounted on the wall across from me. Considering the time was inching closer to six o'clock, no one should've been in the office.

"Where is she?"

"You can't go in there."

The shrilled tone Vince's voice took on is what alarmed me most. Standing, I hurried out of my office and started down the hallway to his desk, but halfway down, I stopped short.

"Are you Syd?" A short woman with a pissed off expression asked.

"Who are you?" I questioned, noticing she began tying her brightly colored unit into a ponytail.

"I'm the chick that's about to beat your ass," she said, looking me in the eye.

Sizing her up, I moved into my defensive stance without thinking about it. "I don't know what the hell your issue with me is, but I bet you won't," I said.

"Syd, I can call the police," Vince said, moving in between the two of us.

"Nah, we don't need the police, but you're lucky as hell you've got all these medical supplies in here, because she's going to need them," this woman shouted.

"Who the hell are you to come into my business and threaten me? Vince, call the police."

"You got him all fucked up over you. Got us jumping out of planes and shit while he should be training for this fight."

"Luke?" I asked, confused. "Is he with you?"

I looked over her head but saw nothing and no one.

"Does it look like he's with me? He's in Vander City, probably ready to drag race or some dumb shit."

I gasped. "He can't do that. He could get hurt." My heart hammered in my chest at the idea of Luke putting himself in that kind of danger.

"Like you care," she yelled, trying to move past Vince.

Blinking, I finally realized who this crazy chick was. "Skittles?"

She narrowed her eyes. "He told you about me, huh?"

"Is he all right?" I asked, ignoring her question. "Is he taking care of himself?" I had to push aside the strangle hold of my jealousy. I hated that this woman knew more about Luke's whereabouts at the moment than I did.

She paused and cocked her head sideways. "You care?"

"Of course, I care." I waved my hand in the air. "If you want to go at it, fine, but let me know how he's doing first. He didn't go to Williamsport with his brother? Is he okay? He's not by himself, is he?"

I wanted to know that more than anything. It pained me to think of him as hurting and alone.

She took a step back and watched me silently for a heartbeat. "He's with his crew," she said before glaring at me for another moment and turning to head out of the office.

I stood there for I don't know how long, waiting for her to come back. When it became apparent she wasn't, I looked at Vince. He looked as confused as I felt. Though, a part of me felt relief in knowing Luke wasn't out there by himself.

CHAPTER THIRTY-ONE

ATVs

Luke

"Whoop," I yelled as I passed Deacon on his left, inside the dirt track we raced around.

"Motherfucker," he yelled to my back.

I threw up a middle finger and chuckled as I revved the engine of my ATV again, speeding up even more. I continued racing by or getting passed by Deacon, Tak, and Skittles over the next thirty minutes, until I caught sight of the low gas level on my ATV. I pulled off the track to where the five gallon fuel containers sat, for times like this.

"You want to tell me what the hell is going on?" Pit asked as I pulled my helmet off my head after climbing off my rented vehicle.

I shrugged. "Ran out of gas. Need to reup," I said casually. I leaned down to pick up one of the containers and moved around to the gas nozzle.

"That's not what I'm talking about and you know it. In the six days you've been here, we've gone skydiving twice, bungee jumping, rock climbing, and today it's ATVs."

I didn't respond as I refueled.

"Don't ignore me."

Waiting until I finished fueling up, I placed the plastic container back on the ground and looked at Pit. I peered over his shoulder, to see Tak climbing on his own ATV. Before he could get on, Deacon stopped him, handing him the same black helmet we all had as part of our rental package for the afternoon.

I snorted, wondering what the hell that was about. Slowly, I looked back at Pit. "What's the damn problem? Your ass getting too old to hang?"

"Motherfucker, you wish. But what you're not going to do is act like you didn't bring your sorry ass back to Vander as a death wish. If a certain trainer has you up in your feelings say that shit. We don't have time for this childish shit."

I narrowed my eyes. "Syd, has nothing to do with this."

He let out the biggest laugh I think I'd ever seen him take. "Lie to yourself but don't try that bullshit this way. Your sad ass has women problems written all over you. Never thought I'd live to see the day you'd get bent out of shape over a broad."

"Syd," I said firmly. "Her fucking name is Syd." My stomach muscles tightened at the mere mentioning of her name, but I hated to hear him call her a *broad.*

He laughed again. "Skittles was right."

"About what?"

He gave me a cocky look. "She thinks *Syd* is actually in love with your grouchy ass, too."

"How the hell would she know that?" I asked, folding my arms over my chest and peering over at where Skittles raced around the dirt track, closely trailed by Tak's ATV.

"She went to visit your girl."

I speared Pit with a look.

He smirked. "Yeah, she was about to beat 'ol girl's ass. You know how she gets about us." He shrugged. "But she came back singing a different tune."

I bit my tongue so damn hard to keep from asking what Skittles said, I nearly bit the tip of it off.

"She didn't touch her, did she?" I finally had to ask, again looking over at Skittles as she sped by again.

Pit chuckled, grating on my nerves. "Maybe. You know how she is. Anyway, you need to get your shit together. You've got a title fight in a week and a half and your ass hasn't been to the gym once since coming back."

"I'm good. I already know how to fight. Besides, I'm tapering."

He pursed his lips. "Be hardheaded if you want. Just don't come crying this way when Rodriguez puts you on your ass."

"I know what I'm doing," I said, staring off in the distance.

"Be sure you do," he replied before walking away.

I watched his back as he headed for Skittles' ATV which was now parked at the center of the track. Something funny moved through my chest, making it difficult to breath when I stared as they shared a kiss.

You do it to everyone.

I thought back to the words she yelled at me in that last argument. They'd been taunting me every day since she first said them. Whenever I slowed down, even a little, they returned to my mind, as if waiting for me right where I'd left them. I couldn't shake the feeling that she was right.

"Are you tapping out?" Deacon asked as he approached, gesturing to the helmet in my hand.

"Not even on my worst day," I replied, putting my helmet back on and climbing back into the driver's seat.

I pushed away thoughts of Syd and even my training. I was there to have fun and hang with my crew before getting back to California for the fight with Rodriguez. Not anything else.

CHAPTER THIRTY-TWO

For The Title

Syd

"I figured you would be here."

Looking up from my laptop in front of me, I peered at Tanisha as she stood in the doorway of my office.

Shrugging, I asked, "Where else am I supposed to be?"

She dropped her arms and entered. "I hear there's a big fight happening tonight."

I frowned as my chest tightened to the point of pain. "Brandi and Cheryl are working the fight," I said and went back to typing out the email I was working on.

"Yup. They've got it covered," she said.

"Good. There are a couple of races coming up in the next few weeks that we need to schedule shifts for."

When Tanisha didn't respond, I paused typing and looked up to find her staring at me, folded arms and head tilted to the side.

"What?"

"You're really going to continue sitting there talking about work?"

I raised my hands. "What else am I supposed to do?"

"Not pretend like you're not hurting right now."

"I'm fine, Tanisha," I said on a sigh, my shoulder slumping.

"Yeah, if by fine you mean doing everything in your power to forget that the love of your life has a major life event happening tonight and you're not there to see it."

I pressed my palm against my chest trying to relieve some of the pain that Tanisha's words reignited.

"Thanks for not denying it."

"What?"

"That he's the love of your life." She shook her head and finally sat down across from me. "Shit, you've got other females coming up here ready to fight you over him. Vince told me all about it."

I rolled my eyes and snorted. "Whatever," I mumbled.

"Don't get flippant with me. I'm only pointing out how important he is to you. And yet, you're sitting here working while he's supposed to take on the biggest fight of his career."

"I'm not his trainer anymore. He fired me, remember?"

"Yeah, and what about being his friend. Can you be that?"

"How?"

"By showing up to support him."

I pushed out a breath, feeling irritated with my best friend. "I can't be in his corner since I've been fired. I couldn't get a seat in the arena even if I wanted to," I mumbled. The truth was, I'd looked up tickets for the fight. They'd sold out months ago.

I considered taking on one of the ParaSquad shifts for the fight to be in the arena but thought better of it. Luke obviously didn't want me there.

"You want to. Which is why I'm going to help you."

I shook my head. "Tanisha, I'm not taking over Brandi or anyone else's shift."

She waved me off. "You don't need to. Here." She stood and placed a ticket for the fight in the center of my laptop.

Blinking, I stared at the ticket and up at Tanisha. I'd forgotten that she purchased a ticket months earlier.

"It's front row. You'll have a clear view of the entire fight. It's not the same as being in his corner but…" She shrugged.

"I can't," I said, staring at the ticket.

Luke

I scanned the room filled with my crew, Lenny, David the yoga instructor hired by Syd, a few months back, and Greyson. Since I was out of town for the past few weeks, I chose him on a whim to be in my corner during the fight.

Whatever.

Despite all the people in the room, I felt a hollowness in my chest that'd been with me for weeks. Jumping out of an airplane, riding ATVs, and all the other shit I did while in Vander City, never fully alleviated the emptiness. Spending time with the crew, doing crazy shit, or focusing on an upcoming fight always worked in the past to get rid of any emptiness brought on by bullshit emotions.

Not that time.

I clenched my jaw and flexed my fists as I surveyed the room, scanning it for the one person I knew wouldn't be there.

"Are you ready for this?" Pit asked as he approached.

I grunted and caught him with a side-eye. "You're starting to act like Lenny. Asking the wrong questions at the last minute."

"Watch your mouth. If you weren't around here looking like a sad puppy for weeks now, I wouldn't have to ask."

"I'm fine," I said, looking over his shoulder. I nodded at Greyson. He approached with the tape and began taping my hands.

"He's got this," Greyson said, looking between Pit and me with a smile on his face.

Pit made a face. "Did I ask you anything?"

Greyson blinked but then looked at me as if expecting me to intervene.

"Did he?" I asked.

Greyson shook his head. "No, but I mean, now that you've taken me on as your trainer, I think—"

"Who said you were my trainer?"

His mouth fell open before saying, "I meant that, now that Syd's out of the picture, you can take some advice from a real trainer. She was cute and all, but she didn't know what she was doing. I even told her—"

"You told her what?" I asked with a harshness in my voice.

Greyson's eyes grew wide and he opened and closed his mouth a few times, not saying anything.

I heard Pit chuckle, but I kept my attention on the dickhead on front of me.

"You approached her? When?"

"A few months ago. She needed to know what she wasn't helping, and she was a distraction to the real training that you needed."

I hopped off the table I sat on and got in Greyson's face. His face reddened.

"You're lucky she never told me about that shit," I cursed. "And if I didn't have a title fight in twenty minutes, I'd beat the shit out of you," I growled. "Get the fuck out of my face and out of this damn arena before I change my mind. You're fired."

"I'd take his advice, before he makes good on his threats," Pit added.

I glared at Greyson as he backed away and grabbed his bags, exiting.

"Idiot," I grunted.

I had my PT step in to finish tapping my hands.

When Pit moved to the other side of the room, I shook off my anger and tried to remember my strategy for the night. It'd been drilled into me for months, but my damn brain was cloudy. Another casualty of that night with Syd, was my ability to zone everything out and focus on the fight.

"Chin up. Even if you lose tonight, you'll still get one hell of a payout," Kelex said as he came up clapping me on the back.

"Don't touch me. What the fuck do you mean even if I lose? Type of talk is that?"

He chuckled. "Just checking to see where your head is at."

"I'm fine."

"That's the second time you said *I'm fine* in the last five minutes," Deacon replied from across the room. "You're fucked."

"Who let you all back here?" I asked.

"Uh, that would be you," Skittles reminded me.

"Note to self, don't invite a bunch of assholes to be your wingmen before a title fight," I mumbled.

"You're asshole enough all by yourself," Tak added.

I grunted, ignoring them as I proceeded with my warmup stretches and shadowboxing. Doing my best to put my attention into the fight, I thought back to all of Rodriguez's fights I watched over the months. I knew his game inside and out. Ordinarily, I walked into a cage confident, certain I'd come out with the W. That had to be my attitude every time I stepped inside, but right then, I just felt numb.

A knock on the door sounded and Lenny entered the room, followed by one of the employees of the arena.

"Jacob and Grace arrived. They're in their seats," Lenny told me.

I nodded.

"It's time, Mr. McConnell," the dude with the headset on, said.

"Let's get this shit over with," was all I could muster to say.

Pit and the rest of the crew headed out to take their seats. Lenny moved behind me and held open my robe for me to slip my arms into. Following Lenny, David, and the arena employee out of the room, I inhaled deeply, expecting for the usual energy to pulse through me. I could always rely on that tingling feeling that started at my toes and spread throughout the rest of my body. Yet, as we entered the arena, nothing.

Not even the cheers and chants from the audience or the lights streaming around the room and down onto the cage could pull a reaction from me. Seeing Rodriguez at the far side of the cage as

I approached stirred nothing inside me. All I felt aside from a deep desire to get this fight over with was that same numbness that accompanied me day and night for weeks.

"Okay, Luke, let your training to take over," David said coming up behind me and massaging my shoulders.

Shaking him off, I said, "Don't touch me."

Lenny removed the robe and I stepped closer to the cage. I bounced up and down on my toes and kept moving to keep my muscles loose and limber.

"You've got this, Luke," Lenny said behind me but not touching me.

Once the announcer stepped inside the cage and gestured for the fighters to enter, I stepped into the cage, still waiting to feel something. Without a conscious thought of doing so, I scanned the audience, looking for the one person missing from my corner. Once I realized what I was doing, I stopped and turned to rest my gaze on Rodriguez.

Mentally, I ran through everything I knew about him and his fighting style. He stared across the cage at me, baring his teeth before putting in his mouth guard. Even that show of aggression didn't pull a reaction from me.

"And fighting in this corner…" The announcer at the center of the ring yelled into the microphone, announcing Rodriguez as the defending heavyweight. Rodriguez's fans roared in applause.

"And standing at, six foot, three inches, Luke Skullcrusher McConnell," the announcer said in a tone that grated on my nerves.

I cracked my neck, rotating my head from side to side, pushing out my annoyance.

"Let's have a clean fight," the ref, Ronnie Smith, said as we approached the center of the cage. He lifted his arm, pausing, giving Rodriguez and I sideways looks before lowering his arm and jumping out of the way. The bell sounded and the fight was on.

We circled the cage, arms in the on-guard position. Rodriguez made the first move by kicking out with his left leg. I quickly sidestepped that attack, but that left me open to the right hook he landed in my ribs.

He grunted and smirked as if he'd proven something.

My usual shit talking didn't come to me. I didn't feel like talking. When Rodriguez left his left side open, trying to hit me with a jab, I went in and caught the tip of his chin. It wasn't a knockout blow, but it caught his attention. He narrowed his eyes and swung wildly with another right hook. That let me go in for a hook of my own with my left. I clipped his chin again and he stumbled backward.

He couldn't match me standing, so I knew eventually he'd go in for the takedown. This early in the fight, my goal was to continue moving, remain on my feet and weaken him with my standing game.

"Son of a bitch," he bellowed when I caught him in the ribs this time with a left uppercut.

For the first time since the fight started, that spark of energy passed through my belly. It was short lived, however, when I missed Rodriguez going in for the takedown. He got low and moved in, wrapping his arms around my legs, toppling the both of us to the ground. Moving fast, I scooted my body back against the cage to prevent him from getting full control of me.

We traded punches and elbows, no one really doing any serious damage. While I didn't lose much ground, the fact that I was the one with my literal back against the cage and Rodriguez was better known for his groundwork, wasn't working in my favor.

It felt like it took forever for that five minute bell to ring. When it did, Rodriguez jumped up, as did I, and we moved to our respective corners. The cutman looked me over and someone, Lenny or David, pressed an icepack to my back.

"That was good," Lenny said, sounding unconvincing.

"Len, shut up," I growled, still staring across the cage. I was off my game and I knew it.

The minute break flew by and Rodriguez and I were soon back in the center of the cage, circling one another. He came out more aggressive that round, as was expected. I held my own and managed to land a few more body blows and chin shots to slow him down.

"Come on, McConnell," he grunted as we tumbled to the floor again. "You can't win this."

"Stop talking, motherfucker, your breath smells like the dump I took this morning," I said right before landing an elbow to the side of his head.

That stunned him but he recovered too fast and I found myself on my back. He attempted to put me in a triangle, locking me up, but I held him off until the bell went off, ending the second round.

"Shit," I cursed, slapping the water bottle out of David's hand when he tried to pass it to me.

"Calm—"

"Don't fucking tell me to calm down," I growled at Lenny. I pushed the cutman away after he pressed that damn enswell to my temple. While I could feel the blood trickling down my eyebrow from one of Rodriguez's elbows, I knew it wasn't enough to worry about. I needed direction and David didn't know my strategy well enough to direct me. In fact, every time he tried to give advice, it pissed me off.

The bell for the third round sounded and Rodriguez and I came out guns blazing this time. Instead of waiting for him to make a move, this round I went in, taking him down. He fell with me on top, but I knew that wasn't necessarily a safe position to be in with someone as skilled as him on the ground. I went in for an elbow, but he slipped it and lifted his hips, maneuvering in a way that had me landing on my stomach.

Shit! I was in trouble when he moved over my back and started going in for the chokehold.

He began applying pressure and within a few heartbeats my vision started to blur. I only had seconds before I made the decision to tap out or pass the fuck out. Either option was a loss for me.

Waltz, Luke!

I blinked and listened for that sound again.

Waltz with him!

The memory of dancing around the cage in San Diego with Syd came to mind.

Waltz.

Syd

I walked into the main entrance of the arena with the rest of the audience members. It pained me to know that I was nothing more than a regular spectator of the fight. While I put in hours as Luke's trainer and wanted to see that dedication all the way through, what hurt most was that I couldn't be there for Luke for emotional support.

He wanted to win another title. He worked his ass off, putting in hours of training and sacrificing literal blood and sweat to win. Selfishly, I wanted to be in his corner when he did.

As the arena attendee handed me my ticket stub and pointed in the direction of my seat, I sighed, feeling the weight of this night. I pushed the sadness aside in order to focus on what was important. At least I would get to see the fight in person.

As took my seat, I glanced around and pulled out my phone to send a 'thank you' text to Tanisha. She really did have a great seat. It gave me a perfect view of the cage. In fact, as I looked down the row, I spotted Skittles taking her seat next to Pit. I'd only met both of them once, but they'd made an impression. From the looks of it, the rest of Luke's crew was with them.

I immediately recognized Tak as the lead singer of Rejected One. There were two other guys. From the looks of it, the one with the tattoos had to be Deacon, leaving the last member to be Kelex. Before I could look away, Skittles caught my eye. Her eyebrows lifted before narrowing slightly and she turned to Pit to say something. He glanced down at me, his eyes narrowing also.

I swallowed the lump that formed in my throat and turned away. My mind began wondering what type of things Luke told them about me. I couldn't imagine it was anything pretty. Thankfully, before I could fully go down that road, the lights went dim and the announcers began welcoming the audience to the fight.

The music signaling the entrance of the athletes into the arena sounded, causing the crowd to ignite in cheers. My heart pounded when I spotted Luke and his corner emerge from the opening into the arena and walk down the aisle toward the cage. Lenny and David were in his corner. That had me releasing a small sigh of relief. At least, he had someone with him. Lenny wasn't much of a corner when it came to fighting but he was a friend, and David had some familiarity with Luke's training.

Straining to get a better glimpse of him, I lifted my gaze to one of the overhead flat screens in the arena. I stared into Luke's eyes, trying to read them. Fear pierced my belly at what I saw there. He didn't look focused on the fight. He almost appeared bored as if he just wanted this over with.

That wasn't a good sign.

"C'mon, Luke," I mumbled.

I twisted my hands in my lap, feeling the energy from the crowd course through me. If Luke could pull it together, after the next twenty-five minutes were up, he would have the title belt. I knew that he could do it but stealing another look into his eyes as he entered the cage, I wasn't fully certain that he believed it.

My heart hammered in my chest from the start of the first bell. I watched intently, mumbling calls that I would've told Luke directly if I were still in his corner. I clasped my hands at my chest, squeezing them while keeping my eyes glued to the action happening in the cage.

"Pull it together, Luke," I said at the end of the second round.

When the bell for the third round went off, both fighters moved with more intention than they'd started off with. Rodriguez was swift, but Luke stayed with him. I gasped when Luke made the first move this time, to take him down. Rodriguez wasn't expecting it and he went down hard. However, he recovered well. Too well.

Luke was suddenly on his stomach, Rodriguez moving in to climb on his back. The worst position for Luke to be in.

"Get up," I shouted, forgetting that I wasn't supposed to be there. Rising to my feet, I yelled for Luke to get up when I saw Rodriguez moving to put him in a chokehold.

Catching a glimpse of Luke's face, my body filled with fear that he was on the verge of giving up.

"Waltz, Luke," I called out, moving as close as I could to the cage before the security stopped me.

"Ma'am step back," the security guard warned.

I did so, but only a few inches, before cupping my hands around my mouth and yelling again.

"Waltz, with him, Luke!"

I breathed heavily, hoping beyond hope he somehow heard me above the rest of the crowd and the chaos in his own mind.

"Waltz," I said again.

I gasped when Luke managed to regain leverage forcing Rodriguez to his right side.

"Yes," I yelled when Luke held onto Rodriguez' left arm and wrapped his leg around his upper waist. "Do it," I said as I waited for Luke to catch his other leg around Rodriguez' body, locking in the triangle.

My belly filled with butterflies when he did. I held my breath, just waiting as Luke tightened the triangle hold around Rodriguez. Seconds went by and eventually, right before the bell signaling the end of the third round, Rodriguez tapped out.

"Fuck yeah," I cheered and raised my arms over my head.

"Skullcrusher. Skullcrusher," those who were fans of Luke's began chanting his fighter name as he rose to his feet with his arms lifted overhead.

He glanced around the outside of the cage, looking for something. I stopped breathing when our eyes connected. He dropped his hands as he continued to heave, his chest rising and lowering rapidly.

His attention became focused on the commentator as two other arena employees wrapped the belt around his waist. I took a step back and then another, until I grabbed my purse from underneath my seat and started for the exit.

I didn't stay to hear the final speeches. I doubted Luke wanted me there. My heart grew heavier with each step I took, but I refused to look back. Luke got his win and that was enough for me. I could go on and nurse my broken heart at home, by myself.

Taking measured steps, I focused my attention on the exit. My vision blurred as the rush of tears I refused to let fall, clouded my eyes. If I could make it to my car, I could allow my release. Only feet away from the exit, however, my escape was halted.

"Hey," Luke's deep voice called, at the same time he pulled my arm, turning me to face him.

I bulged my eyes and opened my mouth in shock. I stared, wordlessly, trying to figure out whether he was real or a figment of my imagination. Around us, I heard the oohs and ahhs of the spectators and fans, surprised to see Luke standing there. Ignoring the onlookers, I continued to stare into his brown eyes.

Finally, words came to me. "What are you doing out here?" I asked, briefly glancing around, noticing the cameras that moved in close, capturing this moment, whatever it was.

"Thanks for the dance lessons," he said, smiling. It was a genuine smile.

My throat tightened at the sparkle in his eyes.

"Y-you're welcome."

He pulled me in closer to his body. He leaned lower, hovering his lips above mine. "Before I tongue you down and take you home to apologize to me all night long, are there any other secrets you need to tell me?"

I opened and closed my mouth a couple of times before nodding.

He lifted an eyebrow.

"I love you."

"Good," he said, before making good on his words and kissing me deeply right there in front of the entire audience spilling out of the arena, cameras, and the entire world to see.

"Shit, I didn't come all this way to watch this dude fall in love," a male voice grunted behind Luke.

Luke lifted his head, brushing his lips against mine and before raising his middle finger to whomever had just spoken.

I peeked over his shoulder to see his entire crew standing there.

"Kelex is a son of a bitch," Luke said, tracing my bottom lip with his thumb.

"I got your son of a bitch," Kelex replied.

Instead of replying to him, Luke said to me, "You still owe me three more blow jobs."

It was my turn to lift an eyebrow. "Three?"

He nodded. "At least. Don't worry, we've got plenty of time and plenty more bets to make, to add on to those."

When he raised his hands to cup my cheeks, I noticed that, save for the tape, his hands were bare.

"Where're your gloves?"

"The cage."

I widened my eyes. "Luke."

"I retired, Syd." He pulled back and tapped the belt around his waist before cupping my face again. "I got the two things I wanted most. I love you, too." He sealed his declaration with a kiss.

CHAPTER THIRTY-THREE

Gravesite

Luke

"Where are we going?" Syd anxiously asked from the passenger seat of my car.

"What'd I say the first seven times you asked me that question?"

She pouted and folded her arms over her breasts, giving me a side-eye.

I chuckled. "Careful with those lips, babe. You know you still owe me another blow job. I might pull over before we get to our destination."

She sucked her teeth. "How do I still owe you another one? My damn jaw has put in overtime this past week."

Grinning, I thought back over the past seven days. It'd been a week since I won the title. And after a rub down and ice bath, which Syd insisted on, I took her home and have barely let her up for air since.

"I lost track somewhere on day three, so I restarted the count," I replied.

She waved me off. "My mouth remains closed until you tell me where we're going."

Frowning, I glance over at her, knowing that comment for the lie it is. If where we were headed weren't so important, I probably would've pulled over in the nearest parking lot and brought us both to a release. Especially since Syd chose to wear a dress that stopped a few inches above the knee.

I bit my lower lip and stifled the groan that threatened to break through.

Focus, Luke. I had to remind myself.

"We'll be there in the next ten minutes."

This was the first time in a long time I was going to visit this place. And it was the first time *ever* I was going with someone not in my crew.

Anyway, my thoughts scrambled as I made the final turn onto the street that led down a long, winding road. We weren't the only car on the road, but we were one of a small few. Beyond the wooded forest, about a mile down the road, the iron gates on both the left and right sides of the road showed we were close to the entrance. In between the metal poles of the gate, the vast greenery lined with cement headstones could be seen.

"A cemetery?" Syd questioned, her voice sounding confused.

I nodded but kept my attention straight ahead as we passed through the main entrance of the cemetery. I continued for some time, until my turn came. I made a right down another short road that led to more headstones and gravesites. About two hundred yards in was where I stopped, parking at the side of the road.

Turning the car off, I turned to Syd.

"What is this, Luke?"

Looking her squarely in the eye, I responded, "Let's go see your father."

She bulged her eyes before biting her lip and staring at me. Confusion reigned supreme out of all the emotions I saw in her eyes.

Took one of her hands into mine and pressed a kiss to it. Releasing her hand, I got out of the car and went around to her side, opening the door and holding out my hand for her to take.

She obliged, allowing me to help her out and close the door behind her. I frowned as I peered down at the four inch heels she wore. Remembering I had an extra pair of shoes in the backseat, I unlocked the car, pulling out the sneakers she'd left in my car weeks earlier.

"You'll need these."

I also grabbed my title belt. I'd made sure to bring it with me for this trip.

Syd changed her shoes and I tossed the heels onto the floor of the passenger side. Taking her hand into mine, I led us both in the direction of Banks' gravesite.

It took only a few minutes for us to reach the headstone that read William Paul Banks.

"This is where he's buried." Her voice was shaky.

I nodded, lifting my arm around her shoulders. She melted into me, her arm going around my waist.

My chest tightened as I stared down at his grave. "Sup, Banks. I've got something to show you. " Releasing Syd, I squatted and held up the belt as if he could see it. "You know how much I hate sharing and shit, but…" I paused and looked up at Syd, who watched me. "This was a team effort. My new trainer and I won this one together."

I turned back to face his headstone. "Oh, also, as it turns out, I'm banging your daughter."

"Oh my God," Syd yelped, smacking me across the shoulder as I rose to my feet, laughing.

I grinned but then got serious. Inhaling I added. "I'm in love with her."

A heartbeat later, Syd lowered her hand to my shoulder. "And I with him," she said above a whisper. She squatted next to me, wrapping her arm around mine and laying her head on my shoulder.

I lowered my head to kiss her forehead.

"He did talk about you a little bit."

Syd lifted her head and turned to me.

I nodded, still staring at the headstone. "Said he had a little girl. He didn't get to see her since her mother left him.

"Was a long time ago. She and her mother are better off without me. Now quit bitching and thinking you're the only one with a fucked up family and go hit the bag."

"He said that to you?"

"Sure as shit. It was right after my father tracked me down at Banks's gym, about a year after I'd been training with him. I'd entered the NFA by then and had made the news for one of my fights. That was how my father was able to find me.

"He tried to guilt me into going back to school, finishing and going on to med school like he and Anna had drilled into me ever since I could remember. After I told him to screw off, I went to Banks complaining about my father. He told me to get my head out of my ass."

"Seems like a charmer."

I stood and brought her to stand with me, my arm around her shoulder. "Where Banks came from there was no room for charm. He didn't talk about you much, but he did tell me shit about his life before you. How he grew up, the times he went to jail for stealing, his younger brother dying. He went through a lot of shit."

"He opened up to you."

"A little. Told me some things about his past, but you and your mother were his sore spot. He kept the both of you to himself. Never even told me your names. He said his ex-wife left him because he was a thug and she wanted to do better. He didn't hate her. In fact, he thought she did the right thing."

"Is that why he never tried to get in contact with me?"

I nodded.

"I was so angry with the both of them for so long. My mother for not telling me about him and him for not trying harder to get to know me."

I moved my gaze back to Syd as she turned and stared at the gravesite. She let out a sigh. "I don't remember much about him except he'd always sit me on his lap to watch boxing. He was the one who encouraged my mom to put me into martial arts when I was so young. After she left him, she did everything to cut ties with him, including trying to make me forget about fighting. That picture on my desk is the only one I have of him and me together."

My nostrils flared. The tremble in Syd's voice as she speaks, pisses me off. I hated that she felt robbed of knowing her history. Moving behind her, I wrapped both my arms around her waist and pull her into me. She laid her head against my chest.

"She put me in piano lessons and ballet, but I rebelled. I snuck out of those sessions and went over to the local Judo school to continue practicing. I saved my weekly allowances to pay for the lessons."

She paused, and turned in my embrace, lifting her head to look me in the eye.

"We fought about it and finally she said if I was going to insist on taking Judo, I'd have to pay for it myself. I guess she thought that would make me quit. But at thirteen, I started walking dogs in my neighborhood to earn money. That was how I continued to pay for lessons all the way up until my senior year."

"You've always been a little entrepreneur, huh?"

She nodded, a sad smile crossing her face. "Maybe I get that from him." She peered down at the headstone.

Considering the thought, I nodded. "Banks always said he hated working for someone else which was why he went into fighting and then training, saving money to open his own gym."

I dropped my hands from her waist when she turned and took a step forward, crouching low in front of Banks' headstone. There was a long pause before Syd's shoulders began shaking. Small whimpers escaped her throat.

My body tightened with the stress of watching her breakdown. Moving closer, I crouched down next to her, pressing my palm to her back as her body continued to shake.

"I spent years wondering what he was like. Trying to figure out if I looked like him. All I had was that picture." She sniffled and wiped away a few tears, but they kept coming. "It was the only thing my mom let me have of his. I was sixteen when I found this in her closet."

She tucks her head, moving her hand to the silver boxing glove pendant around her neck.

"It belonged to him. When I asked her, my mother said he mailed it to her after she left. He wanted her to give it to me to remember him."

Syd turned to stare at me with red eyes and a tear-soaked face. "Do you think he loved me? Did he miss me?" Her bottom lip trembled.

I had to pause and turn to face the headstone. The lump in my own throat threatened to steal my voice. Somehow, I found the words.

Nodding, I responded with, "Yeah. He loved you. I don't know what went on between your mother and him but the few times he mentioned his family he'd get this far off look in his eyes. Like, out of all the shit he'd done in his life, that was his one regret. Not getting to see you grow up."

I turned to face Syd and my damn heart squeezed in my chest. Her pain felt like my own.

"Thank you," she said just above a whisper. "For bringing me here and sharing part of him with me." Her words were barely audible before she completely broke down into tears in my arms.

I held onto her for dear life. The two of us sitting in front of Banks's headstone, Syd's face tucked into my chest as she let out years of anger and pain. I rocked her back and forth as she sobbed. I held on, not allowing her to feel alone in her pain and grief. This woman was mine.

We sat there for a long while before Syd's tears stopped flowing.

"How did he die? Was he alone?" She finally asked.

I shook my head.

"Nine months before he died I went with him to a doctor's visit after he'd had a cough for months that wouldn't go away. He was sure it was a cold he couldn't shake. Turned out it was lung cancer. His two pack a day habit of over thirty years finally caught up with him. He was adamant that I not change anything in my schedule or training. He never wanted me to lose focus."

"He must've cared deeply about you."

I nodded. "He did. He was more than just my trainer. I was twenty-two when I walked into his gym. By most standards I got into MMA late as hell. But he saw potential or whatever because he stayed on my ass. Made sure I trained hard. He did his best to keep me out of trouble." I snorted because that was laughable. Trouble often found me but that wasn't Banks's fault.

"Once he was diagnosed, I knew he was scared shitless."

Syd looked up at me.

"I know fear, Syd. I was raised in it. Learned to fight in it and fight as a result of it. I can smell fear a fucking mile away. Even when it comes with a smile. Banks wasn't afraid of much, but he was scared of dying. He chose to ignore it. Pretend like it wasn't inevitable. And I let him."

Syd wrapped her arm around my waist, leaning her head against my chest again.

"He didn't die alone. He spent the last months of his life still coming into the gym to train me. When he got too weak for that, I moved him into my home, hired a nurse for him 'round the clock." I stopped talking. The memory of Banks's final days overwhelming me.

"I held his hand when he took his last breath."

Syd reached her free hand up, cupping my face. Leaning up, she grazed my lips with her own. Licking mine, I tasted the salt from both our tears. I hadn't even realized I'd been crying.

"Fuck. You're making me soft. I didn't even cry at his funeral." I wiped my tears away.

Syd let out a tiny smile. "You are soft, Skullcrusher."

It was on the tip of my tongue to tell her it was only for her, but I refrained. The look that passed between us, however, spoke for itself.

"He lasted longer than the docs expected, though. I made sure he was comfortable in his last months. He was a tough son of a bitch. One of the last things I wanted to do before he died was win another title. For him, not for me. But I failed."

"You didn't fail," she said, peering down at the belt on the ground in front of us. "It just took a little longer than you expected."

I glanced at the mole at the side of her mouth, before moving to those juicy lips, and I smiled, leaned down for a kiss.

Pulling back, I reached into my left pocket to remove the black ring box I made sure to bring with me.

"Tradition says I'm supposed to go to the father and shit before I ask this question, but Banks is gone and your stepfather's out of town again," I said, looking at Syd as I flipped open the ring box.

She gasped and widened her eyes, looking between me and the box. "Luke," she whispered.

"You were right. I kept everyone at arm's length. I thought life was easier that way. And then you barged your thick ass into my life and refused to leave."

I grunted when she punched my shoulder.

"Is this supposed to be your proposal speech?"

"It gets better," I promised. "I thought you were full of shit, having me go to dance lessons as part of my training."

"I'm waiting for the part where this speech improves," Syd said.

"Patience, babe." I chuckled. "Anyway," I paused and sighed, turning to her. "You need to stand for this part." She rose to her feet while I got on one knee. "You've taught me more than how to be a better fighter. You've shown me that the one thing I went to my mother's funeral to find, I had all along."

She raised an eyebrow, cocking her head to the side.

I covered my chest with my free hand. "My heart."

Her eyes watered.

"But it's no longer mine. It's yours if you'll have it." Holding up the ring, I asked, "Sydney Quinn, will you marry me?"

More tears spilled down her cheeks and she nodded.

After sliding the ring onto her finger, I stood and cupped her face, pulling her in for a kiss.

"Thank you," I said against her lips. For the first time in my life, I felt whole. Not even winning a second title had done that. But this woman before me, she did.

Glancing back over my shoulder, I said, "You might want to cover your eyes from here on out, Banks. I'm about to defile the shit out of your daughter."

Syd gasped. "Oh my—" Her comment was cut off when I pulled her to me, kissing her deeply.

Syd

Mrs. Syd McConnell. I tried the name out again and again in my head as we headed back to Luke's home. His hand rested on my thigh, holding firmly as if he were afraid I'd disappear or something.

The only time his hand left my body was when we needed to part to get out of the car. As soon as we stepped over the threshold, Luke pressed his body against mine, his lips going to my neck. I moaned out in pleasure and anticipation of what was to come next.

Luke groaned when I suddenly pushed him away from me, stepping around him to move further down the hall. Spinning around to face him, I caught the surprised look on his face.

I grinned. "Where should our wedding be?" I asked, holding up my hand with the diamond on it and wiggling my fingers.

Luke frowned. "Wherever the hell you want. Get over here," he took a step forward. I countered, moving back.

"I was thinking maybe a destination wedding. Somewhere in the Caribbean." I cocked my head to the side.

"Syd." His voice was tight and full of warning.

I backed up again, the back of my ankle hitting the first stair of the staircase. "Oh, maybe Vander City?"

"We can figure all that shit out after I coat your pussy walls with my cum."

My nipples pebbled at his vulgar language. I began pushing down the straps of the sleeveless dress and within seconds it pooled at my feet.

Luke's eyes glinted with lust, and most importantly, love.

"I hope you don't write that as part of your vows." I tried to sound teasing but the tremble in my voice gave me away.

"Bring your ass over here," he growled.

"Gotta catch me first," I said before taking off up the stairs as fast as I could.

My foot barely touched the top step before I felt his warm breath barreling down the back of my neck. Before I knew it, a giggle burst from my mouth as he picked me up and carried me the rest of the way down the hall and into his bedroom, slamming the door shut behind us.

"Shit," I cursed when he tossed me like a ragdoll onto the bed. However, when he moved to cover me with his body, I rolled away.

I laughed when he growled in annoyance. Ignoring his frustration, I reached for the belt buckle that held his jeans in place. He stopped reaching for me when I tugged at his jeans, bringing them down past his waist.

"I think I owe you one of these, right?" I asked. I pushed him to lay on the bed. Lowering to my knees, I gleefully covered the tip of his shaft with my mouth.

Luke groaned and my nipples hardened beneath the silk material of my bra. I began stroking the entirety of his length with my mouth. He was so long that he reached all the way to the back of my throat. Tingling sensations began to erupt in my core when Luke moved his hands to the back of my head.

Raising my head, I traced the tip of his member with my tongue, tasting the precum that already began to emerge. He tasted like every dream I'd ever had. The more I captured him with my mouth the hungrier I grew. It didn't take long for him to come in my mouth. His orgasm was powerful, shaking his entire body along with the bed and igniting a fiery need in my own body. I wanted every ounce of liquid he had to offer. I continued to suckle him as if it was for the preservation of my very own life. Swallowing, I felt more satisfied than I'd ever been.

Luke wasn't done. He never was after his first release. So I wasn't surprised when he sat up, easily pulling my body up from the floor to straddle his. He reached over to the nightstand and grabbed a condom, holding it up between us.

"As soon as we're married, these are the first fucking things to go," he growled.

I grinned and took the condom from him and ripped it open with my teeth. Luke watched me carefully as he always did when I used my mouth to sheath him. Slowly and precisely, I lowered my mouth, unraveling the condom bit by bit along his shaft. Raising up, I made sure the condom was securely in place.

"You're taking too fucking long," Luke complained before moving lightning fast and bringing my body beneath his. He pushed my panties down my hips.

"You're so damn imp— *Oooh*," I moaned as he slipped inside of me.

Shit! I cursed in my head because all the air had been stolen from my body, making it impossible for me to verbally express the feeling that surged through me when he entered me. I arched my back off the bed and lifted my arms, going around his neck and pulling his lips forcibly down onto mine. Making love to Luke wasn't anything short of awe-inspiring, mesmerizing, unending passion.

"Luke," I panted over and over, barely able to get his name out in hoarse whispers.

"Fuck, Syd. You're killing me," he groaned, staring me in the eyes. The love he had shone through. A bead of sweat moved down the side of his face and I sat up on my elbows, raising my face to lick the saltwater stream.

Luke let out a wild sound from the back of his throat and I soon found myself on all fours, back arching as he pounded into me from behind. Our yells and moans of pleasure combined to form our own unique chorus of bliss. He reached his hand underneath my body, his palm pressing flat against my belly, holding me in place.

"Luuuke," I shrieked as I came, my fingers tightly holding onto the linens that covered his bed.

His second orgasm was only minutes behind mine. His heavy breathing and groaning low in my ear were his body's telltale signs of his release.

When it was over, he slowly pulled free of my body, turning me over onto my back. He moved to the side, lying on his back and then pulled me over to lie on top of him.

"I love you," I murmured against his chest, feeling dazed.

His arms tightened around my body. "I love the shit out of you."

Leaning up, I pressed a kiss to the middle of his chest before laying my head back down.

"As soon as we're married, I'm filling your womb up with my seed."

I gasped and raised my head. "You know what that could lead to, right?"

"No, what, Syd?" He gave me a deadpan expression.

I plucked his nose, and he caught my hand in his and bit my finger.

"You're such a bully. You want to have a kid with me?" I asked.

"No." He shook his head. "I want to have a gang of those little fuckers with you."

Rolling my eyes, I said, "First, we'll have to work on your calling them little fuckers. Let's start with one."

He shrugged. "If I nut in you enough, maybe we'll get twins on our first try."

"That's not how it works."

"Let's continue practicing to find out," he said, before rolling us over until I was on my back.

"Mmm." I let out a sigh as he licked the outside of my ear.

We practiced for the rest of the night.

Let the Games Begin

Luke

"About damn time you showed up," Deacon called as Syd and I passed through the door Pit held open for me in the penthouse room of the Vegas hotel we'd rented for him for the weekend.

"I had other things to do besides look at your fucking face, Deacon."

He snorted.

"We're late because I was on the phone with the realtor about our new place in Bridge Lake."

I finally went ahead and made a decision on one of the homes my realtor sent. And since Syd agreed to our living half-time in Bridge Lake and the other half of the year on the West Coast, it was a done deal.

"Oh, and because I had my face buried in some pussy," I added.

Syd gasped next to me and punched me in the side.

Laughing, I stepped further inside the hotel room, my arm still wrapped around Syd. "It's okay, though since I'm engaged to this particular pussy."

"Luke, you keep referring to me as pussy and see how fast I stuff this ring down your throat."

"Oh shit," Deacon said, laughing.

"I need a drink," Syd said.

"You come with me," Skittles insisted, taking Syd by the hand and carting her off to the other side of the room where a group of women were dancing and laughing.

I stared after my fiancée. She and Skittles had developed something of a friendship since the night of my title win.

"The hell is wrong with you, not having the decency to be on time for my bachelor party," Pit said, moving next to me.

"Who the fuck has a co-ed bachelor party, anyway?"

"I do. No one here can pretend as if they don't know that woman is psycho. I swear, her little ass sits on my chest watching me sleep. I wasn't getting my balls cut off with a grinder for any of you."

"That's a visual I didn't need," Deacon said.

"Nor did I," I added.

"Speaking of… Deacon, you better have your gun on you. I'm gonna need another tat this weekend."

"Y'all asses are always asking for a tattoo, I have to bring that shit. What're you trying to get?"

I motioned with my head to the part of the room where Syd talked with the other women. "Her name."

"I'm surprised this guy's still got any space on his body left to ink up," Tak said, entering the room.

"There he is." Spreading my arms wide, I moved over to Tak who's ass looked like the lost puppy of the group.

He shrugs me off. "I'm going for a smoke," he grumbled.

"Awe, careful there, pipsqueak…" I ruffled Tak's dark hair and laughed when he flung my arm away. "Don't make me forget who you are to me and kick your ass."

Tak flipped me off before heading out onto the balcony. I shook my head.

"What bug crawled up his ass and died?" I turned, asking the other two.

Pit shrugged.

"What'd you think? You're getting married. Pit's getting married. And Kelex is fucking MIA. He feels left out," Deacon answered.

I looked over my shoulder at Tak staring out on the Vegas skyline before turning back to Pit and Deacon.

"What about you?"

"Me?" Deacon asked.

"Yeah, your ass ain't up to shit?"

Deacon frowned. "Same ol' same ol'. I'm not the one to be tied down."

"Go talk to the kid before this stubborn ass fucker starts talking that shit about never fucking the same pussy," Pit insisted. "Get on my damn nerves."

I nodded and turned toward the balcony. As soon as the door slid open, the sounds from the nightlife happening some twenty-five floors below us floated around us. I pushed the door closed.

"Stare gazing? Really, when we're here to celebrate? How long are you planning on staying out here?" I asked Tak.

"As long as it takes for you fuckers to remember tying your dick to one person is a fucking curse," he said, dropping his cigarette and stomping on it. He half turned, giving me a once over. "But enough about your and Pit's shitty mistake. Is there a reason you're checking on me?"

"Worried about you. You're looking glum for someone who should be happy one of his best friends is getting married."

"Fuck that," he said. "I said I would attend the wedding and party, not fuck her friends. And if I stay in there, one of them is going to get their feelings hurt."

I smirked. "Quit lying. There're at least two pussies in that room you've exchanged bodily fluids with," I said, giving Tak a solid pat on the back. "Don't be shy, you can tell me you're feeling lonely with Pit and me engaged."

I watched as Tak quietly contemplated whatever went on in his head. A sense of unease filled my gut. I didn't like it when he got quiet.

"Come back inside. The champagne's not much but it'll take the edge off," I insisted.

"Nah, I'm going to cut out early. Time to find me a piece of ass to wipe away this nightmare of marital bliss," he replied.

"You're going to miss the best part—the sappy retelling of how they met," I teased.

"I was there for it," he nonchalantly answered. "Tell them my stomach hurts," he added sarcastically, pushing the doors open.

I watched Tak walk off as I re-entered the room. My hand was grabbed as soon as I did.

"Dance with me," Syd purred as someone turned up the music.

"Anytime and anywhere, babe." I leaned down and pressed a kiss to her lips. I spun her around with my left arm, causing her to laugh out loud. My entire chest filled with something warm and comforting. I might've been teasing Tak on the balcony, but I was dead fucking serious about Syd. I knew something the kid had yet to learn. When it's real, you'll be itching to make it official.

Pit, with his arm wrapped around Skittles, inched closer. "Knew there was something about you. Must be crazy as fuck. Good, you're good for him," he said to Syd.

Syd looked up at me and wiggled her hips, dancing with her back to me.

"He's been good for me too."

I dropped a kiss to her lips. Lifting my head, I caught Tak standing in the foyer.

He gave me one last glare before storming out of the room, slamming the door behind him. Rolling my eyes, I turned back to Pit.

"He'll be all right," Pit said, not sounding too sure.

I snorted, looking back at the door. "Let the games begin."

ACKNOWLEDGMENTS

I love this book so much. Luke is a character who's story I've wanted to tell for some time. I'm glad he came to me when he did, and I am truly grateful for him allowing me to share his story with the world. Luke and Syd were not an easy couple by any means. They didn't want to play by my rules. But in the end, what I learned is that I needed to drop my established way of doing things and learn something new.

This book taught me a lot and I will carry it into every story I tell moving forward.

I'd like to thank Blue Saffire for asking me to be a part of this series. You truly are a gift to the literary world, and me personally. Thank you for pushing me to be a better author than I was before I began this story.

To all of my readers who write me emails, DMs or messages asking when the next book is, or telling me your thoughts on my latest release, I appreciate you more than you will ever know. Thank you for your support throughout the years. I look forward to keeping you satisfied with more stories of romance and love for years to come.

Finally, I would like to thank God. It is only through His guidance, strength, and power that I am able to show up day after day and do my best. I am grateful for every ounce of strength I receive.

ABOUT THE AUTHOR

I am an Amazon bestselling author of interracial and African-American romance. My first book debuted in May 2015 and since then I have been lucky enough to publish over 20 more novels. Currently, you can find me sitting at my desk, daydreaming about my characters while I type furiously on my keyboard to get their stories down on paper. I'm a native of the East Coast—New Jersey to be specific, but have recently relocated to San Antonio, Texas. If I'm not working on my next novel, then you'll definitely spot me out on the trails, hiking the hills of Texas Hill Country, or watching the latest True Crime television show.

Wait, there is more to come! You can stay updated with my latest releases, learn more about me, the author, and be a part of contests by subscribing to my newsletter at
www. TiffanyPattersonWrites.com
If you enjoyed Luke, I'd love to hear
your thoughts and please feel free to leave a
review. And when you do, please let me
know by emailing me at TiffanyPattersonWrites@gmail.com
or leave a comment on Facebook
https://www.facebook.com/AuthorTiffanyPatteron or Twitter
@TiffanyPWrites